The Adventure of the Christmas Pudding

HARPER

HARPER

An imprint of HarperCollins*Publishers*
77–85 Fulham Palace Road
Hammersmith, London W6 8JB
www.harpercollins.co.uk

This *Agatha Christie Signature Edition* published 2002
13

First published in Great Britain by
Collins 1960

ISBN 13: 978 0 00 712108 3

Typeset by Palimpsest Book Production Limited,
Grangemouth, Stirlingshire

Printed and bound in Great Britain by
Clays Ltd, St Ives plc

The Adventure of the Christmas Pudding

Agatha Christie is known throughout the world as the Queen of Crime. Her books have sold over a billion copies in English with another billion in 100 foreign countries. She is the most widely published author of all time and in any language, outsold only by the Bible and Shakespeare. She is the author of 80 crime novels and short story collections, 19 plays, and six novels written under the name of Mary Westmacott.

Agatha Christie's first novel, *The Mysterious Affair at Styles*, was written towards the end of the First World War, in which she served as a VAD. In it she created Hercule Poirot, the little Belgian detective who was destined to become the most popular detective in crime fiction since Sherlock Holmes. It was eventually published by The Bodley Head in 1920.

In 1926, after averaging a book a year, Agatha Christie wrote her masterpiece. *The Murder of Roger Ackroyd* was the first of her books to be published by Collins and marked the beginning of an author-publisher relationship which lasted for 50 years and well over 70 books. *The Murder of Roger Ackroyd* was also the first of Agatha Christie's books to be dramatised – under the name *Alibi* – and to have a successful run in London's West End. *The Mousetrap*, her most famous play of all, opened in 1952 and is the longest-running play in history.

Agatha Christie was made a Dame in 1971. She died in 1976, since when a number of books have been published posthumously: the bestselling novel *Sleeping Murder* appeared later that year, followed by her autobiography and the short story collections *Miss Marple's Final Cases*, *Problem at Pollensa Bay* and *While the Light Lasts*. In 1998 *Black Coffee* was the first of her plays to be novelised by another author, Charles Osborne.

The Agatha Christie Collection

The Man In The Brown Suit
The Secret of Chimneys
The Seven Dials Mystery
The Mysterious Mr Quin
The Sittaford Mystery
The Hound of Death
The Listerdale Mystery
Why Didn't They Ask Evans?
Parker Pyne Investigates
Murder Is Easy
And Then There Were None
Towards Zero
Death Comes as the End
Sparkling Cyanide
Crooked House
They Came to Baghdad
Destination Unknown
Spider's Web *
The Unexpected Guest *
Ordeal by Innocence
The Pale Horse
Endless Night
Passenger To Frankfurt
Problem at Pollensa Bay
While the Light Lasts

Poirot
The Mysterious Affair at Styles
The Murder on the Links
Poirot Investigates
The Murder of Roger Ackroyd
The Big Four
The Mystery of the Blue Train
Black Coffee *
Peril at End House
Lord Edgware Dies
Murder on the Orient Express
Three-Act Tragedy
Death in the Clouds
The ABC Murders
Murder in Mesopotamia
Cards on the Table
Murder in the Mews
Dumb Witness
Death on the Nile
Appointment With Death
Hercule Poirot's Christmas
Sad Cypress
One, Two, Buckle My Shoe
Evil Under the Sun
Five Little Pigs

* novelised by Charles Osborne

The Hollow
The Labours of Hercules
Taken at the Flood
Mrs McGinty's Dead
After the Funeral
Hickory Dickory Dock
Dead Man's Folly
Cat Among the Pigeons
The Adventure of the Christmas Pudding
The Clocks
Third Girl
Hallowe'en Party
Elephants Can Remember
Poirot's Early Cases
Curtain: Poirot's Last Case

Marple
The Murder at the Vicarage
The Thirteen Problems
The Body in the Library
The Moving Finger
A Murder is Announced
They Do It With Mirrors
A Pocket Full of Rye
The 4.50 from Paddington
The Mirror Crack'd from Side to Side
A Caribbean Mystery
At Bertram's Hotel
Nemesis
Sleeping Murder
Miss Marple's Final Cases

Tommy & Tuppence
The Secret Adversary
Partners in Crime
N or M?
By the Pricking of My Thumbs
Postern of Fate

Published as Mary Westmacott
Giant's Bread
Unfinished Portrait
Absent in the Spring
The Rose and the Yew Tree
A Daughter's a Daughter
The Burden

Memoirs
An Autobiography
Come, Tell Me How You Live

Play Collections
The Mousetrap and Selected Plays
Witness for the Prosecution and
    Selected Plays

Contents

Foreword

By Agatha Christie

This book of Christmas fare may be described as 'The Chef's Selection'. I am the Chef!

There are two main courses: The Adventure of the Christmas Pudding and The Mystery of the Spanish Chest; a selection of Entrées: Greenshaw's Folly, The Dream and The Under Dog, and a Sorbet: Four-and-Twenty Blackbirds.

The Mystery of the Spanish Chest may be described as a Hercule Poirot Special. It is a case in which he considers he was at his best! Miss Marple, in her turn, has always been pleased with her perspicuity in Greenshaw's Folly.

The Adventure of the Christmas Pudding is an indulgence of my own, since it recalls to me, very pleasurably, the Christmases of my youth. After my father's death, my mother and I always spent Christmas with my brother-in-law's family in the north of England – and what superb Christmases they were for a child to remember! Abney

Agatha Christie

Hall had everything! The garden boasted a waterfall, a stream, and a tunnel under the drive! The Christmas fare was of gargantuan proportions. I was a skinny child, appearing delicate, but actually of robust health and perpetually hungry! The boys of the family and I used to vie with each other as to who could eat most on Christmas Day. Oyster Soup and Turbot went down without undue zest, but then came Roast Turkey, Boiled Turkey and an enormous Sirloin of Beef. The boys and I had two helpings of all three! We then had Plum Pudding, Mince-pies, Trifle and every kind of dessert. During the afternoon we ate chocolates solidly. We neither felt, nor were, sick! How lovely to be eleven years old and greedy!

What a day of delight from 'Stockings' in bed in the morning, Church and all the Christmas hymns, Christmas dinner, Presents, and the final Lighting of the Christmas Tree!

And how deep my gratitude to the kind and hospitable hostess who must have worked so hard to make Christmas Day a wonderful memory to me still in my old age.

So let me dedicate this book to the memory of Abney Hall – its kindness and its hospitality.

And a happy Christmas to all who read this book.

Agatha Christie

The Adventure of the
Christmas Pudding

I

'I regret exceedingly –' said M. Hercule Poirot.

He was interrupted. Not rudely interrupted. The interruption was suave, dexterous, persuasive rather than contradictory.

'Please don't refuse offhand, M. Poirot. There are grave issues of State. Your co-operation will be appreciated in the highest quarters.'

'You are too kind,' Hercule Poirot waved a hand, 'but I really cannot undertake to do as you ask. At this season of the year –'

Again Mr Jesmond interrupted. 'Christmas time,' he said, persuasively. 'An old-fashioned Christmas in the English countryside.'

Hercule Poirot shivered. The thought of the English countryside at this season of the year did not attract him.

'A good old-fashioned Christmas!' Mr Jesmond stressed it.

'Me – I am not an Englishman,' said Hercule Poirot. 'In my country, Christmas, it is for the children. The New Year, that is what we celebrate.'

'Ah,' said Mr Jesmond, 'but Christmas in England is a great institution and I assure you at Kings Lacey you would see it at its best. It's a wonderful old house, you know. Why, one wing of it dates from the fourteenth century.'

Again Poirot shivered. The thought of a fourteenth-century English manor house filled him with apprehension. He had suffered too often in the historic country houses of England. He looked round appreciatively at his comfortable modern flat with its radiators and the latest patent devices for excluding any kind of draught.

'In the winter,' he said firmly, 'I do not leave London.'

'I don't think you quite appreciate, M. Poirot, what a very serious matter this is.' Mr Jesmond glanced at his companion and then back at Poirot.

Poirot's second visitor had up to now said nothing but a polite and formal 'How do you do.' He sat now, gazing down at his well-polished shoes, with an air of the utmost dejection on his coffee-coloured face. He was a young man, not more than twenty-three, and he was clearly in a state of complete misery.

'Yes, yes,' said Hercule Poirot. 'Of course the matter

12

is serious. I do appreciate that. His Highness has my heartfelt sympathy.'

'The position is one of the utmost delicacy,' said Mr Jesmond.

Poirot transferred his gaze from the young man to his older companion. If one wanted to sum up Mr Jesmond in a word, the word would have been discretion. Everything about Mr Jesmond was discreet. His well-cut but inconspicuous clothes, his pleasant, well-bred voice which rarely soared out of an agreeable monotone, his light-brown hair just thinning a little at the temples, his pale serious face. It seemed to Hercule Poirot that he had known not one Mr Jesmond but a dozen Mr Jesmonds in his time, all using sooner or later the same phrase – 'a position of the utmost delicacy'.

'The police,' said Hercule Poirot, 'can be very discreet, you know.'

Mr Jesmond shook his head firmly.

'Not the police,' he said. 'To recover the – er – what we want to recover will almost inevitably invoke taking proceedings in the law courts and we know so little. We *suspect*, but we do not *know*.'

'You have my sympathy,' said Hercule Poirot again.

If he imagined that his sympathy was going to mean anything to his two visitors, he was wrong. They did not want sympathy, they wanted practical help. Mr

13

Jesmond began once more to talk about the delights of an English Christmas.

'It's dying out, you know,' he said, 'the real old-fashioned type of Christmas. People spend it at hotels nowadays. But an English Christmas with all the family gathered round, the children and their stockings, the Christmas tree, the turkey and plum pudding, the crackers. The snowman outside the window –'

In the interests of exactitude, Hercule Poirot intervened.

'To make a snowman one has to have the snow,' he remarked severely. 'And one cannot have snow to order, even for an English Christmas.'

'I was talking to a friend of mine in the meteorological office only today,' said Mr Jesmond, 'and he tells me that it is highly probable there *will* be snow this Christmas.'

It was the wrong thing to have said. Hercule Poirot shuddered more forcefully than ever.

'Snow in the country!' he said. 'That would be still more abominable. A large, cold, stone manor house.'

'Not at all,' said Mr Jesmond. 'Things have changed very much in the last ten years or so. Oil-fired central heating.'

'They have oil-fired central heating at Kings Lacey?' asked Poirot. For the first time he seemed to waver.

Mr Jesmond seized his opportunity. 'Yes, indeed,'

he said, 'and a splendid hot water system. Radiators in every bedroom. I assure you, my dear M. Poirot, Kings Lacey is comfort itself in the winter time. You might even find the house *too* warm.'

'That is most unlikely,' said Hercule Poirot.

With practised dexterity Mr Jesmond shifted his ground a little.

'You can appreciate the terrible dilemma we are in,' he said, in a confidential manner.

Hercule Poirot nodded. The problem was, indeed, not a happy one. A young potentate-to-be, the only son of the ruler of a rich and important native State, had arrived in London a few weeks ago. His country had been passing through a period of restlessness and discontent. Though loyal to the father whose way of life had remained persistently Eastern, popular opinion was somewhat dubious of the younger generation. His follies had been Western ones and as such looked upon with disapproval.

Recently, however, his betrothal had been announced. He was to marry a cousin of the same blood, a young woman who, though educated at Cambridge, was careful to display no Western influence in her own country. The wedding day was announced and the young prince had made a journey to England, bringing with him some of the famous jewels of his house to be reset in appropriate modern settings by Cartier. These had included a very famous ruby which had been removed from its cumbersome old-fashioned necklace and had been given a new look by the famous jewellers. So far so good, but after this came the snag. It was not to be supposed that a young man possessed of much wealth and convivial tastes, should not commit a few follies of the pleasanter type. As to that there would have been no censure. Young princes were supposed to amuse themselves in this fashion. For the prince to take the girl friend of the moment for a walk down Bond Street and bestow upon her an emerald bracelet or a diamond clip as a reward for the pleasure she had afforded him would have been regarded as quite natural and suitable, corresponding in fact to the Cadillac cars which his father invariably presented to his favourite dancing girl of the moment.

But the prince had been far more indiscreet than that. Flattered by the lady's interest, he had displayed to her the famous ruby in its new setting, and had finally been so unwise as to accede to her request to be allowed to wear it – just for one evening!

The sequel was short and sad. The lady had retired from their supper table to powder her nose. Time passed. She did not return. She had left the establishment by another door and since then had disappeared into space. The important and distressing thing was that the ruby in its new setting had disappeared with her.

These were the facts that could not possibly be made public without the most dire consequences. The ruby was something more than a ruby, it was a historical possession of great significance, and the circumstances of its disappearance were such that any undue publicity about them might result in the most serious political consequences.

Mr Jesmond was not the man to put these facts into simple language. He wrapped them up, as it were, in a great deal of verbiage. Who exactly Mr Jesmond was, Hercule Poirot did not know. He had met other Mr Jesmonds in the course of his career. Whether he was connected with the Home Office, the Foreign Secretary or some other discreet branch of public service was not specified. He was acting in the interests of the Commonwealth. The ruby must be recovered.

M. Poirot, so Mr Jesmond delicately insisted, was the man to recover it.

'Perhaps – yes,' Hercule Poirot admitted, 'but you can tell me so little. Suggestion – suspicion – all that is not very much to go upon.'

'Come now, Monsieur Poirot, surely it is not beyond your powers. Ah, come now.'

'I do not always succeed.'

But this was mock modesty. It was clear enough from Poirot's tone that for him to undertake a mission was almost synonymous with succeeding in it.

'His Highness is very young,' Mr Jesmond said. 'It will be sad if his whole life is to be blighted for a mere youthful indiscretion.'

Poirot looked kindly at the downcast young man. 'It is the time for follies, when one is young,' he said encouragingly, 'and for the ordinary young man it does not matter so much. The good papa, he pays up; the family lawyer, he helps to disentangle the inconvenience; the young man, he learns by experience and all ends for the best. In a position such as yours, it is hard indeed. Your approaching marriage –'

'That is it. That is it exactly.' For the first time words poured from the young man. 'You see she is very, very serious. She takes life very seriously. She has acquired at Cambridge many very serious ideas. There is to be education in my country. There are to be schools. There are to be many things. All in the name of progress, you understand, of democracy. It will not be, she says, like it was in my father's time. Naturally she knows that I will have diversions in London, but not the scandal. No! It is the scandal that matters. You see it is very, very famous, this ruby. There is a long trail behind it, a history. Much bloodshed – many deaths!'

'Deaths,' said Hercule Poirot thoughtfully. He looked at Mr Jesmond. 'One hopes,' he said, 'it will not come to that?'

Mr Jesmond made a peculiar noise rather like a

hen who has decided to lay an egg and then thought better of it.

'No, no indeed,' he said, sounding rather prim. 'There is no question, I am sure, of anything of *that* kind.'

'You cannot be sure,' said Hercule Poirot. 'Whoever has the ruby now, there may be others who want to gain possession of it, and who will not stick at a trifle, my friend.'

'I really don't think,' said Mr Jesmond, sounding more prim than ever, 'that we need enter into speculation of that kind. Quite unprofitable.'

'Me,' said Hercule Poirot, suddenly becoming very foreign, 'me, I explore all the avenues, like the politicians.'

Mr Jesmond looked at him doubtfully. Pulling himself together, he said, 'Well, I can take it that is settled, M. Poirot? You will go to Kings Lacey?'

'And how do I explain myself there?' asked Hercule Poirot.

Mr Jesmond smiled with confidence.

'That, I think, can be arranged very easily,' he said. 'I can assure you that it will all seem quite natural. You will find the Laceys most charming. Delightful people.'

'And you do not deceive me about the oil-fired central heating?'

Agatha Christie

'No, no, indeed.' Mr Jesmond sounded quite pained. 'I assure you you will find every comfort.'

'*Tout confort moderne*,' murmured Poirot to himself, reminiscently. '*Eh bien*,' he said, 'I accept.'

II

The temperature in the long drawing-room at Kings Lacey was a comfortable sixty-eight as Hercule Poirot sat talking to Mrs Lacey by one of the big mullioned windows. Mrs Lacey was engaged in needlework. She was not doing *petit point* or embroidered flowers upon silk. Instead, she appeared to be engaged in the prosaic task of hemming dishcloths. As she sewed she talked in a soft reflective voice that Poirot found very charming.

'I hope you will enjoy our Christmas party here, M. Poirot. It's only the family, you know. My granddaughter and a grandson and a friend of his and Bridget who's my great niece, and Diana who's a cousin and David Welwyn who is a very old friend. Just a family party. But Edwina Morecombe said that that's what you really wanted to see. An old-fashioned Christmas. Nothing could be more old-fashioned than we are! My husband, you know, absolutely lives in the past. He likes everything to be just as it was when he was a boy of twelve years old, and used to come here for his holidays.' She smiled to herself. 'All the same old things, the Christmas tree and the stockings hung up and the oyster soup and the turkey – two turkeys, one boiled and one roast – and the plum pudding with the ring and the bachelor's button and all the rest of it in it. We can't have sixpences nowadays because they're not pure silver any more. But all the old desserts, the Elvas plums and Carlsbad plums and almonds and raisins, and crystallized fruit and ginger. Dear me, I sound like a catalogue from Fortnum and Mason!'

'You arouse my gastronomic juices, Madame.'

'I expect we'll all have frightful indigestion by tomorrow evening,' said Mrs Lacey. 'One isn't used to eating so much nowadays, is one?'

She was interrupted by some loud shouts and whoops of laughter outside the window. She glanced out.

'I don't know what they're doing out there. Playing some game or other, I suppose. I've always been so afraid, you know, that these young people would be bored by our Christmas here. But not at all, it's just the opposite. Now my own son and daughter and their friends, they used to be rather sophisticated about Christmas. Say it was all nonsense and too much fuss and it would be far better to go out to a hotel somewhere and dance. But the younger generation seem to find all this terribly attractive. Besides,' added Mrs Lacey practically, 'schoolboys and schoolgirls are always hungry, aren't they? I think they must starve them at these schools. After all, one does know children of that age each eat about as much as three strong men.'

Poirot laughed and said, 'It is most kind of you and your husband, Madame, to include me in this way in your family party.'

'Oh, we're both delighted, I'm sure,' said Mrs Lacey. 'And if you find Horace a little gruff,' she continued, 'pay no attention. It's just his manner, you know.'

What her husband, Colonel Lacey, had actually said was: 'Can't think why you want one of these damned foreigners here cluttering up Christmas? Why can't we have him some other time? Can't stick foreigners! All right, all right, so Edwina Morecombe wished him on us. What's it got to do with *her*, I should like to know? Why doesn't *she* have him for Christmas?'

'Because you know very well,' Mrs Lacey had said, 'that Edwina always goes to Claridge's.'

Her husband had looked at her piercingly and said, 'Not up to something, are you, Em?'

'Up to something?' said Em, opening very blue eyes. 'Of course not. Why should I be?'

Old Colonel Lacey laughed, a deep, rumbling laugh. 'I wouldn't put it past you, Em,' he said. 'When you look your most innocent is when you *are* up to something.'

Revolving these things in her mind, Mrs Lacey went on: 'Edwina said she thought perhaps you might help us . . . I'm sure I don't know quite how, but she said that friends of yours had once found you very helpful in – in a case something like ours. I – well, perhaps you don't know what I'm talking about?'

Poirot looked at her encouragingly. Mrs Lacey was close on seventy, as upright as a ramrod, with snow-white hair, pink cheeks, blue eyes, a ridiculous nose and a determined chin.

'If there is anything I can do I shall only be too happy to do it,' said Poirot. 'It is, I understand, a rather unfortunate matter of a young girl's infatuation.'

Mrs Lacey nodded. 'Yes. It seems extraordinary that I should – well, want to talk to you about it. After all, you *are* a perfect stranger . . .'

'*And* a foreigner,' said Poirot, in an understanding manner.

'Yes,' said Mrs Lacey, 'but perhaps that makes it easier, in a way. Anyhow, Edwina seemed to think that you might perhaps know something – how shall I put it – something useful about this young Desmond Lee-Wortley.'

Poirot paused a moment to admire the ingenuity of Mr Jesmond and the ease with which he had

23

made use of Lady Morecombe to further his own purposes.

'He has not, I understand, a very good reputation, this young man?' he began delicately.

'No, indeed, he hasn't! A very bad reputation! But that's no help so far as Sarah is concerned. It's never any good, is it, telling young girls that men have a bad reputation? It – it just spurs them on!'

'You are so very right,' said Poirot.

'In my young day,' went on Mrs Lacey. ('Oh dear, that's a very long time ago!') We used to be warned, you know, against certain young men, and of course it *did* heighten one's interest in them, and if one could possibly manage to dance with them, or to be alone with them in a dark conservatory –' She laughed. 'That's why I wouldn't let Horace do any of the things he wanted to do.'

'Tell me,' said Poirot, 'exactly what is it that troubles you?'

'Our son was killed in the war,' said Mrs Lacey. 'My daughter-in-law died when Sarah was born so that she has always been with us, and we've brought her up. Perhaps we've brought her up unwisely – I don't know. But we thought we ought always to leave her as free as possible.'

'That is desirable, I think,' said Poirot. 'One cannot go against the spirit of the times.'

'No,' said Mrs Lacey, 'that's just what I felt about it. And, of course, girls nowadays do these sort of things.'

Poirot looked at her inquiringly.

'I think the way one expresses it,' said Mrs Lacey, 'is that Sarah has got in with what they call the coffee-bar set. She won't go to dances or come out properly or be a deb or anything of that kind. Instead she has two rather unpleasant rooms in Chelsea down by the river and wears these funny clothes that they like to wear, and black stockings or bright green ones. Very thick stockings. (So prickly, I always think!) And she goes about without washing or combing her hair.'

'*Ça, c'est tout à fait naturelle*,' said Poirot. 'It is the fashion of the moment. They grow out of it.'

'Yes, I know,' said Mrs Lacey. 'I wouldn't worry about *that* sort of thing. But you see she's taken up with this Desmond Lee-Wortley and he really has a *very* unsavoury reputation. He lives more or less on well-to-do girls. They seem to go quite mad about him. He very nearly married the Hope girl, but her people got her made a ward in court or something. And of course that's what Horace wants to do. He says he must do it for her protection. But I don't think it's really a good idea, M. Poirot. I mean, they'll just run away together and go to Scotland or Ireland or the Argentine or somewhere and either get married or else live together without getting married. And although it may be contempt of court and all that – well, it isn't really an answer, is it, in the end? Especially if a baby's coming. One has to give in then, and let them get married. And then, nearly always, it seems to me, after a year or two there's a divorce. And then the girl comes home and usually after a year or two she marries someone so nice he's almost dull and settles down. But it's particularly sad, it seems to me, if there is a child, because it's not the same thing, being brought up by a stepfather, however nice. No, I think it's much better if we did as we did in my young days. I mean the first young man one fell in love with was *always* someone undesirable. I remember I had a horrible passion for a young man called – now what was his name now? – how strange it is, I can't remember his Christian name at all! Tibbitt, that was his surname. Young Tibbitt. Of course, my father more or less forbade him the house, but he used to get asked to the same dances, and we used to dance together. And sometimes we'd escape and sit out together and occasionally friends would arrange picnics to which we both went. Of course, it was all very exciting and forbidden and one enjoyed it enormously. But one didn't go to the – well, to the *lengths* that girls go nowadays. And so, after a while, the Mr Tibbitts faded out. And do you know, when I saw him four years later I was surprised what

I could *ever* have seen in him! He seemed to be such a *dull* young man. Flashy, you know. No interesting conversation.'

'One always thinks the days of one's own youth are best,' said Poirot, somewhat sententiously.

'I know,' said Mrs Lacey. 'It's tiresome, isn't it? I mustn't be tiresome. But all the same I *don't* want Sarah, who's a dear girl really, to marry Desmond Lee-Wortley. She and David Welwyn, who is staying here, were always such friends and so fond of each other, and we did hope, Horace and I, that they would grow up and marry. But of course she just finds him dull now, and she's absolutely infatuated with Desmond.'

'I do not quite understand, Madame,' said Poirot. 'You have him here now, staying in the house, this Desmond Lee-Wortley?'

'That's *my* doing,' said Mrs Lacey. 'Horace was all for forbidding her to see him and all that. Of course, in Horace's day, the father or guardian would have called round at the young man's lodgings with a horse whip! Horace was all for forbidding the fellow the house, and forbidding the girl to see him. I told him that was quite the wrong attitude to take. "No," I said. "Ask him down here. We'll have him down for Christmas with the family party." Of course, my husband said I was mad! But I said, "At any rate, dear, let's *try* it. Let

her see him in *our* atmosphere and *our* house and we'll
be very nice to him and very polite, and perhaps then
he'll seem less interesting to her"!'

'I think, as they say, you *have* something there,
Madame,' said Poirot. 'I think your point of view is
very wise. Wiser than your husband's.'

'Well, I hope it is,' said Mrs Lacey doubtfully. 'It
doesn't seem to be working much yet. But of course
he's only been here a couple of days.' A sudden dimple
showed in her wrinkled cheek. 'I'll confess something
to you, M. Poirot. I myself can't help liking him. I
don't mean I *really* like him, with my *mind*, but I can
feel the charm all right. Oh yes, I can see what Sarah
sees in him. But I'm an old enough woman and have
enough experience to know that he's absolutely no
good. Even if I *do* enjoy his company. Though I do
think,' added Mrs Lacey, rather wistfully, 'he has *some*
good points. He asked if he might bring his sister here,
you know. She's had an operation and was in hospital.
He said it was so sad for her being in a nursing home
over Christmas and he wondered if it would be too
much trouble if he could bring her with him. He said
he'd take all her meals up to her and all that. Well now,
I do think that *was* rather nice of him, don't you, M.
Poirot?'

'It shows a consideration,' said Poirot, thoughtfully,
'which seems almost out of character.'

'Oh, I don't know. You can have family affections at the same time as wishing to prey on a rich young girl. Sarah will be *very* rich, you know, not only with what we leave her – and of course that won't be very much because most of the money goes with the place to Colin, my grandson. But her mother was a very rich woman and Sarah will inherit all her money when she's twenty-one. She's only twenty now. No, I do think it was nice of Desmond to mind about his sister. And he didn't pretend she was anything very wonderful or that. She's a shorthand typist, I gather – does secretarial work in London. And he's been as good as his word and does carry up trays to her. Not all the time, of course, but quite often. So I think he has some nice points. But all the same,' said Mrs Lacey with great decision, 'I don't want Sarah to marry him.'

'From all I have heard and been told,' said Poirot, 'that would indeed be a disaster.'

'Do you think it would be possible for you to help us in any way?' asked Mrs Lacey.

'I think it is possible, yes,' said Hercule Poirot, 'but I do not wish to promise too much. For the Mr Desmond Lee-Wortleys of this world are clever, Madame. But do not despair. One can, perhaps, do a little something. I shall at any rate put forth my best endeavours, if only in gratitude for your kindness in asking me here for this Christmas festivity.' He looked round him. 'And it cannot be so easy these days to have Christmas festivities.'

'No, indeed,' Mrs Lacey sighed. She leaned forward. 'Do you know, M. Poirot, what I really dream of – what I would love to have?'

'But tell me, Madame.'

'I simply long to have a small, modern bungalow. No, perhaps not a bungalow exactly, but a small, modern, easy to run house built somewhere in the park here, and live in it with an absolute up-to-date kitchen and no long passages. Everything easy and simple.'

'It is a very practical idea, Madame.'

'It's not practical for me,' said Mrs Lacey. 'My husband *adores* this place. He *loves* living here. He doesn't mind being slightly uncomfortable, he doesn't mind the inconveniences and he would hate, simply *hate*, to live in a small modern house in the park!'

'So you sacrifice yourself to his wishes?'

Mrs Lacey drew herself up. 'I do not consider it a sacrifice, M. Poirot,' she said. 'I married my husband with the wish to make him happy. He has been a good husband to me and made me very happy all these years, and I wish to give happiness to him.'

'So you will continue to live here,' said Poirot.

'It's not really too uncomfortable,' said Mrs Lacey.

'No, no,' said Poirot, hastily. 'On the contrary, it is most comfortable. Your central heating and your bath water are perfection.'

'We spent a lot of money on making the house comfortable to live in,' said Mrs Lacey. 'We were able to sell some land. Ripe for development, I think they call it. Fortunately right out of sight of the house on the other side of the park. Really rather an ugly bit of ground with no nice view, but we got a very good price for it. So that we have been able to have as many improvements as possible.'

'But the service, Madame?'

'Oh, well, that presents less difficulty than you might think. Of course, one cannot expect to be looked after and waited upon as one used to be. Different people come in from the village. Two women in the morning, another two to cook lunch and wash it up, and different ones again in the evening. There are plenty of people who want to come and work for a few hours a day. Of course for Christmas we are very lucky. My dear Mrs Ross always comes in every Christmas. She is a wonderful cook, really first-class. She retired about ten years ago, but she comes in to help us in any emergency. Then there is dear Peverell.'

'Your butler?'

'Yes. He is pensioned off and lives in the little house

31

near the lodge, but he is so devoted, and he insists on coming to wait on us at Christmas. Really, I'm terrified, M. Poirot, because he's so old and so shaky that I feel certain that if he carries anything heavy he will drop it. It's really an agony to watch him. And his heart is not good and I'm afraid of his doing too much. But it would hurt his feelings dreadfully if I did not let him come. He hems and hahs and makes disapproving noises when he sees the state our silver is in and within three days of being here, it is all wonderful again. Yes. He is a dear faithful friend.' She smiled at Poirot. 'So you see, we are all set for a happy Christmas. A white Christmas, too,' she added as she looked out of the window. 'See? It is beginning to snow. Ah, the children are coming in. You must meet them, M. Poirot.'

Poirot was introduced with due ceremony. First, to Colin and Michael, the schoolboy grandson and his friend, nice polite lads of fifteen, one dark, one fair. Then to their cousin, Bridget, a black-haired girl of about the same age with enormous vitality.

'And this is my granddaughter, Sarah,' said Mrs Lacey.

Poirot looked with some interest at Sarah, an attractive girl with a mop of red hair; her manner seemed to him nervy and a trifle defiant, but she showed real affection for her grandmother.

'And this is Mr Lee-Wortley.'

Mr Lee-Wortley wore a fisherman's jersey and tight black jeans; his hair was rather long and it seemed doubtful whether he had shaved that morning. In contrast to him was a young man introduced as David Welwyn, who was solid and quiet, with a pleasant smile, and rather obviously addicted to soap and water. There was one other member of the party, a handsome, rather intense-looking girl who was introduced as Diana Middleton.

Tea was brought in. A hearty meal of scones, crumpets, sandwiches and three kinds of cake. The younger members of the party appreciated the tea. Colonel Lacey came in last, remarking in a non-committal voice:

'Hey, tea? Oh yes, tea.'

He received his cup of tea from his wife's hand, helped himself to two scones, cast a look of aversion at Desmond Lee-Wortley and sat down as far away from him as he could. He was a big man with bushy eyebrows and a red, weather-beaten face. He might have been taken for a farmer rather than the lord of the manor.

'Started to snow,' he said. 'It's going to be a white Christmas all right.'

After tea the party dispersed.

'I expect they'll go and play with their tape recorders

33

now,' said Mrs Lacey to Poirot. She looked indulgently after her grandson as he left the room. Her tone was that of one who says 'The children are going to play with their toy soldiers.'

'They're frightfully technical, of course,' she said, 'and very grand about it all.'

The boys and Bridget, however, decided to go along to the lake and see if the ice on it was likely to make skating possible.

'*I* thought we could have skated on it this morning,' said Colin. 'But old Hodgkins said no. He's always so terribly careful.'

'Come for a walk, David,' said Diana Middleton, softly.

David hesitated for half a moment, his eyes on Sarah's red head. She was standing by Desmond Lee-Wortley, her hand on his arm, looking up into his face.

'All right,' said David Welwyn, 'yes, let's.'

Diana slipped a quick hand through his arm and they turned towards the door into the garden. Sarah said:

'Shall we go, too, Desmond? It's fearfully stuffy in the house.'

'Who wants to walk?' said Desmond. 'I'll get my car out. We'll go along to the Speckled Boar and have a drink.'

Sarah hesitated for a moment before saying:

'Let's go to Market Ledbury to the White Hart. It's much more fun.'

Though for all the world she would not have put it into words, Sarah had an instinctive revulsion from going down to the local pub with Desmond. It was, somehow, not in the tradition of Kings Lacey. The women of Kings Lacey had never frequented the bar of the Speckled Boar. She had an obscure feeling that to go there would be to let old Colonel Lacey and his wife down. And why not? Desmond Lee-Wortley would have said. For a moment of exasperation Sarah felt that he ought to know why not! One didn't upset such old darlings as Grandfather and dear old Em unless it was necessary. They'd been very sweet, really, letting her lead her own life, not understanding in the least why she wanted to live in Chelsea in the way she did, but accepting it. That was due to Em of course. Grandfather would have kicked up no end of a row.

Sarah had no illusions about her grandfather's attitude. It was not his doing that Desmond had been asked to stay at Kings Lacey. That was Em, and Em was a darling and always had been.

When Desmond had gone to fetch his car, Sarah popped her head into the drawing-room again.

'We're going over to Market Ledbury,' she said.

'We thought we'd have a drink there at the White Hart.'

There was a slight amount of defiance in her voice, but Mrs Lacey did not seem to notice it.

'Well, dear,' she said. 'I'm sure that will be very nice. David and Diana have gone for a walk, I see. I'm so glad. I really think it was a brainwave on my part to ask Diana here. So sad being left a widow so young – only twenty-two – I do hope she marries again *soon*.'

Sarah looked at her sharply. 'What are you up to, Em?'

'It's my little plan,' said Mrs Lacey gleefully. 'I think she's just right for David. Of course I know he was terribly in love with *you*, Sarah dear, but you'd no use for him and I realize that he isn't your type. But I don't want him to go on being unhappy, and I think Diana will really suit him.'

'What a matchmaker you are, Em,' said Sarah.

'I know,' said Mrs Lacey. 'Old women always are. Diana's quite keen on him already, I think. Don't you think she'd be just right for him?'

'I shouldn't say so,' said Sarah. 'I think Diana's far too – well, too intense, too serious. I should think David would find it terribly boring being married to her.'

'Well, we'll see,' said Mrs Lacey. 'Anyway, *you* don't want him, do you, dear?'

'No, indeed,' said Sarah, very quickly. She added, in a sudden rush, 'You *do* like Desmond, don't you, Em?'

'I'm sure he's very nice indeed,' said Mrs Lacey.

'Grandfather doesn't like him,' said Sarah.

'Well, you could hardly expect him to, could you?' said Mrs Lacey reasonably, 'but I dare say he'll come round when he gets used to the idea. You mustn't rush him, Sarah dear. Old people are very slow to change their minds and your grandfather *is* rather obstinate.'

'I don't care what Grandfather thinks or says,' said Sarah. 'I shall get married to Desmond whenever I like!'

'I know, dear, I know. But do try and be realistic about it. Your grandfather could cause a lot of trouble, you know. You're not of age yet. In another year you can do as you please. I expect Horace will have come round long before that.'

'You're on my side aren't you, darling?' said Sarah. She flung her arms round her grandmother's neck and gave her an affectionate kiss.

'I want you to be happy,' said Mrs Lacey. 'Ah! there's your young man bringing his car round. You know, I like these very tight trousers these young men wear nowadays. They look so smart – only, of course, it does accentuate knock knees.'

Yes, Sarah thought, Desmond *had* got knock knees, she had never noticed it before . . .

'Go on, dear, enjoy yourself,' said Mrs Lacey.

She watched her go out to the car, then, remembering her foreign guest, she went along to the library. Looking in, however, she saw that Hercule Poirot was taking a pleasant little nap and, smiling to herself, she went across the hall and out into the kitchen to have a conference with Mrs Ross.

'Come on, beautiful,' said Desmond. 'Your family cutting up rough because you're coming out to a pub? Years behind the times here, aren't they?'

'Of course they're not making a fuss,' said Sarah, sharply as she got into the car.

'What's the idea of having that foreign fellow down? He's a detective, isn't he? What needs detecting here?'

'Oh, he's not here professionally,' said Sarah. 'Edwina Morecombe, my grandmother, asked us to have him. I think he's retired from professional work long ago.'

'Sounds like a broken-down old cab horse,' said Desmond.

'He wanted to see an old-fashioned English Christmas, I believe,' said Sarah vaguely.

Desmond laughed scornfully. 'Such a lot of tripe, that sort of thing,' he said. 'How you can stand it I don't know.'

Sarah's red hair was tossed back and her aggressive chin shot up.

'I enjoy it!' she said defiantly.

'You can't, baby. Let's cut the whole thing tomorrow. Go over to Scarborough or somewhere.'

'I couldn't possibly do that.'

'Why not?'

'Oh, it would hurt their feelings.'

'Oh, bilge! You know you don't enjoy this childish sentimental bosh.'

'Well, not really perhaps, but –' Sarah broke off. She realized with a feeling of guilt that she was looking forward a good deal to the Christmas celebration. She enjoyed the whole thing, but she was ashamed to admit that to Desmond. It was not the thing to enjoy Christmas and family life. Just for a moment she wished that Desmond had not come down here at Christmas time. In fact, she almost wished that Desmond had not come down here at all. It was much more fun seeing Desmond in London than here at home.

In the meantime the boys and Bridget were walking back from the lake, still discussing earnestly the problems of skating. Flecks of snow had been falling, and looking up at the sky it could be prophesied that before long there was going to be a heavy snowfall.

'It's going to snow all night,' said Colin. 'Bet you by Christmas morning we have a couple of feet of snow.'

The prospect was a pleasurable one.

Agatha Christie

'Let's make a snowman,' said Michael.

'Good lord,' said Colin, 'I haven't made a snowman since – well, since I was about four years old.'

'I don't believe it's a bit easy to do,' said Bridget. 'I mean, you have to know how.'

'We might make an effigy of M. Poirot,' said Colin. 'Give it a big black moustache. There is one in the dressing-up box.'

'I don't see, you know,' said Michael thoughtfully, 'how M. Poirot could ever have been a detective. I don't see how he'd ever be able to disguise himself.'

'I know,' said Bridget, 'and one can't imagine him running about with a microscope and looking for clues or measuring footprints.'

'I've got an idea,' said Colin. 'Let's put on a show for him!'

'What do you mean, a show?' asked Bridget.

'Well, arrange a murder for him.'

'What a gorgeous idea,' said Bridget. 'Do you mean a body in the snow – that sort of thing?'

'Yes. It would make him feel at home, wouldn't it?'

Bridget giggled.

'I don't know that I'd go as far as that.'

'If it snows,' said Colin, 'we'll have the perfect setting. A body and footprints – we'll have to think that out rather carefully and pinch one of Grandfather's daggers and make some blood.'

They came to a halt and, oblivious to the rapidly falling snow, entered into an excited discussion.

'There's a paintbox in the old schoolroom. We could mix up some blood – crimson-lake, I should think.'

'Crimson-lake's a bit too pink, *I* think,' said Bridget. 'It ought to be a bit browner.'

'Who's going to be the body?' asked Michael.

'I'll be the body,' said Bridget quickly.

'Oh, look here,' said Colin, '*I* thought of it.'

'Oh, no, no,' said Bridget, 'it must be me. It's got to be a girl. It's more exciting. Beautiful girl lying lifeless in the snow.'

'Beautiful girl! Ah-ha,' said Michael in derision.

'I've got black hair, too,' said Bridget.

'What's that got to do with it?'

'Well, it'll show up so well on the snow and I shall wear my red pyjamas.'

'If you wear red pyjamas, they won't show the bloodstains,' said Michael in a practical manner.

'But they'd look so effective against the snow,' said Bridget, 'and they've got white facings, you know, so the blood could be on that. Oh, won't it be gorgeous? Do you think he will really be taken in?'

'He will if we do it well enough,' said Michael. 'We'll have just your footprints in the snow and one other person's going to the body and coming away from it –

a man's, of course. He won't want to disturb them, so he won't know that you're not really dead. You don't think,' Michael stopped, struck by a sudden idea. The others looked at him. 'You don't think he'll be *annoyed* about it?'

'Oh, I shouldn't think so,' said Bridget, with facile optimism. 'I'm sure he'll understand that we've just done it to entertain him. A sort of Christmas treat.'

'I don't think we ought to do it on Christmas Day,' said Colin reflectively. 'I don't think Grandfather would like that very much.'

'Boxing Day then,' said Bridget.

'Boxing Day would be just right,' said Michael.

'And it'll give us more time, too,' pursued Bridget. 'After all, there are a lot of things to arrange. Let's go and have a look at all the props.'

They hurried into the house.

III

The evening was a busy one. Holly and mistletoe had been brought in in large quantities and a Christmas tree had been set up at one end of the dining-room. Everyone helped to decorate it, to put up the branches of holly behind pictures and to hang mistletoe in a convenient position in the hall.

'I had no idea anything so archaic still went on,' murmured Desmond to Sarah with a sneer.

'We've always done it,' said Sarah, defensively.

'What a reason!'

'Oh, don't be tiresome, Desmond. *I* think it's fun.'

'Sarah my sweet, you *can't*!'

'Well, not – not really perhaps but – I do in a way.'

'Who's going to brave the snow and go to midnight mass?' asked Mrs Lacey at twenty minutes to twelve.

'Not me,' said Desmond. 'Come on, Sarah.'

With a hand on her arm he guided her into the library and went over to the record case.

'There are limits, darling,' said Desmond. 'Midnight mass!'

'Yes,' said Sarah. 'Oh yes.'

With a good deal of laughter, donning of coats and stamping of feet, most of the others got off. The two boys, Bridget, David and Diana set out for the ten minutes' walk to the church through the falling snow. Their laughter died away in the distance.

'Midnight mass!' said Colonel Lacey, snorting. 'Never went to midnight mass in my young days. *Mass*, indeed! Popish, that is! Oh, I beg your pardon, M. Poirot.'

Poirot waved a hand. 'It is quite all right. Do not mind me.'

43

'Matins is good enough for anybody, I should say,' said the colonel. 'Proper Sunday morning service. "Hark the herald angels sing," and all the good old Christmas hymns. And then back to Christmas dinner. That's right, isn't it, Em?'

'Yes, dear,' said Mrs Lacey. 'That's what *we* do. But the young ones enjoy the midnight service. And it's nice, really, that they *want* to go.'

'Sarah and that fellow don't want to go.'

'Well, there dear, I think you're wrong,' said Mrs Lacey. 'Sarah, you know, *did* want to go, but she didn't like to say so.'

'Beats me why she cares what that fellow's opinion is.'

'She's very young, really,' said Mrs Lacey placidly. 'Are you going to bed, M. Poirot? Good night. I hope you'll sleep well.'

'And you, Madame? Are you not going to bed yet?'

'Not just yet,' said Mrs Lacey. 'I've got the stockings to fill, you see. Oh, I know they're all practically grown up, but they do *like* their stockings. One puts jokes in them! Silly little things. But it all makes for a lot of fun.'

'You work very hard to make this a happy house at Christmas time,' said Poirot. 'I honour you.'

He raised her hand to his lips in a courtly fashion.

'Hm,' grunted Colonel Lacey, as Poirot departed. 'Flowery sort of fellow. Still – he appreciates you.'

Mrs Lacey dimpled up at him. 'Have you noticed, Horace, that I'm standing under the mistletoe?' she asked with the demureness of a girl of nineteen.

Hercule Poirot entered his bedroom. It was a large room well provided with radiators. As he went over towards the big four-poster bed he noticed an envelope lying on his pillow. He opened it and drew out a piece of paper. On it was a shakily printed message in capital letters.

DON'T EAT NONE OF THE PLUM PUDDING. ONE AS WISHES YOU WELL.

Hercule Poirot stared at it. His eyebrows rose. 'Cryptic,' he murmured, 'and most unexpected.'

IV

Christmas dinner took place at 2 p.m. and was a feast indeed. Enormous logs crackled merrily in the wide fireplace and above their crackling rose the babel of many tongues talking together. Oyster soup had been consumed, two enormous turkeys had come and gone, mere carcasses of their former selves. Now, the supreme moment, the Christmas pudding was brought in, in state! Old Peverell, his hands and his knees shaking with the weakness of eighty years, permitted no one but himself to bear it in. Mrs Lacey sat, her hands pressed together in nervous apprehension. One Christmas, she felt sure, Peverell would fall down dead. Having either to take the risk of letting him fall down dead or of hurting his feelings to such an extent that he would probably prefer to be dead than alive, she had so far chosen the former alternative. On a silver dish the Christmas pudding reposed in its glory. A large football of a pudding, a piece of holly stuck in it like a triumphant flag and glorious flames of blue and red rising round it. There was a cheer and cries of 'Ooh-ah.'

One thing Mrs Lacey had done: prevailed upon Peverell to place the pudding in front of her so that she could help it rather than hand it in turn round the table. She breathed a sigh of relief as it was deposited safely in front of her. Rapidly the plates were passed round, flames still licking the portions.

'Wish, M. Poirot,' cried Bridget. 'Wish before the flame goes. Quick, Gran darling, quick.'

Mrs Lacey leant back with a sigh of satisfaction. Operation Pudding had been a success. In front of everyone was a helping with flames still licking it. There was a momentary silence all round the table as everyone wished hard.

There was nobody to notice the rather curious expression on the face of M. Poirot as he surveyed the portion of pudding on his plate. '*Don't eat none of the plum pudding.*' What on earth did that sinister warning mean? There could be nothing different about his portion of plum pudding from that of everyone else! Sighing as he admitted himself baffled – and Hercule Poirot never liked to admit himself baffled – he picked up his spoon and fork.

'Hard sauce, M. Poirot?'

Poirot helped himself appreciatively to hard sauce.

'Swiped my best brandy again, eh Em?' said the colonel good-humouredly from the other end of the table. Mrs Lacey twinkled at him.

'Mrs Ross insists on having the best brandy, dear,' she said. 'She says it makes all the difference.'

'Well, well,' said Colonel Lacey, 'Christmas comes but once a year and Mrs Ross is a great woman. A great woman and a great cook.'

'She is indeed,' said Colin. 'Smashing plum pudding, this. Mmmm.' He filled an appreciative mouth.

Gently, almost gingerly, Hercule Poirot attacked his portion of pudding. He ate a mouthful. It was delicious! He ate another. Something tinkled faintly on his plate. He investigated with a fork. Bridget, on his left, came to his aid.

'You've got something, M. Poirot,' she said. 'I wonder what it is'

Poirot detached a little silver object from the surrounding raisins that clung to it.

'Oooh,' said Bridget, 'it's the bachelor's button! M. Poirot's got the bachelor's button!'

Hercule Poirot dipped the small silver button into the finger-glass of water that stood by his plate, and washed it clear of pudding crumbs.

'It is very pretty,' he observed.

'That means you're going to be a bachelor, M. Poirot,' explained Colin helpfully.

'That is to be expected,' said Poirot gravely. 'I have been a bachelor for many long years and it is unlikely that I shall change that status now.'

'Oh, never say die,' said Michael. 'I saw in the paper that someone of ninety-five married a girl of twenty-two the other day.'

'You encourage me,' said Hercule Poirot.

Colonel Lacey uttered a sudden exclamation. His face became purple and his hand went to his mouth.

'Confound it, Emmeline,' he roared, 'why on earth do you let the cook put glass in the pudding?'

'Glass!' cried Mrs Lacey, astonished.

Colonel Lacey withdrew the offending substance from his mouth. 'Might have broken a tooth,' he grumbled. 'Or swallowed the damn' thing and had appendicitis.'

He dropped the piece of glass into the finger-bowl, rinsed it and held it up.

'God bless my soul,' he ejaculated. 'It's a red stone out of one of the cracker brooches.' He held it aloft.

'You permit?'

Very deftly M. Poirot stretched across his neighbour, took it from Colonel Lacey's fingers and examined it attentively. As the squire had said, it was an enormous red stone the colour of a ruby. The light gleamed from its facets as he turned it about. Somewhere around the table a chair was pushed sharply back and then drawn in again.

'Phew!' cried Michael. 'How wizard it would be if it was *real*.'

'Perhaps it is real,' said Bridget hopefully.

'Oh, don't be an ass, Bridget. Why a ruby of that size would be worth thousands and thousands and thousands of pounds. Wouldn't it, M. Poirot?'

'It would indeed,' said Poirot.

'But what *I* can't understand,' said Mrs Lacey, 'is how it got into the pudding.'

'Oooh,' said Colin, diverted by his last mouthful, 'I've got the pig. It isn't fair.'

Bridget chanted immediately, 'Colin's got the pig! Colin's got the pig! Colin is the greedy guzzling *pig*!'

'I've got the ring,' said Diana in a clear, high voice.

'Good for you, Diana. You'll be married first, of us all.'

'I've got the thimble,' wailed Bridget.

'Bridget's going to be an old maid,' chanted the two boys. 'Yah, Bridget's going to be an old maid.'

'Who's got the money?' demanded David. 'There's a real ten-shilling piece, gold, in this pudding. I know. Mrs Ross told me so.'

'I think I'm the lucky one,' said Desmond Lee-Wortley.

Colonel Lacey's two next-door neighbours heard him mutter, 'Yes, you would be.'

'*I*'ve got a ring, too,' said David. He looked across at Diana. 'Quite a coincidence, isn't it?'

The laughter went on. Nobody noticed that M. Poirot carelessly, as though thinking of something else, had dropped the red stone into his pocket.

Mince-pies and Christmas dessert followed the pudding. The older members of the party then retired for a welcome siesta before the tea-time ceremony of the lighting of the Christmas tree. Hercule Poirot, however, did not take a siesta. Instead, he made his way to the enormous old-fashioned kitchen.

'It is permitted,' he asked, looking round and beaming, 'that I congratulate the cook on this marvellous meal that I have just eaten?'

There was a moment's pause and then Mrs Ross came forward in a stately manner to meet him. She was a large woman, nobly built with all the dignity of a stage duchess. Two lean grey-haired women were beyond in the scullery washing up and a tow-haired girl was moving to and fro between the scullery and the kitchen. But these were obviously mere myrmidons. Mrs Ross was the queen of the kitchen quarters.

'I am glad to hear you enjoyed it, sir,' she said graciously.

'Enjoyed it!' cried Hercule Poirot. With an extravagant foreign gesture he raised his hand to his lips, kissed it, and wafted the kiss to the ceiling. 'But you are a genius, Mrs Ross! A genius! *Never* have I tasted such a wonderful meal. The oyster soup –' he made an expressive noise with his lips '– and the stuffing. The chestnut stuffing in the turkey, that was quite unique in my experience.'

'Well, it's funny that you should say that, sir,' said Mrs Ross graciously. 'It's a very special recipe, that stuffing. It was given me by an Austrian chef that I worked with many years ago. But all the rest,' she added, 'is just good, plain English cooking.'

'And is there anything better?' demanded Hercule Poirot.

'Well, it's nice of you to say so, sir. Of course, you being a foreign gentleman might have preferred the continental style. Not but what I can't manage continental dishes too.'

'I am sure, Mrs Ross, you could manage anything!

Agatha Christie

But you must know that English cooking – *good* English cooking, not the cooking one gets in the second-class hotels or the restaurants – is much appreciated by *gourmets* on the continent, and I believe I am correct in saying that a special expedition was made to London in the early eighteen hundreds, and a report sent back to France of the wonders of the English puddings. "We have nothing like that in France," they wrote. "It is worth making a journey to London just to taste the varieties and excellencies of the English puddings." And above all puddings,' continued Poirot, well launched now on a kind of rhapsody, 'is the Christmas plum pudding, such as we have eaten today. That was a home-made pudding, was it not? Not a bought one?'

'Yes, indeed, sir. Of my own making and my own recipe such as I've made for many years. When I came here Mrs Lacey said that she'd ordered a pudding from a London store to save me the trouble. But no, Madam, I said, that may be kind of you but no bought pudding from a store can equal a home-made Christmas one. Mind you,' said Mrs Ross, warming to her subject like the artist she was, 'it was made too soon before the day. A good Christmas pudding should be made some weeks before and allowed to wait. The longer they're kept, within reason, the better they are. I mind now that when I was a child and we went to church every Sunday, we'd start listening for the collect that begins "Stir up O Lord we beseech thee" because that collect was the signal, as it were, that the puddings should be made that week. And so they always were. We had the collect on the Sunday, and that week sure enough my mother would make the Christmas puddings. And so it should have been here this year. As it was, that pudding was only made three days ago, the day before you arrived, sir. However, I kept to the old custom. Everyone in the house had to come out into the kitchen and have a stir and make a wish. That's an old custom, sir, and I've always held to it.'

'Most interesting,' said Hercule Poirot. 'Most interesting. And so everyone came out into the kitchen?'

'Yes, sir. The young gentlemen, Miss Bridget and the London gentleman who's staying here, and his sister and Mr David and Miss Diana – Mrs Middleton, I should say – All had a stir, they did.'

'How many puddings did you make? Is this the only one?'

'No, sir, I made four. Two large ones and two smaller ones. The other large one I planned to serve on New Year's Day and the smaller ones were for Colonel and Mrs Lacey when they're alone like and not so many in the family.'

'I see, I see,' said Poirot.

'As a matter of fact, sir,' said Mrs Ross, 'it was the wrong pudding you had for lunch today.'

'The wrong pudding?' Poirot frowned. 'How is that?'

'Well, sir, we have a big Christmas mould. A china mould with a pattern of holly and mistletoe on top and we always have the Christmas Day pudding boiled in that. But there was a most unfortunate accident. This morning, when Annie was getting it down from the shelf in the larder, she slipped and dropped it and it broke. Well, sir, naturally I couldn't serve that, could I? There might have been splinters in it. So we had to use the other one – the New Year's Day one, which was in a plain bowl. It makes a nice round but it's not so decorative as the Christmas mould. Really, where we'll get another mould like that I don't know. They don't make things in that size nowadays. All tiddly bits of things. Why, you can't even buy a breakfast dish that'll take a proper eight to ten eggs and bacon. Ah, things aren't what they were.'

'No, indeed,' said Poirot. 'But today that is not so. This Christmas Day has been like the Christmas Days of old, is that not true?'

Mrs Ross sighed. 'Well, I'm glad you say so, sir, but of course I haven't the *help* now that I used to have. Not skilled help, that is. The girls nowadays –'

she lowered her voice slightly, '– they mean very well and they're very willing but they've not been *trained*, sir, if you understand what I mean.'

'Times change, yes,' said Hercule Poirot. 'I too find it sad sometimes.'

'This house, sir,' said Mrs Ross, 'it's too large, you know, for the mistress and the colonel. The mistress, she knows that. Living in a corner of it as they do, it's not the same thing at all. It only comes alive, as you might say, at Christmas time when all the family come.'

'It is the first time, I think, that Mr Lee-Wortley and his sister have been here?'

'Yes, sir.' A note of slight reserve crept into Mrs Ross's voice. 'A very nice gentleman he is but, well – it seems a funny friend for Miss Sarah to have, according to our ideas. But there – London ways are different! It's sad that his sister's so poorly. Had an operation, she had. She seemed all right the first day she was here, but that very day, after we'd been stirring the puddings, she was took bad again and she's been in bed ever since. Got up too soon after her operation, I expect. Ah, doctors nowadays, they have you out of hospital before you can hardly stand on your feet. Why, my very own nephew's wife . . .' And Mrs Ross went into a long and spirited tale of hospital treatment as accorded to her relations, comparing it unfavourably with the consideration that had been lavished upon them in older times.

Poirot duly commiserated with her. 'It remains,' he said, 'to thank you for this exquisite and sumptuous meal. You permit a little acknowledgement of my appreciation?' A crisp five-pound note passed from his hand into that of Mrs Ross who said perfunctorily:

'You really shouldn't do *that*, sir.'

'I insist. I insist.'

'Well, it's very kind of you indeed, sir.' Mrs Ross accepted the tribute as no more than her due. 'And I wish you, sir, a very happy Christmas and a prosperous New Year.'

V

The end of Christmas Day was like the end of most Christmas Days. The tree was lighted, a splendid Christmas cake came in for tea, was greeted with approval but was partaken of only moderately. There was cold supper.

Both Poirot and his host and hostess went to bed early.

'Good night, M. Poirot,' said Mrs Lacey. 'I hope you've enjoyed yourself.'

'It has been a wonderful day, Madame, wonderful.'

'You're looking very thoughtful,' said Mrs Lacey.

'It is the English pudding that I consider.'

'You found it a little heavy, perhaps?' asked Mrs Lacey delicately.

'No, no, I do not speak gastronomically. I consider its significance.'

'It's traditional, of course,' said Mrs Lacey. 'Well, good night, M. Poirot, and don't dream too much of Christmas puddings and mince-pies.'

'Yes,' murmured Poirot to himself as he undressed. 'It is a problem certainly, that Christmas plum pudding. There is here something that I do not understand at all.' He shook his head in a vexed manner. 'Well – we shall see.'

After making certain preparations, Poirot went to bed, but not to sleep.

It was some two hours later that his patience was rewarded. The door of his bedroom opened very gently. He smiled to himself. It was as he had thought it would be. His mind went back fleetingly to the cup of coffee so politely handed him by Desmond Lee-Wortley. A little later, when Desmond's back was turned, he had laid the cup down for a few moments on a table. He had then apparently picked it up again and Desmond had had the satisfaction, if satisfaction it was, of seeing him drink the coffee to the last drop. But a little smile lifted Poirot's moustache as he reflected that it was not he but someone else who was sleeping a good sound sleep tonight. 'That pleasant young David,' said Poirot to himself, 'he is worried, unhappy. It will do him no harm to have a night's really sound sleep. And now, let us see what will happen?'

He lay quite still, breathing in an even manner with occasionally a suggestion, but the very faintest suggestion, of a snore.

Someone came up to the bed and bent over him. Then, satisfied, that someone turned away and went to the dressing-table. By the light of a tiny torch the visitor was examining Poirot's belongings neatly arranged on top of the dressing-table. Fingers explored the wallet, gently pulled open the drawers of the dressing-table, then extended the search to the pockets of Poirot's clothes. Finally the visitor approached the bed and with great caution slid his hand under the pillow. Withdrawing his hand, he stood for a moment or two as though uncertain what to do next. He walked round the room looking inside ornaments, went into the adjoining bathroom from whence he presently returned. Then, with a faint exclamation of disgust, he went out of the room.

'Ah,' said Poirot, under his breath. 'You have a

disappointment. Yes, yes, a serious disappointment. Bah! To imagine, even, that Hercule Poirot would hide something where you could find it!' Then, turning over on his other side, he went peacefully to sleep.

He was aroused next morning by an urgent soft tapping on his door.

'*Qui est là?* Come in, come in.'

The door opened. Breathless, red-faced, Colin stood upon the threshold. Behind him stood Michael.

'Monsieur Poirot, Monsieur Poirot.'

'But yes?' Poirot sat up in bed. 'It is the early tea? But no. It is you, Colin. What has occurred?'

Colin was, for a moment, speechless. He seemed to be under the grip of some strong emotion. In actual fact it was the sight of the nightcap that Hercule Poirot wore that affected for the moment his organs of speech. Presently he controlled himself and spoke.

'I think – M. Poirot, could you help us? Something rather awful has happened.'

'Something has happened? But what?'

'It's – it's Bridget. She's out there in the snow. I think – she doesn't move or speak and – oh, you'd better come and look for yourself. I'm terribly afraid – she may be *dead*.'

'What?' Poirot cast aside his bed covers. 'Mademoiselle Bridget – dead!'

'I think – I think somebody's killed her. There's – there's blood and – oh do come!'

'But certainly. But certainly. I come on the instant.'

With great practicality Poirot inserted his feet into his outdoor shoes and pulled a fur-lined overcoat over his pyjamas.

'I come,' he said. 'I come on the moment. You have aroused the house?'

'No. No, so far I haven't told anyone but you. I thought it would be better. Grandfather and Gran aren't up yet. They're laying breakfast downstairs, but I didn't say anything to Peverell. She – Bridget – she's round the other side of the house, near the terrace and the library window.'

'I see. Lead the way. I will follow.'

Turning away to hide his delighted grin, Colin led the way downstairs. They went out through the side door. It was a clear morning with the sun not yet high over the horizon. It was not snowing now, but it had snowed heavily during the night and everywhere around was an unbroken carpet of thick snow. The world looked very pure and white and beautiful.

'There!' said Colin breathlessly. 'I – it's – *there*!' He pointed dramatically.

The scene was indeed dramatic enough. A few yards away Bridget lay in the snow. She was wearing scarlet pyjamas and a white wool wrap thrown round her shoulders. The white wool wrap was stained with crimson. Her head was turned aside and hidden by the mass of her outspread black hair. One arm was under her body, the other lay flung out, the fingers clenched, and standing up in the centre of the crimson stain was the hilt of a large curved Kurdish knife which Colonel Lacey had shown to his guests only the evening before.

'*Mon Dieu!*' ejaculated M. Poirot. 'It is like something on the stage!'

There was a faint choking noise from Michael. Colin thrust himself quickly into the breach.

'I know,' he said. 'It – it doesn't seem *real* somehow, does it. Do you see those footprints – I suppose we mustn't disturb them?'

'Ah yes, the footprints. No, we must be careful not to disturb those footprints.'

'That's what I thought,' said Colin. 'That's why I wouldn't let anyone go near her until we got you. I thought you'd know what to do.'

'All the same,' said Hercule Poirot briskly, 'first, we must see if she is still alive? Is not that so?'

'Well – yes – of course,' said Michael, a little doubtfully. 'but you see, we thought – I mean, we didn't like –'

'Ah, you have the prudence! You have read the detective stories. It is most important that nothing

61

Agatha Christie

should be touched and that the body should be left as it is. But we cannot be sure as yet if it *is* a body, can we? After all, though prudence is admirable, common humanity comes first. We must think of the doctor, must we not, before we think of the police?'

'Oh yes. Of course,' said Colin, still a little taken aback.

'We only thought – I mean – we thought we'd better get you before we did anything,' said Michael hastily.

'Then you will both remain here,' said Poirot. 'I will approach from the other side so as not to disturb these footprints. Such excellent footprints, are they not – so very clear? The footprints of a man and a girl going out together to the place where she lies. And then the man's footsteps come back but the girl's – do not.'

'They must be the footprints of the murderer,' said Colin, with bated breath.

'Exactly,' said Poirot. 'The footprints of the murderer. A long narrow foot with rather a peculiar type of shoe. Very interesting. Easy, I think, to recognize. Yes, those footprints will be very important.'

At that moment Desmond Lee-Wortley came out of the house with Sarah and joined them.

'What on earth are you all doing here?' he demanded

in a somewhat theatrical manner. 'I saw you from my bedroom window. What's up? Good lord, what's this? It – it looks like –'

'Exactly,' said Hercule Poirot. 'It looks like murder, does it not?'

Sarah gave a gasp, then shot a quick suspicious glance at the two boys.

'You mean someone's killed the girl – what's-her-name – Bridget?' demanded Desmond. 'Who on earth would want to kill her? It's unbelievable!'

'There are many things that are unbelievable,' said Poirot. 'Especially before breakfast, is it not? That is what one of your classics says. Six impossible things before breakfast.' He added: 'Please wait here, all of you.'

Carefully making a circuit, he approached Bridget and bent for a moment down over the body. Colin and Michael were now both shaking with suppressed laughter. Sarah joined them, murmuring 'What have you two been up to?'

'Good old Bridget,' whispered Colin. 'Isn't she wonderful? Not a twitch!'

'I've never seen anything look so dead as Bridget does,' whispered Michael.

Hercule Poirot straightened up again.

'This is a terrible thing,' he said. His voice held an emotion it had not held before.

Overcome by mirth, Michael and Colin both turned away. In a choked voice Michael said:

'What – what must we do?'

'There is only one thing to do,' said Poirot. 'We must send for the police. Will one of you telephone or would you prefer me to do it?'

'I think,' said Colin, 'I think – what about it, Michael?'

'Yes,' said Michael, 'I think the jig's up now.' He stepped forward. For the first time he seemed a little unsure of himself. 'I'm awfully sorry,' he said, 'I hope you won't mind too much. It – er – it was a sort of joke for Christmas and all that, you know. We thought we'd – well, lay on a murder for you.'

'You thought you would lay on a murder for me? Then this – then this –'

'It's just a show we put on,' explained Colin, 'to – to make you feel at home, you know.'

'Aha,' said Hercule Poirot. 'I understand. You make of me the April fool, is that it? But today is not April the first, it is December the twenty-sixth.'

'I suppose we oughtn't to have done it really,' said Colin, 'but – but – you don't mind very much, do you, M. Poirot? Come on, Bridget,' he called, 'get up. You must be half-frozen to death already.'

The figure in the snow, however, did not stir.

'It is odd,' said Hercule Poirot, 'she does not seem

to hear you.' He looked thoughtfully at them. 'It is a joke, you say? You are sure this is a joke?'

'Why, yes.' Colin spoke uncomfortably. 'We – we didn't mean any harm.'

'But why then does Mademoiselle Bridget not get up?'

'I can't imagine,' said Colin.

'Come on, Bridget,' said Sarah impatiently. 'Don't go on lying there playing the fool.'

'We really are very sorry, M. Poirot,' said Colin apprehensively. 'We do really apologize.'

'You need not apologize,' said Poirot, in a peculiar tone.

'What do you mean?' Colin stared at him. He turned again. 'Bridget! Bridget! What's the matter? Why doesn't she get up? Why does she go on lying there?'

Poirot beckoned to Desmond. '*You*, Mr Lee-Wortley. Come here –'

Desmond joined him.

'Feel her pulse,' said Poirot.

Desmond Lee-Wortley bent down. He touched the arm – the wrist.

'There's no pulse . . .' He stared at Poirot. 'Her arm's still. Good God, she really *is* dead!'

Poirot nodded. 'Yes, she is dead,' he said. 'Someone has turned the comedy into a tragedy.'

'Someone – who?'

'There is a set of footprints going and returning. A set of footprints that bears a strong resemblance to the footprints *you* have just made, Mr Lee-Wortley, coming from the path to this spot.'

Desmond Lee-Wortley wheeled round.

'What on earth – Are you accusing me? *ME?* You're crazy! Why on earth should I want to kill the girl?'

'Ah – why? I wonder . . . Let us see . . .'

He bent down and very gently prised open the stiff fingers of the girl's clenched hand.

Desmond drew a sharp breath. He gazed down unbelievingly. In the palm of the dead girl's hand was what appeared to be a large ruby.

'It's that damn' thing out of the pudding!' he cried.

'Is it?' said Poirot. 'Are you sure?'

'Of course it is.'

With a swift movement Desmond bent down and plucked the red stone out of Bridget's hand.

'You should not do that,' said Poirot reproachfully. 'Nothing should have been disturbed.'

'I haven't disturbed the body, have I? But this thing might – might get lost and it's evidence. The great thing is to get the police here as soon as possible. I'll go at once and telephone.'

He wheeled round and ran sharply towards the house. Sarah came swiftly to Poirot's side.

'I don't understand,' she whispered. Her face was dead white. 'I don't *understand*.' She caught at Poirot's arm. 'What did you mean about – about the footprints?'

'Look for yourself, Mademoiselle.'

The footprints that led to the body and back again were the same as the ones just made accompanying Poirot to the girl's body and back.

'You mean – that it was Desmond? Nonsense!'

Suddenly the noise of a car came through the clear air. They wheeled round. They saw the car clearly enough driving at a furious pace down the drive and Sarah recognized what car it was.

'It's Desmond,' she said. 'It's Desmond's car. He – he must have gone to fetch the police instead of telephoning.'

Diana Middleton came running out of the house to join them.

'What's happened?' she cried in a breathless voice. 'Desmond just came rushing into the house. He said something about Bridget being killed and then he rattled the telephone but it was dead. He couldn't get an answer. He said the wires must have been cut. He said the only thing was to take a car and go for the police. Why the police? . . .'

Poirot made a gesture.

'Bridget?' Diana stared at him. 'But surely – isn't it

a joke of some kind? I heard something – something last night. I thought that they were going to play a joke on you, M. Poirot?'

'Yes,' said Poirot, 'that was the idea – to play a joke on me. But now come into the house, all of you. We shall catch our deaths of cold here and there is nothing to be done until Mr Lee-Wortley returns with the police.'

'But look here,' said Colin, 'we can't – we can't leave Bridget here alone.'

'You can do her no good by remaining,' said Poirot gently. 'Come, it is a sad, a very sad tragedy, but there is nothing we can do any more to help Mademoiselle Bridget. So let us come in and get warm and have perhaps a cup of tea or of coffee.'

They followed him obediently into the house. Peverell was just about to strike the gong. If he thought it extraordinary for most of the household to be outside and for Poirot to make an appearance in pyjamas and an overcoat, he displayed no sign of it. Peverell in his old age was still the perfect butler. He noticed nothing that he was not asked to notice. They went into the dining-room and sat down. When they all had a cup of coffee in front of them and were sipping it, Poirot spoke.

'I have to recount to you,' he said, 'a little history. I cannot tell you all the details, no. But I can give you the main outline. It concerns a young princeling who came to this country. He brought with him a famous jewel which he was to have reset for the lady he was going to marry, but unfortunately before that he made friends with a very pretty young lady. This pretty young lady did not care very much for the man, but she did care for his jewel – so much so that one day she disappeared with this historic possession which had belonged to his house for generations. So the poor young man, he is in a quandary, you see. Above all he cannot have a scandal. Impossible to go to the police. Therefore he comes to me, to Hercule Poirot. "Recover for me," he says, "my historic ruby." *Eh bien*, this young lady, she has a friend, and the friend, he has put through several very questionable transactions. He has been concerned with blackmail and he has been concerned with the sale of jewellery abroad. Always he has been very clever. He is suspected, yes, but nothing can be proved. It comes to my knowledge that this very clever gentleman, he is spending Christmas here in this house. It is important that the pretty young lady, once she has acquired the jewel, should disappear for a while from circulation, so that no pressure can be put upon her, no questions can be asked her. It is arranged, therefore, that she comes here to Kings Lacey, ostensibly as the sister of the clever gentleman –'

Sarah drew a sharp breath.

'Oh, no. Oh, no, not *here*! Not with me here!'

'But so it is,' said Poirot. 'And by a little manipulation I, too, become a guest here for Christmas. This young lady, she is supposed to have just come out of hospital. She is much better when she arrives here. But then comes the news that I, too, arrive, a detective – a well-known detective. At once she has what you call the wind up. She hides the ruby in the first place she can think of, and then very quickly she has a relapse and takes to her bed again. She does not want that I should see her, for doubtless I have a photograph and I shall recognize her. It is very boring for her, yes, but she has to stay in her room and her brother, he brings her up the trays.'

'And the ruby?' demanded Michael.

'I think,' said Poirot, 'that at the moment it is mentioned I arrive, the young lady was in the kitchen with the rest of you, all laughing and talking and stirring the Christmas puddings. The Christmas puddings are put into bowls and the young lady she hides the ruby, pressing it down into one of the pudding bowls. Not the one that we are going to have on Christmas Day. Oh no, that one she knows is in a special mould. She put it in the other one, the one that is destined to be eaten on New Year's Day. Before then she will be ready to leave, and when she leaves no doubt that Christmas pudding will go with her. But see how fate takes a hand. On the very morning of Christmas Day there is an accident. The Christmas pudding in its fancy mould is dropped on the stone floor and the mould is shattered to pieces. So what can be done? The good Mrs Ross, she takes the other pudding and sends it in.'

'Good lord,' said Colin, 'do you mean that on Christmas Day when Grandfather was eating his pudding that that was a *real* ruby he'd got in his mouth?'

'Precisely,' said Poirot, 'and you can imagine the emotions of Mr Desmond Lee-Wortley when he saw that. *Eh bien*, what happens next? The ruby is passed round. I examine it and I manage unobtrusively to slip it in my pocket. In a careless way as though I were not interested. But one person at least observes what I have done. When I lie in bed that person searches my room. He searches me. He does not find the ruby. Why?'

'Because,' said Michael breathlessly, 'you had given it to Bridget. That's what you mean. And so that's why – but I don't understand quite – I mean – Look here, what *did* happen?'

Poirot smiled at him.

'Come now into the library,' he said, 'and look out of the window and I will show you something that may explain the mystery.'

He led the way and they followed him.

'Consider once again,' said Poirot, 'the scene of the crime.'

He pointed out of the window. A simultaneous gasp broke from the lips of all of them. There was no body lying on the snow, no trace of the tragedy seemed to remain except a mass of scuffled snow.

'It wasn't all a dream, was it?' said Colin faintly. 'I – has someone taken the body away?'

'Ah,' said Poirot. 'You see? The Mystery of the Disappearing Body.' He nodded his head and his eyes twinkled gently.

'Good lord,' cried Michael. 'M. Poirot, you are – you haven't – oh, look here, he's been having us on all this time!'

Poirot twinkled more than ever.

'It is true, my children, I also have had my little joke. I knew about your little plot, you see, and so I arranged a counter-plot of my own. Ah, *voilà* Mademoiselle Bridget. None the worse, I hope, for your exposure in the snow? Never should I forgive myself if you attrapped *une fluxion de poitrine*.'

Bridget had just come into the room. She was wearing a thick skirt and a woollen sweater. She was laughing.

'I sent a *tisane* to your room,' said Poirot severely. 'You have drunk it?'

'One sip was enough!' said Bridget. '*I*'m all right.

Did I do it well, M. Poirot? Goodness, my arm hurts still after that tourniquet you made me put on it.'

'You were splendid, my child,' said Poirot. 'Splendid. But see, all the others are still in the fog. Last night I went to Mademoiselle Bridget. I told her that I knew about your little *complot* and I asked her if she would act a part for me. She did it very cleverly. She made the footprints with a pair of Mr Lee-Wortley's shoes.'

Sarah said in a harsh voice:

'But what's the point of it all, M. Poirot? What's the point of sending Desmond off to fetch the police? They'll be very angry when they find out it's nothing but a hoax.'

Poirot shook his head gently.

'But I do not think for one moment, Mademoiselle, that Mr Lee-Wortley went to fetch the police,' he said. 'Murder is a thing in which Mr Lee-Wortley does not want to be mixed up. He lost his nerve badly. All he could see was his chance to get the ruby. He snatched that, he pretended the telephone was out of order and he rushed off in a car on the pretence of fetching the police. I think myself it is the last you will see of him for some time. He has, I understand, his own ways of getting out of England. He has his own plane, has he not, Mademoiselle?'

Sarah nodded. 'Yes,' she said. 'We were thinking of –' She stopped.

73

'He wanted you to elope with him that way, did he not? *Eh bien*, that is a very good way of smuggling a jewel out of the country. When you are eloping with a girl, and that fact is publicized, then you will not be suspected of also smuggling a historic jewel out of the country. Oh yes, that would have made a very good camouflage.'

'I don't believe it,' said Sarah. 'I don't believe a word of it!'

'Then ask his sister,' said Poirot, gently nodding his head over her shoulder. Sarah turned her head sharply.

A platinum blonde stood in the doorway. She wore a fur coat and was scowling. She was clearly in a furious temper.

'Sister my foot!' she said, with a short unpleasant laugh. 'That swine's no brother of mine! So he's beaten it, has he, and left me to carry the can? The whole thing was *his* idea! *He* put me up to it! Said it was money for jam. They'd never prosecute because of the scandal. I could always threaten to say that Ali had *given* me his historic jewel. Des and I were to have shared the swag in Paris – and now the swine runs out on me! I'd like to murder him!' She switched abruptly. 'The sooner I get out of here – Can someone telephone for a taxi?'

'A car is waiting at the front door to take you to the station, Mademoiselle,' said Poirot.

'Think of everything, don't you?'

'Most things,' said Poirot complacently.

But Poirot was not to get off so easily. When he returned to the dining-room after assisting the spurious Miss Lee-Wortley into the waiting car, Colin was waiting for him.

There was a frown on his boyish face.

'But look here, M. Poirot. *What about the ruby?* Do you mean to say you've let him get away with it?'

Poirot's face fell. He twirled his moustaches. He seemed ill at ease.

'I shall recover it yet,' he said weakly. 'There are other ways. I shall still –'

'Well, I do think!' said Michael. 'To let that swine get away with the ruby!'

Bridget was sharper.

'He's having us on again,' she cried. 'You are, aren't you, M. Poirot?'

'Shall we do a final conjuring trick, Mademoiselle? Feel in my left-hand pocket.'

Bridget thrust her hand in. She drew it out again with a scream of triumph and held aloft a large ruby blinking in crimson splendour.

'You comprehend,' explained Poirot, 'the one that was clasped in your hand was a paste replica. I brought it from London in case it was possible to make a substitute. You understand? We do not want the

75

scandal. Monsieur Desmond will try and dispose of that ruby in Paris or in Belgium or wherever it is that he has his contacts, and then it will be discovered that the stone is not real! What could be more excellent? All finishes happily. The scandal is avoided, my princeling receives his ruby back again, he returns to his country and makes a sober and we hope a happy marriage. All ends well.'

'Except for me,' murmured Sarah under her breath.

She spoke so low that no one heard her but Poirot. He shook his head gently.

'You are in error, Mademoiselle Sarah, in what you say there. You have gained experience. All experience is valuable. Ahead of you I prophesy there lies happiness.'

'That's what *you* say,' said Sarah.

'But look here, M. Poirot.' Colin was frowning. 'How did you know about the show we were going to put on for you?'

'It is my business to know things,' said Hercule Poirot. He twirled his moustache.

'Yes, but I don't see how you could have managed it. Did someone split – did someone come and tell you?'

'No, no, not that.'

'Then how? Tell us how?'

They all chorused, 'Yes, tell us how.'

'But no,' Poirot protested. 'But no. If I tell you how I deduced that, you will think nothing of it. It is like the conjurer who shows how his tricks are done!'

'Tell us, M. Poirot! Go on. Tell us, tell us!'

'You really wish that I should solve for you this last mystery?'

'Yes, go on. Tell us.'

'Ah, I do not think I can. You will be so disappointed.'

'Now, come on, M. Poirot, tell us. *How did you know?*'

'Well, you see, I was sitting in the library by the window in a chair after tea the other day and I was reposing myself. I had been asleep and when I awoke you were discussing your plans just outside the window close to me, and the window was open at the top.'

'Is that all?' cried Colin, disgusted. 'How simple!'

'Is it not?' said Hercule Poirot, smiling. 'You see? You *are* disappointed!'

'Oh well,' said Michael, 'at any rate we know everything now.'

'Do we?' murmured Hercule Poirot to himself. '*I* do not. *I*, whose business it is to know things.'

He walked out into the hall, shaking his head a little. For perhaps the twentieth time he drew from his pocket a rather dirty piece of paper.

'DON'T EAT NONE OF THE PLUM PUDDING. ONE AS
WISHES YOU WELL.'

Hercule Poirot shook his head reflectively. He who could
explain everything could not explain this! Humiliating.
Who had written it? *Why* had it been written? Until
he found that out he would never know a moment's
peace. Suddenly he came out of his reverie to be aware
of a peculiar gasping noise. He looked sharply down.
On the floor, busy with a dustpan and brush was a tow-
headed creature in a flowered overall. She was staring
at the paper in his hand with large round eyes.

'Oh sir,' said this apparition. 'Oh, *sir. Please*, sir.'

'And who may you be, *mon enfant*?' inquired M.
Poirot genially.

'Annie Bates, sir, please sir. I come here to help
Mrs Ross. I didn't mean, sir, I didn't mean to – to
do anything what I shouldn't do. I did mean it well,
sir. For your good, I mean.'

Enlightenment came to Poirot. He held out the dirty
piece of paper.

'Did you write that, Annie?'

'I didn't mean any harm, sir. Really I didn't.'

'Of course you didn't, Annie.' He smiled at her.
'But tell me about it. Why did you write this?'

'Well, it was them two, sir. Mr Lee-Wortley and his
sister. Not that she *was* his sister, I'm sure. None of

us thought so! And she wasn't ill a bit. We could all tell *that*. We thought – we all thought – something queer was going on. I'll tell you straight, sir. I was in her bathroom taking in the clean towels, and I listened at the door. *He* was in her room and they were talking together. I heard what they said plain as plain. "This detective," he was saying. "This fellow Poirot who's coming here. We've got to do something about it. We've got to get him out of the way as soon as possible." And then he says to her in a nasty, sinister sort of way, lowering his voice, "Where did you put it?" And she answered him, "*In the pudding*." Oh, sir, my heart gave such a leap I thought it would stop beating. I thought they meant to poison you in the Christmas pudding. I didn't know *what* to do! Mrs Ross, she wouldn't listen to the likes of me. Then the idea came to me as I'd write you a warning. And I did and I put it on your pillow where you'd find it when you went to bed.' Annie paused breathlessly.

Poirot surveyed her gravely for some minutes.

'You see too many sensational films, I think, Annie,' he said at last, 'or perhaps it is the television that affects you? But the important thing is that you have the good heart and a certain amount of ingenuity. When I return to London I will send you a present.'

'Oh thank you, sir. Thank you very much, sir.'

'What would you like, Annie, as a present?'

'Anything I like, sir? Could I have anything I like?'

'Within reason,' said Hercule Poirot prudently, 'yes.'

'Oh sir, could I have a vanity box? A real posh slap-up vanity box like the one Mr Lee-Wortley's sister, wot wasn't his sister, had?'

'Yes,' said Poirot, 'yes, I think that could be managed.

'It is interesting,' he mused. 'I was in a museum the other day observing some antiquities from Babylon or one of those places, thousands of years old – and among them were cosmetic boxes. The heart of woman does not change.'

'Beg your pardon, sir?' said Annie.

'It is nothing,' said Poirot. 'I reflect. You shall have your vanity box, child.'

'Oh thank you, sir. Oh thank you very much indeed, sir.'

Annie departed ecstatically. Poirot looked after her, nodding his head in satisfaction.

'Ah,' he said to himself. 'And now – I go. There is nothing more to be done here.'

A pair of arms slipped round his shoulders unexpectedly.

'If you *will* stand just under the mistletoe –' said Bridget.

VI

Hercule Poirot enjoyed it. He enjoyed it very much. He said to himself that he had had a very good Christmas.

The Mystery of
the Spanish Chest

I

Punctual to the moment, as always, Hercule Poirot entered the small room where Miss Lemon, his efficient secretary, awaited her instructions for the day.

At first sight Miss Lemon seemed to be composed entirely of angles – thus satisfying Poirot's demand for symmetry.

Not that where women were concerned Hercule Poirot carried his passion for geometrical precision so far. He was, on the contrary, old-fashioned. He had a continental prejudice for curves – it might be said for voluptuous curves. He liked women to *be* women. He liked them lush, highly coloured, exotic. There had been a certain Russian countess – but that was long ago now. A folly of earlier days.

But Miss Lemon he had never considered as a woman. She was a human machine – an instrument of precision. Her efficiency was terrific. She was forty-eight years of age, and was fortunate enough to have no imagination whatever.

'Good morning, Miss Lemon.'

'Good morning, M. Poirot.'

Poirot sat down and Miss Lemon placed before him the morning's mail, neatly arranged in categories. She resumed her seat and sat with pad and pencil at the ready.

But there was to be this morning a slight change in routine. Poirot had brought in with him the morning newspaper, and his eyes were scanning it with interest. The headlines were big and bold.

SPANISH CHEST MYSTERY. LATEST DEVELOPMENTS.

'You have read the morning papers, I presume, Miss Lemon?'

'Yes, M. Poirot. The news from Geneva is not very good.'

Poirot waved away the news from Geneva in a comprehensive sweep of the arm.

'A Spanish chest,' he mused. 'Can you tell me, Miss Lemon, what exactly is a Spanish chest?'

'I suppose, M. Poirot, that it is a chest that came originally from Spain.'

'One might reasonably suppose so. You have then, no expert knowledge?'

'They are usually of the Elizabethan period, I believe. Large, and with a good deal of brass decoration on them. They look very nice when well kept and polished. My sister bought one at a sale. She keeps household linen in it. It looks very nice.'

'I am sure that in the house of any sister of yours, all the furniture would be well kept,' said Poirot, bowing gracefully.

Miss Lemon replied sadly that servants did not seem to know what elbow grease *was* nowadays. Poirot looked a little puzzled, but decided not to inquire into the inward meaning of the mysterious phrase 'elbow grease'.

He looked down again at the newspaper, conning over the names: Major Rich, Mr and Mrs Clayton, Commander McLaren, Mr and Mrs Spence. Names, nothing but names to him; yet all possessed of human personalities, hating, loving, fearing. A drama, this, in which he, Hercule Poirot, had no part. And he would have liked to have a part in it! Six people at an evening party, in a room with a big Spanish chest against the wall, six people, five of them talking, eating a buffet supper, putting records on the gramophone, dancing, and the sixth *dead, in the Spanish chest . . .*

Ah, thought Poirot. How my dear friend, Hastings, would have enjoyed this! What romantic flights of imagination he would have had. What ineptitudes he would have uttered! Ah, *ce cher Hastings*, at this moment, today, I miss him . . . Instead –

He sighed and looked at Miss Lemon. Miss Lemon, intelligently perceiving that Poirot was in no mood to dictate letters, had uncovered her typewriter and was awaiting her moment to get on with certain arrears of work. Nothing could have interested her less than sinister Spanish chests containing dead bodies.

Poirot sighed and looked down at a photographed face. Reproductions in newsprint were never very good, and this was decidedly smudgy – but what a face!

Mrs Clayton, the wife of the murdered man . . .

On an impulse, he thrust the paper at Miss Lemon. 'Look,' he demanded. 'Look at that face.'

Miss Lemon looked at it obediently, without emotion.

'What do you think of her, Miss Lemon? That is Mrs Clayton.'

Miss Lemon took the paper, glanced casually at the picture and remarked:

'She's a little like the wife of our bank manager when we lived at Croydon Heath.'

'Interesting,' said Poirot. 'Recount to me, if you will be so kind, the history of your bank manager's wife.'

'Well, it's not really a very pleasant story, M. Poirot.'

'It was in my mind that it might not be. Continue.'

'There was a good deal of talk – about Mrs Adams and a young artist. Then Mr Adams shot himself. But Mrs Adams wouldn't marry the other man and he took some kind of poison – but they pulled him through all right; and finally Mrs Adams married a young solicitor. I believe there was more trouble after that, only of course we'd left Croydon Heath by then so I didn't hear very much more about it.'

Hercule Poirot nodded gravely.

'She was beautiful?'

'Well – not really what you'd call beautiful – But there seemed to be something about her –'

'Exactly. What is that something that they possess – the sirens of this world! The Helens of Troy, the Cleopatras –?'

Miss Lemon inserted a piece of paper vigorously into her typewriter.

'Really, M. Poirot, I've never thought about it. It seems all very silly to me. If people would just go on with their jobs and didn't think about such things it would be much better.'

Having thus disposed of human frailty and passion, Miss Lemon let her fingers hover over the keys of the typewriter, waiting impatiently to be allowed to begin her work.

'That is your view,' said Poirot. 'And at this moment it is your desire that *you* should be allowed to get on with *your* job. But your job, Miss Lemon, is not only to take down my letters, to file my papers, to deal with my telephone calls, to typewrite my letters – All these things you do admirably. But me, I deal not only with documents but with human beings. And there, too, I need assistance.'

'Certainly, M. Poirot,' said Miss Lemon patiently. 'What is it you want me to do?'

'This case interests me. I should be glad if you would make a study of this morning's report of it in all the papers and also of any additional reports in the evening papers – Make me a précis of the facts.'

'Very good, M. Poirot.'

Poirot withdrew to his sitting-room, a rueful smile on his face.

'It is indeed the irony,' he said to himself, 'that after my dear friend Hastings I should have Miss Lemon. What greater contrast can one imagine? *Ce cher Hastings* – how he would have enjoyed himself. How he would have walked up and down talking about it, putting the most romantic construction on every incident, believing as gospel truth every word the papers have printed about it. And my poor Miss Lemon, what I have asked her to do, she will not enjoy at all!'

Miss Lemon came to him in due course with a type-written sheet.

'I've got the information you wanted, M. Poirot. I'm afraid though, it can't be regarded as reliable. The papers vary a good deal in their accounts. I shouldn't like to guarantee that the facts as stated are more than sixty per cent accurate.'

'That is probably a conservative estimate,' murmured Poirot. 'Thank you, Miss Lemon, for the trouble you have taken.'

The facts were sensational, but clear enough. Major Charles Rich, a well-to-do bachelor, had given an evening party to a few of his friends, at his apartment. These friends consisted of Mr and Mrs Clayton, Mr and Mrs Spence, and a Commander McLaren. Commander McLaren was a very old friend of both Rich and the Claytons, Mr and Mrs Spence, a younger couple, were fairly recent acquaintances. Arnold Clayton was in the Treasury. Jeremy Spence was a junior Civil Servant. Major Rich was forty-eight, Arnold Clayton was fifty-five, Commander McLaren was forty-six, Jeremy Spence was thirty-seven. Mrs Clayton was said to be 'some years younger than her husband'. One person was unable to attend the party. At the last moment, Mr Clayton was called away to Scotland on urgent business, and was supposed to have left King's Cross by the 8.15 train.

The party proceeded as such parties do. Everyone appeared to be enjoying themselves. It was neither a wild party nor a drunken one. It broke up about 11.45. The four guests left together and shared a taxi. Commander McLaren was dropped first at his club and then the Spences dropped Margharita Clayton at Cardigan Gardens just off Sloane Street and went on themselves to their house in Chelsea.

The gruesome discovery was made on the following morning by Major Rich's manservant, William Burgess. The latter did not live in. He arrived early so as to clear up the sitting-room before calling Major Rich with his early morning tea. It was whilst clearing up that Burgess was startled to find a big stain discolouring the light-coloured rug on which stood the Spanish chest. It seemed to have seeped through from the chest, and the valet immediately lifted up the lid of the chest and looked inside. He was horrified to find there the body of Mr Clayton, stabbed through the neck.

Obeying his first impulse, Burgess rushed out into the street and fetched the nearest policeman.

Such were the bald facts of the case. But there were further details. The police had immediately broken the news to Mrs Clayton who had been 'completely prostrated'. She had seen her husband for the last time at a little after six o'clock on the evening before. He had come home much annoyed, having been summoned to Scotland on urgent business in connection with some property that he owned. He had urged his wife to go to the party without him. Mr Clayton had then called in at his and Commander McLaren's club, had had a drink with his friend, and had explained the position. He had then said, looking at his watch, that he had just time on his way to King's Cross, to call in on Major Rich and explain. He had already tried to telephone him, but the line had seemed to be out of order.

According to William Burgess, Mr Clayton arrived at the flat at about 7.55. Major Rich was out but was due to return any moment, so Burgess suggested that Mr Clayton should come in and wait. Clayton said he had no time, but would come in and write a note. He explained that he was on his way to catch a train at King's Cross. The valet showed him into the sitting-room and himself returned to the kitchen where he was engaged in the preparation of canapés for the party. The valet did not hear his master return but, about ten minutes later, Major Rich looked into the kitchen and told Burgess to hurry out and get some Turkish cigarettes which were Mrs Spence's favourite smoking. The valet did so and brought them to his master in the sitting-room. Mr Clayton was not there, but the valet naturally thought he had already left to catch his train.

Major Rich's story was short and simple. Mr Clayton was not in the flat when he himself came in and he had no idea that he had been there. No note had been left for him and the first he heard of Mr Clayton's journey to Scotland was when Mrs Clayton and the others arrived.

There were two additional items in the evening papers. Mrs Clayton who was 'prostrated with shock' had left her flat in Cardigan Gardens and was believed to be staying with friends.

The second item was in the stop press. Major Charles Rich had been charged with the murder of Arnold Clayton and had been taken into custody.

'So that is that,' said Poirot, looking up at Miss Lemon. 'The arrest of Major Rich was to be expected. But what a remarkable case. What a *very* remarkable case! Do you not think so?'

'I suppose such things do happen, M. Poirot,' said Miss Lemon without interest.

'Oh certainly! They happen every day. Or nearly every day. But usually they are quite understandable – though distressing.'

'It is certainly a very unpleasant business.'

'To be stabbed to death and stowed away in a Spanish chest is certainly unpleasant for the victim – supremely so. But when I say this is a remarkable case, I refer to the remarkable behaviour of Major Rich.'

Miss Lemon said with faint distaste:

'There seems to be a suggestion that Major Rich and Mrs Clayton were very close friends . . . It was a suggestion and not a proved fact, so I did not include it.'

'That was very correct of you. But it is an inference that leaps to the eye. Is that all you have to say?'

Miss Lemon looked blank. Poirot sighed, and missed the rich colourful imagination of his friend Hastings. Discussing a case with Miss Lemon was uphill work.

'Consider for a moment this Major Rich. He is in love with Mrs Clayton – granted . . . He wants to dispose of her husband – that, too, we grant, though if Mrs Clayton is in love with him, and they are having the affair together, where is the urgency? It is, perhaps, that Mr Clayton will not give his wife the divorce? But it is not of all this that I talk. Major Rich, he is a retired soldier, and it is said sometimes that soldiers are not brainy. But, *tout de même*, this Major Rich, is he, can he be, a complete imbecile?'

Miss Lemon did not reply. She took this to be a purely rhetorical question.

'Well,' demanded Poirot. 'What do *you* think about it all?'

'What do *I* think?' Miss Lemon was startled.

'*Mais oui* – you!'

Miss Lemon adjusted her mind to the strain put

95

upon it. She was not given to mental speculation of any kind unless asked for it. In such leisure moments as she had, her mind was filled with the details of a superlatively perfect filing-system. It was her only mental recreation.

'Well –' she began, and paused.

'Tell me just what happened – what you think happened, on that evening. Mr Clayton is in the sitting-room writing a note, Major Rich comes back – what then?'

'He finds Mr Clayton there. They – I suppose they have a quarrel. Major Rich stabs him. Then, when he sees what he has done, he – he puts the body in the chest. After all, the guests, I suppose, might be arriving any minute.'

'Yes, yes. The guests arrive! The body is in the chest. The evening passes. The guests depart. And then –'

'Well, then, I suppose Major Rich goes to bed and – Oh!'

'Ah,' said Poirot. 'You see it now. You have murdered a man. You have concealed his body in a chest. And then – you go peacefully to bed, quite unperturbed by the fact that your valet will discover the crime in the morning.'

'I suppose it's possible that the valet might never have looked inside the chest?'

'With an enormous pool of blood on the carpet underneath it?'

'Perhaps Major Rich didn't realize that the blood was there.'

'Was it not somewhat careless of him not to look and see?'

'I dare say he was upset,' said Miss Lemon.

Poirot threw up his hands in despair.

Miss Lemon seized the opportunity to hurry from the room.

II

The Mystery of the Spanish chest was, strictly speaking, no business of Poirot's. He was engaged at the moment in a delicate mission for one of the large oil companies where one of the high ups was possibly involved in some questionable transaction. It was hush-hush, important and exceedingly lucrative. It was sufficiently involved to command Poirot's attention, and had the great advantage that it required very little physical activity. It was sophisticated and bloodless. Crime at the highest levels.

The mystery of the Spanish chest was dramatic and emotional; two qualities which Poirot had often declared to Hastings could be much overrated – and indeed frequently were so by the latter. He had been severe with *ce cher Hastings* on this point, and now here he was, behaving much as his friend might have done, obsessed with beautiful women, crimes of passion, jealousy, hatred and all the other romantic causes of murder! He wanted to *know* about it all. He wanted to know what Major Rich was like, and what his manservant, Burgess, was like, and what Margharita Clayton was like (though that, he thought, he knew) and what the late Arnold Clayton had been like (since he held that the character of the victim was of the first importance in a murder case), and even what Commander McLaren, the faithful friend, and Mr and Mrs Spence, the recently acquired acquaintances, were like.

And he did not see exactly how he was going to gratify his curiosity!

He reflected on the matter later in the day.

Why did the whole business intrigue him so much? He decided, after reflection, that it was because – as the facts were related – the whole thing was more or less impossible! Yes, there was a Euclidean flavour.

Starting from what one could accept, there had been a quarrel between two men. Cause, presumably, a woman. One man killed the other in the heat of rage. Yes, that happened – though it would be more acceptable if the husband had killed the lover. Still – the lover had killed the husband, stabbed him with a dagger (?) – somehow a rather unlikely weapon. Perhaps Major Rich had had an Italian mother? Somewhere – surely – there should be something to explain the choice of a dagger as a weapon. Anyway, one must accept the dagger (some papers called it a stiletto!). It was to hand and was used. The body was concealed in the chest. That was common sense and inevitable. The crime had not been premeditated, and as the valet was returning at any moment, and four guests would be arriving before very long, it seemed the only course indicated.

The party is held, the guests depart, the manservant is already gone – and – Major Rich goes to bed!

To understand how that could happen, one must see Major Rich and find out what kind of a man acts in that way.

Could it be that, overcome with horror at what he had done and the long strain of an evening trying to appear his normal self, he had taken a sleeping-pill of some kind or a tranquilizer which had put him into a heavy slumber which lasted long beyond his usual hour of waking? Possible. Or was it a case, rewarding to a psychologist, where Major Rich's feeling of subconscious guilt made him *want* the crime to be discovered? To make up one's mind on that point one would have to see Major Rich. It all came back to –

The telephone rang. Poirot let it ring for some moments, until he realized that Miss Lemon after bringing him his letters to sign, had gone home some time ago, and that George had probably gone out.

He picked up the receiver.

'M. Poirot?'

'Speaking!'

'Oh how splendid.' Poirot blinked slightly at the fervour of the charming female voice. 'It's Abbie Chatterton.'

'Ah, Lady Chatterton. How can I serve you?'

'By coming over as quickly as you can right away to a simply frightful cocktail party I am giving. Not just for the cocktail party – it's for something quite different really. I *need* you. It's absolutely *vital*. Please, *please, please* don't let me down! *Don't* say you can't manage it.'

Poirot had not been going to say anything of the kind. Lord Chatterton, apart from being a peer of the realm and occasionally making a very dull speech in the House of Lords, was nobody in particular. But Lady Chatterton was one of the brightest jewels in what Poirot called *le haut monde*. Everything she did or said was news. She had brains, beauty, originality and enough vitality to activate a rocket to the moon.

She said again:

'I *need* you. Just give that wonderful moustache of yours a lovely twirl, and *come!*'

It was not quite so quick as that. Poirot had first to make a meticulous toilet. The twirl to the moustaches was added and he then set off.

The door of Lady Chatterton's delightful house in Cheriton Street was ajar and a noise as of animals mutinying at the zoo sounded from within. Lady Chatterton who was holding two ambassadors, an international rugger player and an American evangelist in play, neatly jettisoned them with the rapidity of sleight of hand and was at Poirot's side.

'M. Poirot, how wonderful to see you! No, don't have that nasty Martini. I've got something special for you – a kind of *sirop* that the sheikhs drink in Morocco. It's in my own little room upstairs.'

She led the way upstairs and Poirot followed her. She paused to say over her shoulder:

'I didn't put these people off, because it's absolutely essential that no one should know there's anything special going on here, and I've promised the servants enormous bonuses if not a word leaks out. After all, one doesn't want one's house besieged by reporters. And, poor darling, she's been through so much already.'

Lady Chatterton did not stop at the first-floor landing, instead she swept on up to the floor above.

Gasping for breath and somewhat bewildered, Hercule Poirot followed.

Lady Chatterton paused, gave a rapid glance downwards over the banisters, and then flung open a door, exclaiming as she did so:

'I've got him, Margharita! I've got him! Here he is!'

She stood aside in triumph to let Poirot enter, then performed a rapid introduction.

'This is Margharita Clayton. She's a very, very dear friend of mine. You'll help her, won't you? Margharita, this is that wonderful Hercule Poirot. He'll do just everything you want – you will, won't you, dear M. Poirot?'

And without waiting for the answer which she obviously took for granted (Lady Chatterton had not been a spoilt beauty all her life for nothing), she dashed out of the door and down the stairs, calling back rather indiscreetly, 'I've got to go back to all these awful people . . .'

The woman who had been sitting in a chair by the window rose and came towards him. He would have recognized her even if Lady Chatterton had not mentioned her name. Here was that wide, that very wide brow, the dark hair that sprang away from it like wings, the grey eyes set far apart. She wore a close-fitting, high-necked gown of dull black that showed up the beauty of her body and the magnolia-whiteness of her skin. It was an unusual face, rather than a beautiful one – one of those oddly proportioned faces that one sometimes sees in an Italian primitive. There was about her a kind of medieval simplicity – a strange innocence that could be, Poirot thought, more devastating than any voluptuous sophistication. When she spoke it was with a kind of childlike candour.

'Abbie says you will help me . . .'

She looked at him gravely and inquiringly.

For a moment he stood quite still, scrutinizing her closely. There was nothing ill-bred in his manner of doing it. It was more the kind but searching look that a famous consultant gives a new patient.

'Are you sure, Madame,' he said at last, 'that I *can* help you?'

A little flush rose to her cheeks.

'I don't know what you mean.'

'What is it, Madame, that you want me to do?'

'Oh,' she seemed surprised. 'I thought – you knew who I was?'

'I know who you are. Your husband was killed – stabbed, and a Major Rich has been arrested and charged with his murder.'

The flush heightened.

'Major Rich did *not* kill my husband.'

Quick as a flash Poirot said:

'Why not?'

She stared, puzzled. 'I – I beg your pardon?'

'I have confused you – because I have not asked the question that everybody asks – the police – the lawyers . . . "Why should Major Rich kill Arnold Clayton?" But I ask the opposite. I ask you, Madame, why you are sure that Major Rich did *not* kill him?'

'Because,' she paused a moment – 'because I know Major Rich so well.'

'You know Major Rich so well,' repeated Poirot tonelessly.

He paused and then said sharply:

'How well?'

Whether she understood his meaning, he could not guess. He thought to himself: Here is either a woman of great simplicity or of great subtlety . . . Many people, he thought, must have wondered that about Margharita Clayton . . .

'How well?' She was looking at him doubtfully. 'Five years – no, nearly six.'

'That was not precisely what I meant . . . You must understand, Madame, that I shall have to ask you the impertinent questions. Perhaps you will speak the truth, perhaps you will lie. It is very necessary for a woman to lie sometimes. Women must defend themselves, and the lie, it can be a good weapon. But there are three people, Madame, to whom a woman should speak the truth. To her Father confessor, to her hairdresser, and to her private detective – if she trusts him. Do you trust me, Madame?'

Margharita Clayton drew a deep breath.

'Yes,' she said. 'I do.' And added: 'I must.'

'Very well, then. What is it you want me to do – find out who killed your husband?'

'I suppose so – yes.'

'But it is not essential? You want me, then, to clear Major Rich from suspicion?'

She nodded quickly – gratefully.

'That – and that only?'

It was, he saw, an unnecessary question. Margharita Clayton was a woman who saw only one thing at a time.

'And now,' he said, 'for the impertinence. You and Major Rich, you are lovers, yes?'

'Do you mean, were we having an affair together? No.'

'But he was in love with you?'

'Yes.'

'And you – were in love with him?'

'I think so.'

'You do not seem quite sure?'

'I *am* sure – now.'

'Ah! You did not, then, love your husband?'

'No.'

Agatha Christie

'You reply with an admirable simplicity. Most women would wish to explain at great length just exactly what their feelings were. How long had you been married?'

'Eleven years.'

'Can you tell me a little about your husband – what kind of a man he was?'

She frowned.

'It's difficult. I don't really know what kind of a man Arnold was. He was very quiet – very reserved. One didn't know what he was thinking. He was clever, of course – everyone said he was brilliant – in his work, I mean . . . He didn't – how can I put it – he never explained himself at all . . .'

'Was he in love with you?'

'Oh, yes. He must have been. Or he wouldn't have minded so much –' She came to a sudden stop.

'About other men? That is what you were going to say? He was jealous?'

Again she said:

'He must have been.' And then, as though feeling that the phrase needed explanation, she went on. 'Sometimes, for days, he wouldn't speak . . .'

Poirot nodded thoughtfully.

'This violence – that has come into your life. Is it the first that you have known?'

'Violence?' She frowned, then flushed. 'Is it – do you mean – that poor boy who shot himself?'

'Yes,' said Poirot. 'I expect that is what I mean.'

'I'd no idea he felt like that . . . I was sorry for him – he seemed so shy – so lonely. He must have been very neurotic, I think. And there were two Italians – a duel – It was ridiculous! Anyway, nobody was killed, thank goodness . . . And honestly, I didn't care about *either* of them! I never even pretended to care.'

'No. You were just – there! And where you are – things happen! I have seen that before in my life. It is *because* you do not care that men are driven mad. But for Major Rich you do care. So – we must do what we can . . .'

He was silent for a moment or two.

She sat there gravely, watching him.

'We turn from personalities, which are often the really important things, to plain facts. I know only what has been in the papers. On the facts as given there, only two persons had the opportunity of killing your husband, only two persons *could* have killed him – Major Rich and Major Rich's manservant.'

She said, stubbornly:

'I *know* Charles didn't kill him.'

'So, then, it must have been the valet. You agree?'

She said doubtfully:

'I see what you mean . . .'

'But you are dubious about it?'

'It just seems – fantastic!'

107

'Yet the *possibility* is there. Your husband undoubt-edly came to the flat, since his body was found there. If the valet's story is true, Major Rich killed him. But if the valet's story is false? Then, the valet killed him and hid the body in the chest before his master returned. An excellent way of disposing of the body from his point of view. He has only got to "notice the bloodstain" the next morning and "discover" it. Suspicion will immediately fall on Rich.'

'But why should he want to kill Arnold?'

'Ah why? The motive cannot be an obvious one – or the police would have investigated it. It is possible that your husband knew something to the valet's discredit, and was about to acquaint Major Rich with the facts. Did your husband ever say anything to you about this man Burgess?'

She shook her head.

'Do you think he would have done so – if that had indeed been the case?'

She frowned.

'It's difficult to say. Possibly not. Arnold never talked much about people. I told you he was reserved. He wasn't – he was never – a *chatty* man.'

'He was a man who kept his own counsel . . . Yes, now what is your opinion of Burgess?'

'He's not the kind of man you notice very much. A fairly good servant. Adequate but not polished.'

'What age?'

'About thirty-seven or -eight, I should think. He'd been a batman in the army during the war, but he wasn't a regular soldier.'

'How long had he been with Major Rich?'

'Not very long. About a year and a half, I think.'

'You never noticed anything odd about his manner towards your husband?'

'We weren't there so very often. No, I noticed nothing at all.'

'Tell me now about the events of that evening. What time were you invited?'

'Eight-fifteen for half past.'

'And just what kind of a party was it to be?'

'Well, there would be drinks, and a kind of buffet supper – usually a very good one. *Foie gras* and hot toast. Smoked salmon. Sometimes there was a hot rice dish – Charles had a special recipe he'd got in the Near East – but that was more for winter. Then we used to have music – Charles had got a very good stereophonic gramophone. Both my husband and Jock McLaren were very fond of classical records. And we had dance music – the Spences were very keen dancers. It was that sort of thing – a quiet informal evening. Charles was a very good host.'

'And this particular evening – it was like other

evenings there? You noticed nothing unusual – nothing out of place?'

'Out of place?' She frowned for a moment. 'When you said that I – no, it's gone. There was something . . .' She shook her head again. 'No. To answer your question, there was nothing unusual at all about that evening. We enjoyed ourselves. Everybody seemed relaxed and happy.' She shivered. 'And to think that all the time –'

Poirot held up a quick hand.

'Do not think. This business that took your husband to Scotland, how much do you know about that?'

'Not very much. There was some dispute over the restrictions on selling a piece of land which belonged to my husband. The sale had apparently gone through and then some sudden snag turned up.'

'What did your husband tell you exactly?'

'He came in with a telegram in his hand. As far as I remember, he said: "This is most annoying. I shall have to take the night mail to Edinburgh and see Johnston first thing tomorrow morning . . . Too bad when one thought the thing was going through smoothly at last." Then he said: "Shall I ring up Jock and get him to call for you," and I said "Nonsense, I'll just take a taxi," and he said that Jock or the Spences would see me home. I said did he want anything packed and he said he'd just throw a few things into a bag, and have a quick snack at the club, before catching the train. Then he went off and – and that's the last time I saw him.'

Her voice broke a little on the last words.

Poirot looked at her very hard.

'Did he show you the telegram?'

'No.'

'A pity.'

'Why do you say that?'

He did not answer that question. Instead he said briskly:

'Now to business. Who are the solicitors acting for Major Rich?'

She told him and he made a note of the address.

'Will you write a few words to them and give it to me? I shall want to make arrangements to see Major Rich.'

'He – it's been remanded for a week.'

'Naturally. That is the procedure. Will you also write a note to Commander McLaren and to your friends the Spences? I shall want to see all of them, and it is essential that they do not at once show me the door.'

When she rose from the writing-desk, he said:

'One thing more. I shall register my own impressions, but I also want yours – of Commander McLaren and of Mr and Mrs Spence.'

'Jock is one of our oldest friends. I've known him ever since I was a child. He appears to be quite a dour person, but he's really a dear – always the same – always to be relied upon. He's not gay and amusing but he's a tower of strength – both Arnold and I relied on his judgement a lot.'

'And he, also, is doubtless in love with you?' Poirot's eyes twinkled slightly.

'Oh yes,' said Margharita happily. 'He's always been in love with me – but by now it's become a kind of habit.'

'And the Spences?'

'They're amusing – and very good company. Linda Spence is really rather a clever girl. Arnold enjoyed talking with her. She's attractive, too.'

'You are friends?'

'She and I? In a way. I don't know that I *really* like her. She's too malicious.'

'And her husband?'

'Oh, Jeremy is delightful. Very musical. Knows a good deal about pictures, too. He and I go to picture shows a good deal together . . .'

'Ah, well, I shall see for myself.' He took her hand in his, 'I hope, Madame, you will not regret asking for my help.'

'Why should I regret it?' Her eyes opened wide.

'One never knows,' said Poirot cryptically.

'And I – I do not know,' he said to himself, as he went down the stairs. The cocktail party was still in full spate, but he avoided being captured and reached the street.

'No,' he repeated. 'I do not know.'

It was of Margharita Clayton he was thinking.

That apparently childlike candour, that frank inno-cence – Was it just that? Or did it mask something else? There had been women like that in medieval days – women on whom history had not been able to agree. He thought of Mary Stuart, the Scottish Queen. Had she known, that night in Kirk o' Fields, of the deed that was to be done? Or was she completely innocent? Had the conspirators told her nothing? Was she one of those childlike simple women who can say to themselves 'I do not know' and believe it? He felt the spell of Margharita Clayton. But he was not entirely sure about her . . .

Such women could be, though innocent themselves, the cause of crimes.

Such women could be, in intent and design, crim-inals themselves, though not in action.

Theirs was never the hand that held the knife –

As to Margharita Clayton – no – he did not know!

Agatha Christie

III

Hercule Poirot did not find Major Rich's solicitors very helpful. He had not expected to do so.

They managed to indicate, though without saying so, that it would be in their client's best interest if Mrs Clayton showed no sign of activity on his behalf.

His visit to them was in the interests of 'correctness'. He had enough pull with the Home Office and the CID to arrange his interview with the prisoner.

Inspector Miller, who was in charge of the Clayton case, was not one of Poirot's favourites. He was not, however, hostile on this occasion, merely contemptuous.

'Can't waste much time over the old dodderer,' he had said to his assisting sergeant before Poirot was shown in. 'Still, I'll have to be polite.'

'You'll really have to pull some rabbits out of a hat if you're going to do anything with this one, M. Poirot,' he remarked cheerfully. 'Nobody else but Rich *could* have killed the bloke.'

'Except the valet.'

'Oh, I'll give you the valet! As a possibility, that is. But you won't find anything there. No motives whatever.'

'You cannot be entirely sure of that. Motives are very curious things.'

'Well, he wasn't acquainted with Clayton in any way. He's got a perfectly innocuous past. And he seems to be perfectly right in his head. I don't know what more you want?'

'I want to find out that Rich did not commit the crime.'

'To please the lady, eh?' Inspector Miller grinned wickedly. 'She's been getting at you, I suppose. Quite something, isn't she? *Cherchez la femme* with a vengeance. If she'd had the opportunity, you know, she might have done it herself.'

'That, *no*!'

'You'd be surprised. I once knew a woman like that. Put a couple of husbands out of the way without a blink of her innocent blue eyes. Broken-hearted each time, too. The jury would have acquitted her if they'd had half a chance – which they hadn't, the evidence being practically cast iron.'

'Well, my friend, let us not argue. What I make so bold as to ask is a few reliable details on the facts. What a newspaper prints is news – but not always truth!'

'They have to enjoy themselves. What do you want?'

'Time of death as near as can be.'

'Which can't be very near because the body wasn't

115

examined until the following morning. Death is estimated to have taken place from thirteen to ten hours previously. That is, between seven and ten o'clock the night before . . . He was stabbed through the jugular vein – Death must have been a matter of moments.'

'And the weapon?'

'A kind of Italian stiletto – quite small – razor sharp. Nobody has ever seen it before, or knows where it comes from. But we shall know – in the end . . . It's a matter of time and patience.'

'It could not have been picked up in the course of a quarrel.'

'No. The valet says no such thing was in the flat.'

'What interests me is the telegram,' said Poirot. 'The telegram that called Arnold Clayton away to Scotland . . . Was that summons genuine?'

'No. There was no hitch or trouble up there. The land transfer, or whatever it was, was proceeding normally.'

'Then who sent that telegram – I am presuming there *was* a telegram?'

'There must have been . . . Not that we'd necessarily believe Mrs Clayton. But Clayton told the valet he was called by wire to Scotland. And he also told Commander McLaren.'

'What time did he see Commander McLaren?'

'They had a snack together at their club – Combined

Services – that was at about a quarter past seven. Then Clayton took a taxi to Rich's flat, arriving there just before eight o'clock. After that –' Miller spread his hands out.

'Anybody notice anything at all odd about Rich's manner that evening?'

'Oh well, you know what people are. Once a thing has happened, people think they noticed a lot of things I bet they never saw at all. Mrs Spence, now, she says he was *distrait* all the evening. Didn't always answer to the point. As though he had "something on his mind". I bet he had, too, if he had a body in the chest! Wondering how the hell to get rid of it!'

'Why didn't he get rid of it?'

'Beats me. Lost his nerve, perhaps. But it was madness to leave it until next day. He had the best chance he'd ever have that night. There's no night porter on. He could have got his car round – packed the body in the boot – it's a big boot – driven out in the country and parked it somewhere. He might have been seen getting the body into the car, but the flats are in a side street and there's a courtyard you drive a car through. At, say, three in the morning, he had a reasonable chance. And what does he do? Goes to bed, sleeps late the next morning and wakes up to find the police in the flat!'

'He went to bed and slept well as an innocent man might do.'

'Have it that way if you like. But do you really believe that yourself?'

'I shall have to leave that question until I have seen the man myself.'

'Think you know an innocent man when you see one? It's not so easy as that.'

'I know it is not easy – and I should not attempt to say I could do it. What I want to make up my mind about is whether the man is as stupid as he seems to be.'

IV

Poirot had no intention of seeing Charles Rich until he had seen everyone else.

He started with Commander McLaren.

McLaren was a tall, swarthy, uncommunicative man. He had a rugged but pleasant face. He was a shy man and not easy to talk to. But Poirot persevered.

Fingering Margharita's note, McLaren said almost reluctantly:

'Well, if Margharita wants me to tell you all I can, of course I'll do so. Don't know what there is to tell, though. You've heard it all already. But whatever Margharita wants – I've always done what she wanted – ever since she was sixteen. She's got a way with her, you know.'

'I know,' said Poirot. He went on: 'First I should like you to answer a question quite frankly. Do you think Major Rich is guilty?'

'Yes, I do. I wouldn't say so to Margharita if she wants to think he's innocent, but I simply can't see it any other way. Hang it all, the fellow's *got* to be guilty.'

'Was there bad feeling between him and Mr Clayton?'

'Not in the least. Arnold and Charles were the best of friends. That's what makes the whole thing so extraordinary.'

'Perhaps Major Rich's friendship with Mrs Clayton –'

He was interrupted.

'Faugh! All that stuff. All the papers slyly hinting at it . . . Damned innuendoes! Mrs Clayton and Rich were good friends and that's all! Margharita's got lots of friends. *I'm* her friend. Been one for years. And nothing the whole world mighn't know about it. Same with Charles and Margharita.'

'You do not then consider that they were having an affair together?'

'Certainly *NOT*!' McLaren was wrathful. 'Don't go listening to that hell-cat Spence woman. She'd say anything.'

'But perhaps Mr Clayton suspected there *might* be something between his wife and Major Rich.'

'You can take it from me he did nothing of the sort! I'd have known if so. Arnold and I were very close.'

'What sort of man was he? You, if anyone, should know.'

'Well, Arnold was a quiet sort of chap. But he was clever – quite brilliant, I believe. What they call a first-class financial brain. He was quite high up in the Treasury, you know.'

'So I have heard.'

'He read a good deal. And he collected stamps. And he was extremely fond of music. He didn't dance, or care much for going out.'

'Was it, do you think, a happy marriage?'

Commander McLaren's answer did not come quickly. He seemed to be puzzling it out.

'That sort of thing's very hard to say . . . Yes, I think they were happy. He was devoted to her in his quiet way. I'm sure she was fond of him. They weren't likely to split up, if that's what you're thinking. They hadn't, perhaps, a lot in common.'

Poirot nodded. It was as much as he was likely to get. He said: 'Now tell me about that last evening. Mr Clayton dined with you at the club. What did he say?'

'Told me he'd got to go to Scotland. Seemed vexed

about it. We didn't have dinner, by the way. No time. Just sandwiches and a drink. For him, that is. I only had the drink. I was going out to a buffet supper, remember.'

'Mr Clayton mentioned a telegram?'

'Yes.'

'He did not actually show you the telegram?'

'No.'

'Did he say he was going to call on Rich?'

'Not definitely. In fact he said he doubted if he'd have time. He said "Margharita can explain or you can." And then he said: "See she gets home all right, won't you?" Then he went off. It was all quite natural and easy.'

'He had no suspicion at all that the telegram wasn't genuine?'

'Wasn't it?' Commander McLaren looked startled.

'Apparently not.'

'How very odd . . .' Commander McLaren went into a kind of coma, emerging suddenly to say:

'But that really *is* odd. I mean, what's the point? Why should anybody *want* him to go to Scotland?'

'It is a question that needs answering, certainly.'

Hercule Poirot left, leaving the commander apparently still puzzling on the matter.

V

The Spences lived in a minute house in Chelsea.

Linda Spence received Poirot with the utmost delight.

'Do tell me,' she said. 'Tell me *all* about Margharita! Where is she?'

'That I am not at liberty to state, Madame.'

'She *has* hidden herself well! Margharita is very clever at that sort of thing. But she'll be called to give evidence at the trial, I suppose? She can't wiggle herself out of that.'

Poirot looked at her appraisingly. He decided grudgingly that she was attractive in the modern style (which at that moment resembled an underfed orphan child). It was not a type he admired. The artistically disordered hair fluffed out round her head, a pair of shrewd eyes watched him from a slightly dirty face devoid of make-up save for a vivid cerise mouth. She wore an enormous pale-yellow sweater hanging almost to her knees, and tight black trousers.

'What's your part in all this?' demanded Mrs Spence. 'Get the boy-friend out of it somehow? Is that it? What a hope!'

'You think then, that he is guilty?'

'Of course. Who else?'

That, Poirot thought, was very much the question. He parried it by asking another question.

'What did Major Rich seem to you like on that fatal evening? As usual? Or not as usual?'

Linda Spence screwed up her eyes judicially.

'No, he wasn't himself. He was – different.'

'How, different?'

'Well, surely, if you've just stabbed a man in cold blood –'

'But you were not aware at the time that he had just stabbed a man in cold blood, were you?'

'No, of course not.'

'So how did you account for his being "different"? In what way?'

'Well – *distrait*. Oh, I don't know. But thinking it over afterwards I decided that there had definitely been *something*.'

Poirot sighed.

'Who arrived first?'

'We did, Jim and I. And then Jock. And finally Margharita.'

'When was Mr Clayton's departure for Scotland first mentioned?'

'When Margharita came. She said to Charles: "Arnold's terribly sorry. He's had to rush off to Edinburgh by the night train." And Charles said: "Oh, that's too bad." And then Jock said: "Sorry. Thought you already knew." And then we had drinks.'

'Major Rich at no time mentioned seeing Mr Clayton that evening? He said nothing of his having called in on his way to the station?'

'Not that I heard.'

'It was strange, was it not,' said Poirot, 'about that telegram?'

'What was strange?'

'It was a fake. Nobody in Edinburgh knows anything about it.'

'So that's it. I wondered at the time.'

'You have an idea about the telegram?'

'I should say it rather leaps to the eye.'

'How do you mean exactly?'

'My dear man,' said Linda. 'Don't play the inno-cent. Unknown hoaxer gets the husband out of the way! For that night, at all events, the coast is clear.'

'You mean that Major Rich and Mrs Clayton planned to spend the night together.'

'You have heard of such things, haven't you?' Linda looked amused.

'And the telegram was sent by one or the other of them?'

'It wouldn't surprise me.'

'Major Rich and Mrs Clayton were having an affair together you think?'

'Let's say I shouldn't be surprised if they were. I

don't know it for a fact.'

'Did Mr Clayton suspect?'

'Arnold was an extraordinary person. He was all bottled up, if you know what I mean. I think he *did* know. But he was the kind of man who would never have let on. Anyone would think he was a dry stick with no feelings at all. But I'm pretty sure he wasn't like that underneath. The queer thing is that I should have been much less surprised if Arnold had stabbed Charles than the other way about. I've an idea Arnold was really an insanely jealous person.'

'That is interesting.'

'Though it's more likely, really, that he'd have done in Margharita. Othello – that sort of thing. Margharita, you know, had an extraordinary effect on men.'

'She is a good-looking woman,' said Poirot with judicious understatement.

'It was more than that. She *had* something. She would get men all het up – mad about her – and turn round and look at them with a sort of wide-eyed surprise that drove them barmy.'

'*Une femme fatale.*'

'That's probably the foreign name for it.'

'You know her well?'

'My dear, she's one of my best friends – and I wouldn't trust her an inch!'

'Ah,' said Poirot and shifted the subject to Commander McLaren.

'Jock? Old faithful? He's a pet. Born to be the friend of the family. He and Arnold were really close friends. I think Arnold unbent to him more than to anyone else. And of course he was Margharita's tame cat. He'd been devoted to her for years.'

'And was Mr Clayton jealous of him, too?'

'Jealous of Jock? What an idea! Margharita's genuinely fond of Jock, but she's never given him a thought of that kind. I don't think, really, that one ever would . . . I don't know why . . . It seems a shame. He's so nice.'

Poirot switched to consideration of the valet. But beyond saying vaguely that he mixed a very good side car, Linda Spence seemed to have no ideas about Burgess, and indeed seemed barely to have noticed him.

But she was quite quick in the uptake.

'You're thinking, I suppose, that *he* could have killed Arnold just as easily as Charles could? It seems to me madly unlikely.'

'That remark depresses me, Madame. But then, it seems to me (though you will probably not agree) that it is madly unlikely – not that Major Rich should kill Arnold Clayton – but that he should kill him in just the way he did.'

'Stiletto stuff? Yes, definitely not in character. More

likely the blunt instrument. Or he might have strangled him, perhaps?'

Poirot sighed.

'We are back at Othello. Yes, Othello . . . you have given me there a little idea . . .'

'Have I? What –' There was the sound of a latchkey and an opening door. 'Oh, here's Jeremy. Do you want to talk to him, too?'

Jeremy Spence was a pleasant-looking man of thirty-odd, well groomed, and almost ostentatiously discreet. Mrs Spence said that she had better go and have a look at a casserole in the kitchen and went off, leaving the two men together.

Jeremy Spence displayed none of the engaging candour of his wife. He was clearly disliking very much being mixed up in the case at all, and his remarks were carefully non-informative. They had known the Claytons some time, Rich not so well. Had seemed a pleasant fellow. As far as he could remember, Rich had seemed absolutely as usual on the evening in question. Clayton and Rich always seemed on good terms. The whole thing seemed quite unaccountable.

Throughout the conversation Jeremy Spence was making it clear that he expected Poirot to take his departure. He was civil, but only just so.

'I am afraid,' said Poirot, 'that you do not like these questions?'

'Well, we've had quite a session of this with the police. I rather feel that's enough. We've told all we know or saw. Now – I'd like to forget it.'

'You have my sympathy. It is most unpleasant to be mixed up in this. To be asked not only what you know or what you saw but perhaps even what you think?'

'Best not to think.'

'But can one avoid it? Do you think, for instance, that Mrs Clayton was in it, too. Did she plan the death of her husband with Rich?'

'Good lord, no.' Spence sounded shocked and dismayed. 'I'd no idea that there was any question of such a thing?'

'Has your wife not suggested such a possibility?'

'Oh Linda! You know what women are – always got their knife into each other. Margharita never gets much of a show from her own sex – a darned sight too attractive. But surely this theory about Rich and Margharita planning murder – that's fantastic!'

'Such things have been known. The weapon, for instance. It is the kind of weapon a woman might possess, rather than a man.'

'Do you mean the police have traced it to her – They can't have! I mean –'

'I know nothing,' said Poirot truthfully, and escaped hastily.

From the consternation on Spence's face, he judged

that he had left that gentleman something to think about!

VI

'You will forgive my saying, M. Poirot, that I cannot see how you can be of assistance to me in any way.'

Poirot did not answer. He was looking thoughtfully at the man who had been charged with the murder of his friend, Arnold Clayton.

He was looking at the firm jaw, the narrow head. A lean brown man, athletic and sinewy. Something of the greyhound about him. A man whose face gave nothing away, and who was receiving his visitor with a marked lack of cordiality.

'I quite understand that Mrs Clayton sent you to see me with the best intentions. But quite frankly, I think she was unwise. Unwise both for her own sake and mine.'

'You mean?'

Rich gave a nervous glance over his shoulder. But the attendant warder was the regulation distance away. Rich lowered his voice.

'They've got to find a motive for this ridiculous accusation. They'll try to bring that there was an – association between Mrs Clayton and myself. That, as

Agatha Christie

I know Mrs Clayton will have told you, is quite untrue. We are friends, nothing more. But surely it is advisable that she should make no move on my behalf?'

Hercule Poirot ignored the point. Instead he picked out a word.

'You said this "ridiculous" accusation. But it is not that, you know.'

'I did *not* kill Arnold Clayton.'

'Call it then a false accusation. Say the accusation is not true. But it is not *ridiculous*. On the contrary, it is highly plausible. You must know that very well.'

'I can only tell you that to me it seems fantastic.'

'Saying that will be of very little use to you. We must think of something more useful than that.'

'I am represented by solicitors. They have briefed, I understand, eminent counsel to appear for my defence. I cannot accept your use of the word "we".'

Unexpectedly Poirot smiled.

'Ah,' he said, in his most foreign manner, 'that is the flea in the ear you give me. Very well. I go. I wanted to see you. I have seen you. Already I have looked up your career. You passed high up into Sandhurst. You passed into the Staff College. And so on and so on. I have made my own judgement of you today. You are not a stupid man.'

'And what has all that got to do with it?'

'Everything! It is impossible that a man of your ability should commit a murder in the way this one was committed. Very well. You are innocent. Tell me now about your manservant Burgess.'

'Burgess?'

'Yes. If you didn't kill Clayton, Burgess must have done so. The conclusion seems inescapable. But why? There must *be* a "why?" You are the only person who knows Burgess well enough to make a guess at it. Why, Major Rich, why?'

'I can't imagine. I simply can't see it. Oh, I've followed the same line of reasoning as you have. Yes, Burgess had opportunity – the only person who had except myself. The trouble is, I just can't believe it. Burgess is not the sort of man you can imagine murdering anybody.'

'What do your legal advisers think?'

Rich's lips set in a grim line.

'My legal advisers spend their time asking me, in a persuasive way, if it isn't true that I have suffered all my life from blackouts when I don't really know what I am doing!'

'As bad as that,' said Poirot. 'Well, perhaps we shall find it is Burgess who is subject to blackouts. It is always an idea. The weapon now. They showed it to you and asked you if it was yours?'

'It was not mine. I had never seen it before.'

'It was not yours, no. But are you quite sure you had never seen it before?'

'No.' Was there a faint hesitation? 'It's a kind of ornamental toy – really – One sees things like that lying about in people's houses.'

'In a woman's drawing-room, perhaps. Perhaps in Mrs Clayton's drawing-room?'

'Certainly NOT!'

The last word came out loudly and the warder looked up.

'*Très bien*. Certainly not – and there is no need to shout. But somewhere, at some time, you *have* seen something very like it. Eh? I am right?'

'I do not think so . . . In some curio shop . . . perhaps.'

'Ah, very likely.' Poirot rose. 'I take my leave.'

VII

'And now,' said Hercule Poirot, 'for Burgess. Yes, at long last, for Burgess.'

He had learnt something about the people in the case, from themselves and from each other. But nobody had given him any knowledge of Burgess. No clue, no hint, of what kind of a man he was.

When he saw Burgess he realized why.

The valet was waiting for him at Major Rich's flat, apprised of his arrival by a telephone call from Commander McLaren.

'I am M. Hercule Poirot.'

'Yes, sir, I was expecting you.'

Burgess held back the door with a deferential hand and Poirot entered. A small square entrance hall, a door on the left, open, leading into the sitting-room. Burgess relieved Poirot of his hat and coat and followed him into the sitting-room.

'Ah,' said Poirot looking round. 'It was here, then, that it happened?'

'Yes, sir.'

A quiet fellow, Burgess, white-faced, a little weedy. Awkward shoulders and elbows. A flat voice with a provincial accent that Poirot did not know. From the east coast, perhaps. Rather a nervous man, perhaps – but otherwise no definite characteristics. It was hard to associate him with positive action of any kind. Could one postulate a negative killer?

He had those pale blue, rather shifty eyes, that unobservant people often equate with dishonesty. Yet a liar can look you in the face with a bold and confident eye.

'What is happening to the flat?' Poirot inquired.

'I'm still looking after it, sir. Major Rich arranged for my pay and to keep it nice until – until –'

Agatha Christie

The eyes shifted uncomfortably.

'Until –' agreed Poirot.

He added in a matter of fact manner: 'I should say that Major Rich will almost certainly be committed for trial. The case will come up probably within three months.'

Burgess shook his head, not in denial, simply in perplexity.

'It really doesn't seem possible,' he said.

'That Major Rich should be a murderer?'

'The whole thing. That chest –'

His eyes went across the room.

'Ah, so that is the famous chest?'

It was a mammoth piece of furniture of very dark polished wood, studded with brass, with a great brass hasp and antique lock.

'A handsome affair.' Poirot went over to it.

It stood against the wall near the window, next to a modern cabinet for holding records. On the other side of it was a door, half ajar. The door was partly masked by a big painted leather screen.

'That leads into Major Rich's bedroom,' said Burgess.

Poirot nodded. His eyes travelled to the other side of the room. There were two stereophonic record players, each on a low table, trailing cords of snake-like flex. There were easy chairs – a big table. On the walls were a set of Japanese prints. It was a handsome room, comfortable, but not luxurious.

He looked back at William Burgess.

'The discovery,' he said kindly, 'must have been a great shock to you.'

'Oh it was, sir. I'll never forget it.' The valet rushed into speech. Words poured from him. He felt, perhaps, that by telling the story often enough, he might at last expunge it from his mind.

'I'd gone round the room, sir. Clearing up. Glasses and so on. I'd just stooped to pick up a couple of olives off the floor – and I saw it – on the rug, a rusty dark stain. No, the rug's gone now. To the cleaners. The police had done with it. Whatever's that? I thought. Saying to myself, almost in joke like: "Really it might be blood! But where does it come from? What got spilt?" And then I saw it was from the chest – down the side, here, where there's a crack. And I said, still not thinking anything, "Well whatever –?" And I lifted up the lid like this' (he suited the action to the word) 'and there it was – the body of a man lying on his side doubled up – like he might be asleep. And that nasty foreign knife or dagger thing sticking up out of his neck. I'll never forget it – never! Not as long as I live! The shock – not expecting it, you understand . . .'

He breathed deeply.

'I let the lid fall and I ran out of the flat and down

135

to the street. Looking for a policeman – and lucky, I found one – just round the corner.'

Poirot regarded him reflectively. The performance, if it was a performance, was very good. He began to be afraid that it was not a performance – that it was just how things had happened.

'You did not think of awakening first Major Rich?' he asked.

'It never occurred to me, sir. What with the shock. I – I just wanted to get out of here –' he swallowed 'and – and get help.'

Poirot nodded.

'Did you realize that it was Mr Clayton?' he asked.

'I ought to have, sir, but you know, I don't believe I did. Of course, as soon as I got back with the police officer, I said "Why, it's Mr Clayton!" And he says "Who's Mr Clayton?" And I says "He was here last night."'

'Ah,' said Poirot, 'last night . . . Do you remember exactly when it was Mr Clayton arrived here?'

'Not to the minute. But as near as not a quarter to eight, I'd say . . .'

'You knew him well?'

'He and Mrs Clayton had been here quite frequently during the year and a half I've been employed here.'

'Did he seem quite as usual?'

'I think so. A little out of breath – but I took it

he'd been hurrying. He was catching a train, or so he said.'

'He had a bag with him, I suppose, as he was going to Scotland?'

'No, sir. I imagine he was keeping a taxi down below.'

'Was he disappointed to find that Major Rich was out?'

'Not to notice. Just said he'd scribble a note. He came in here and went over to the desk and I went back to the kitchen. I was a little behindhand with the anchovy eggs. The kitchen's at the end of the passage and you don't hear very well from there. I didn't hear him go out or the master come in – but then I wouldn't expect to.'

'And the next thing?'

'Major Rich called me. He was standing in the door here. He said he'd forgotten Mrs Spence's Turkish cigarettes. I was to hurry out and get them. So I did. I brought them back and put them on the table in here. Of course I took it that Mr Clayton had left by then to get his train.'

'And nobody else came to the flat during the time Major Rich was out, and you were in the kitchen?'

'No, sir – no one.'

'Can you be sure of that?'

'How could anyone, sir? They'd have had to ring the bell.'

Poirot shook his head. How could anyone? The Spences and McLaren and also Mrs Clayton could, he already knew, account for every minute of their time. McLaren had been with acquaintances at the club, the Spences had had a couple of friends in for a drink before starting. Margharita Clayton had talked to a friend on the telephone at just that period. Not that he thought of any of them as possibilities. There would have been better ways of killing Arnold Clayton than following him to a flat with a manservant there and the host returning any moment. No, he had had a last minute hope of a 'mysterious stranger'! Someone out of Clayton's apparently impeccable past, recognizing him in the street, following him here. Attacking him with the stiletto, thrusting the body into the chest, and fleeing. Pure melodrama, unrelated to reason or to probabilities! In tune with romantic historical fictions – matching the Spanish chest.

He went back across the room to the chest. He raised the lid. It came up easily, noiselessly.

In a faint voice, Burgess said: 'It's been scrubbed out, sir, I saw to that.'

Poirot bent over it. With a faint exclamation he bent lower. He explored with his fingers.

'These holes – at the back and one side – they look

– they feel, as though they had been made quite recently.'

'Holes, sir?' The valet bent to see. 'I really couldn't say. I've never noticed them particularly.'

'They are not very obvious. But they are there. What is their purpose, would you say?'

'I really wouldn't know, sir. Some animal, perhaps – I mean a beetle, something of that kind. Something that gnaws wood?'

'Some animal?' said Poirot. 'I wonder.'

He stepped back across the room.

'When you came in here with the cigarettes, was there anything at all about this room that looked different? Anything at all? Chairs moved, table, something of that kind?'

'It's odd your saying that, sir . . . Now you come to mention it, there was. That screen there that cuts off the draught from the bedroom door, it was moved over a bit more to the left.'

'Like this?' Poirot moved swiftly.

'A little more still . . . That's right.'

The screen had already masked about half of the chest. The way it was now arranged, it almost hid the chest altogether.

'Why did you think it had been moved?'

'I didn't think, sir.'

(Another Miss Lemon!)

Burgess added doubtfully:

'I suppose it leaves the way into the bedroom clearer – if the ladies wanted to leave their wraps.'

'Perhaps. But there might be another reason.' Burgess looked inquiring. 'The screen hides the chest now, and it hides the rug below the chest. If Major Rich stabbed Mr Clayton, blood would presently start dripping through the cracks at the base of the chest. Someone might notice – as you noticed the next morning. So – the screen was moved.'

'I never thought of that, sir.'

'What are the lights like here, strong or dim?'

'I'll show you, sir.'

Quickly, the valet drew the curtains and switched on a couple of lamps. They gave a soft mellow light, hardly strong enough even to read by. Poirot glanced up at a ceiling light.

'That wasn't on, sir. It's very little used.'

Poirot looked round in the soft glow.

The valet said:

'I don't believe you'd see any bloodstains, sir, it's too dim.'

'I think you are right. So, then, why was the screen moved?'

Burgess shivered.

'It's awful to think of – a nice gentleman like Major Rich doing a thing like that.'

'You've no doubt that he did do it? Why did he do it, Burgess?'

'Well, he'd been through the war, of course. He might have had a head wound, mightn't he? They do say as sometimes it all flares up years afterwards. They suddenly go all queer and don't know what they're doing. And they say as often as not, it's their nearest and dearest as they goes for. Do you think it could have been like that?'

Poirot gazed at him. He sighed. He turned away.

'No,' he said, 'it was not like that.'

With the air of a conjuror, a piece of crisp paper was insinuated into Burgess's hand.

'Oh thank you, sir, but really I don't –'

'You have helped me,' said Poirot. 'By showing me this room. By showing me what is in the room. By showing me what took place that evening. The impossible is never impossible! Remember that. I said that there were only two possibilities – I was wrong. There is a third possibility.' He looked round the room again and gave a little shiver. 'Pull back the curtains. Let in the light and the air. This room needs it. It needs cleansing. It will be a long time, I think, before it is purified from what afflicts it – the lingering memory of hate.'

Burgess, his mouth open, handed Poirot his hat and coat. He seemed bewildered. Poirot, who enjoyed

making incomprehensible statements, went down to
the street with a brisk step.

VIII

When Poirot got home, he made a telephone call to
Inspector Miller.

'What happened to Clayton's bag? His wife said he
had packed one.'

'It was at the club. He left it with the porter. Then
he must have forgotten it and gone off without it.'

'What was in it?'

'What you'd expect. Pyjamas, extra shirt, washing-
things.'

'Very thorough.'

'What did you expect would be in it?'

Poirot ignored that question. He said:

'About the stiletto. I suggest that you get hold
of whatever cleaning woman attends Mrs Spence's
house. Find out if she ever saw anything like it lying
about there.'

'Mrs Spence?' Miller whistled. 'Is that the way your
mind is working? The Spences were shown the stiletto.
They didn't recognize it.'

'Ask them again.'

'Do you mean –'

'And then let me know what they say –'

'I can't imagine what you think you have got hold of!'

'Read *Othello*, Miller. Consider the characters in *Othello*. We've missed out one of them.'

He rang off. Next he dialled Lady Chatterton. The number was engaged.

He tried again a little later. Still no success. He called for George, his valet, and instructed him to continue ringing the number until he got a reply. Lady Chatterton, he knew, was an incorrigible telephoner.

He sat down in a chair, carefully eased off his patent leather shoes, stretched his toes and leaned back.

'I am old,' said Hercule Poirot. 'I tire easily . . .' He brightened. 'But the cells – they still function. Slowly – but they function . . . *Othello*, yes. Who was it said that to me? Ah yes, Mrs Spence. The bag . . . The screen . . . The body, lying there like a man asleep. A clever murder. Premeditated, planned . . . I think, *enjoyed*! . . .'

George announced to him that Lady Chatterton was on the line.

'Hercule Poirot here, Madame. May I speak to your guest?'

'Why, of course! Oh M. Poirot, have you done something wonderful?'

'Not yet,' said Poirot. 'But possibly, it marches.'

Presently Margharita's voice – quiet, gentle.

'Madame, when I asked you if you noticed anything out of place that evening at the party, you frowned, as though you remembered something – and then it escaped you. Would it have been the position of the screen that night?'

'The screen? Why, of course, yes. It was not quite in its usual place.'

'Did you dance that night?'

'Part of the time.'

'Who did you dance with mostly?'

'Jeremy Spence. He's a wonderful dancer. Charles is good but not spectacular. He and Linda danced and now and then we changed. Jock McLaren doesn't dance. He got out the records and sorted them and arranged what we'd have.'

'You had serious music later?'

'Yes.'

There was a pause. Then Margharita said:

'M. Poirot, what is – all this? Have you – is there – *hope*?'

'Do you ever know, Madame, what the people around you are feeling?'

Her voice, faintly surprised said:

'I – suppose so.'

'I suppose not. I think you have no idea. I think that

144

is the tragedy of your life. But the tragedy is for other people – not for you.

'Someone today mentioned to me Othello. I asked you if your husband was jealous, and you said you thought he must be. But you said it quite lightly. You said it as Desdemona might have said it not realizing danger. She, too, recognized jealousy, but she did not understand it, because she herself never had, and never could, experience jealousy. She was, I think, quite unaware of the force of acute physical passion. She loved her husband with the romantic fervour of hero worship, she loved her friend Cassio, quite innocently, as a close companion . . . I think that because of her immunity to passion, she herself drove men mad . . . Am I making sense to you, Madame?'

There was a pause – and then Margharita's voice answered. Cool, sweet, a little bewildered:

'I don't – I don't really understand what you are saying . . .'

Poirot sighed. He spoke in matter of fact tones.

'This evening,' he said, 'I pay you a visit.'

Agatha Christie

IX

Inspector Miller was not an easy man to persuade. But equally Hercule Poirot was not an easy man to shake off until he had got his way. Inspector Miller grumbled, but capitulated.

'– though what Lady Chatterton's got to do with this –'

'Nothing, really. She has provided asylum for a friend, that is all.'

'About those Spences – how did you know?'

'That stiletto came from there? It was a mere guess. Something Jeremy Spence said gave me the idea. I suggested that the stiletto belonged to Margharita Clayton. He showed that he knew positively that it did *not*.' He paused. 'What did they say?' he asked with some curiosity.

'Admitted that it was very like a toy dagger they'd once had. But it had been mislaid some weeks ago, and they had really forgotten about it. I suppose Rich pinched it from there.'

'A man who likes to play safe, Mr Jeremy Spence,' said Hercule Poirot. He muttered to himself: 'Some weeks ago . . . Oh yes, the planning began a long time ago.'

'Eh, what's that?'

'We arrive,' said Poirot. The taxi drew up at Lady Chatterton's house in Cheriton Street. Poirot paid the fare.

Margharita Clayton was waiting for them in the room upstairs. Her face hardened when she saw Miller.

'I didn't know –'

'You did not know who the friend was I proposed to bring?'

'Inspector Miller is not a friend of mine.'

'That rather depends on whether you want to see justice done or not, Mrs Clayton. Your husband was murdered –'

'And now we have to talk of who killed him,' said Poirot quickly. 'May we sit down, Madame?'

Slowly Margharita sat down in a high-backed chair facing the two men.

'I ask,' said Poirot, addressing both his hearers, 'to listen to me patiently. I think I now know what happened on that fatal evening at Major Rich's flat . . . We started, all of us, by an assumption that was not true – the assumption that there were only two persons who had the opportunity of putting the body in the chest – that is to say, Major Rich, or William Burgess. But we were wrong – there was a third person at the flat that evening who had an equally good opportunity to do so.'

'And who was that?' demanded Miller sceptically. 'The lift boy?'

'No. *Arnold Clayton.*'

'What? Concealed his own dead body? You're crazy.'

'Naturally not a dead body – a live one. In simple terms, he hid himself in the chest. A thing that has often been done throughout the course of history. The dead bride in the *Mistletoe Bough*, Iachimo with designs on the virtue of Imogen and so on. I thought of it as soon as I saw that there had been holes bored in the chest quite recently. Why? They were made so that there might be a sufficiency of air in the chest. Why was the screen moved from its usual position that evening? So as to hide the chest from the people in the room. So that the hidden man could lift the lid from time to time and relieve his cramp, and hear better what went on.'

'But why?' demanded Margharita, wide-eyed with astonishment. 'Why should Arnold want to hide in the chest?'

'Is it you who ask that, Madame? Your husband was a jealous man. He was also an inarticulate man. "Bottled up", as your friend Mrs Spence put it. His jealousy mounted. It tortured him! Were you or were you not Rich's mistress? He did not know! He *had* to know! So – a "telegram from Scotland", the telegram that was never sent and that no one ever saw! The overnight bag is packed and conveniently forgotten at the club. He goes to the flat at a time when he has probably ascertained Rich will be out – He tells the valet he will write a note. As soon as he is left alone, he bores the holes in the chest, moves the screen, and climbs inside the chest. Tonight he will know the truth. Perhaps his wife will stay behind the others, perhaps she will go, but come back again. That night the desperate, jealousy-racked man will *know* . . .'

'You're not saying he stabbed *himself*?' Miller's voice was incredulous. 'Nonsense!'

'Oh no, someone else stabbed him. Somebody who knew he was there. It was murder all right. Carefully planned, long premeditated, murder. Think of the other characters in *Othello*. It is Iago we should have remembered. Subtle poisoning of Arnold Clayton's mind; hints, suspicions. Honest Iago, the faithful friend, the man you always believe! Arnold Clayton believed him. Arnold Clayton let his jealousy be played upon, be roused to fever pitch. Was the plan of hiding in the chest Arnold's own idea? He may have thought it was – probably he did think so! And so the scene is set. The stiletto, quietly abstracted some weeks earlier, is ready. The evening comes. The lights are low, the gramophone is playing, two couples dance, the odd man out is busy at the record cabinet, close to the Spanish chest and its masking screen. To slip behind the screen, lift the lid and strike – Audacious, but quite easy!'

'Clayton would have cried out!'

'Not if he were drugged,' said Poirot. 'According to the valet, the body was "lying like a man asleep". Clayton was asleep, drugged by the only man who *could* have drugged him, the man he had had a drink with at the club.'

'Jock?' Margharita's voice rose high in childlike surprise. 'Jock? Not dear old Jock. Why, I've known Jock all my life! Why on earth should Jock . . . ?'

Poirot turned on her.

'Why did two Italians fight a duel? Why did a young man shoot himself? Jock McLaren is an inarticulate man. He has resigned himself, perhaps, to being the faithful friend to you and your husband, but then comes Major Rich as well. It is too much! In the darkness of hate and desire, he plans what is well nigh the perfect murder – a double murder, for Rich is almost certain to be found guilty of it. And with Rich and your husband both out of the way – he thinks that at last you may turn to *him*. And perhaps. Madame, you would have done . . . Eh?'

She was staring at him, wide eyed horror struck . . .

Almost unconsciously she breathed:

'Perhaps . . . I don't – know . . .'

Inspector Miller spoke with sudden authority.

'This is all very well, Poirot. It's a theory, nothing more. There's not a shred of evidence. Probably not a word of it is true.'

'It is all true.'

'But there's no *evidence*. There's nothing we can act on.'

'You are wrong. I think that McLaren, if this is put to him, will admit it. That is, if it is made clear to him that Margharita Clayton knows . . .'

Poirot paused and added:

'Because, once he knows *that*, he has lost . . . The perfect murder has been in vain.'

The Under Dog

I

Lily Margrave smoothed her gloves out on her knee with a nervous gesture, and darted a glance at the occupant of the big chair opposite her.

She had heard of M. Hercule Poirot, the well-known investigator, but this was the first time she had seen him in the flesh.

The comic, almost ridiculous, aspect that he presented disturbed her conception of him. Could this funny little man, with the egg-shaped head and the enormous moustaches, really do the wonderful things that were claimed for him? His occupation at the moment struck her as particularly childish. He was piling small blocks of coloured wood one upon the other, and seemed far more interested in the result than in the story she was telling.

At her sudden silence, however, he looked sharply across at her.

'Mademoiselle, continue, I pray of you. It is not that I do not attend; I attend very carefully, I assure you.'

He began once more to pile the little blocks of wood one upon the other, while the girl's voice took up the tale again. It was a gruesome tale, a tale of violence and tragedy, but the voice was so calm and unemotional, the recital was so concise that something of the savour of humanity seemed to have been left out of it.

She stopped at last.

'I hope,' she said anxiously, 'that I have made everything clear.'

Poirot nodded his head several times in emphatic assent. Then he swept his hand across the wooden blocks, scattering them over the table, and, leaning back in his chair, his fingertips pressed together and his eyes on the ceiling, he began to recapitulate.

'Sir Reuben Astwell was murdered ten days ago. On Wednesday, the day before yesterday, his nephew, Charles Leverson, was arrested by the police. The facts against him as far as you know are: – you will correct me if I am wrong, Mademoiselle – Sir Reuben was sitting up late writing in his own special sanctum, the Tower room. Mr Leverson came in late, letting himself in with a latch-key. He was overheard quarrelling with his uncle by the butler, whose room is directly below the Tower room. The quarrel ended with a sudden thud as of a chair being thrown over and a half-smothered cry.

'The butler was alarmed, and thought of getting up to see what was the matter, but as a few seconds later he heard Mr Leverson leave the room gaily whistling a tune, he thought nothing more of it. On the following morning, however, a housemaid discovered Sir Reuben dead by his desk. He had been struck down by some heavy instrument. The butler, I gather, did not at once tell his story to the police. That was natural, I think, eh, Mademoiselle?'

The sudden question made Lily Margrave start.

'I beg your pardon?' she said.

'One looks for humanity in these matters, does one not?' said the little man. 'As you recited the story to me – so admirably, so concisely – you made of the actors in the drama machines – puppets. But me, I look always for human nature. I say to myself, this butler, this – what did you say his name was?'

'His name is Parsons.'

'This Parsons, then, he will have the characteristics of his class, he will object very strongly to the police, he will tell them as little as possible. Above all, he will say nothing that might seem to incriminate a member of the household. A house-breaker, a burglar, he will cling to that idea with all the strength of extreme

157

obstinacy. Yes, the loyalties of the servant class are an interesting study.'

He leaned back beaming.

'In the meantime,' he went on, 'everyone in the household has told his or her tale, Mr Leverson among the rest, and his tale was that he had come in late and gone up to bed without seeing his uncle.'

'That is what he said.'

'And no one saw reason to doubt that tale,' mused Poirot, 'except, of course, Parsons. Then there comes down an inspector from Scotland Yard, Inspector Miller you said, did you not? I know him, I have come across him once or twice in the past. He is what they call the sharp man, the ferret, the weasel.

'Yes, I know him! And the sharp Inspector Miller, he sees what the local inspector has not seen, that Parsons is ill at ease and uncomfortable, and knows something that he has not told. *Eh bien*, he makes short work of Parsons. By now it has been clearly proved that no one broke into the house that night, that the murderer must be looked for inside the house and not outside. And Parsons is unhappy and frightened, and feels very relieved to have his secret knowledge drawn out of him.

'He has done his best to avoid scandal, but there are limits; and so Inspector Miller listens to Parsons' story, and asks a question or two, and then makes some private investigations of his own. The case he builds up is very strong – very strong.

'Blood-stained fingers rested on the corner of the chest in the Tower room, and the fingerprints were those of Charles Leverson. The housemaid told him she emptied a basin of blood-stained water in Mr Leverson's room the morning after the crime. He explained to her that he had cut his finger, and he *had* a little cut there, oh yes, but such a very little cut! The cuff of his evening shirt had been washed, but they found blood-stains in the sleeve of his coat. He was hard pressed for money, and he inherited money at Sir Reuben's death. Oh, yes, a very strong case, Mademoiselle.' He paused.

'And yet you come to me today.'

Lily Margrave shrugged her slender shoulders.

'As I told you, M. Poirot, Lady Astwell sent me.'

'You would not have come of your own accord, eh?'

The little man glanced at her shrewdly. The girl did not answer.

'You do not reply to my question.'

Lily Margrave began smoothing her gloves again.

'It is rather difficult for me, M. Poirot. I have my loyalty to Lady Astwell to consider. Strictly speaking, I am only her paid companion, but she has treated me more as though I were a daughter or a niece.

Agatha Christie

She has been extraordinarily kind and, whatever her faults, I should not like to appear to criticize her actions, or – well, to prejudice you against taking up the case.'

'Impossible to prejudice Hercule Poirot, *cela ne ce fait pas*,' declared the little man cheerily. 'I perceive that you think Lady Astwell has in her bonnet the buzzing bee. Come now, is it not so?'

'If I must say –'

'Speak, Mademoiselle.'

'I think the whole thing is simply silly.'

'It strikes you like that, eh?'

'I don't want to say anything against Lady Astwell –'

'I comprehend,' murmured Poirot gently. 'I comprehend perfectly.' His eyes invited her to go on.

'She really is a very good sort, and frightfully kind, but she isn't – how can I put it? She isn't an educated woman. You know she was an actress when Sir Reuben married her, and she has all sorts of prejudices and superstitions. If she says a thing, it must be so, and she simply won't listen to reason. The inspector was not very tactful with her, and it put her back up. She says it is nonsense to suspect Mr Leverson and just the sort of stupid, pig-headed mistake the police would make, and that, of course, dear Charles did not do it.'

'But she has no reasons, eh?'

'None whatever.'

'Ha! Is that so? Really, now.'

'I told her,' said Lily, 'that it would be no good coming to you with a mere statement like that and nothing to go on.'

'You told her that,' said Poirot, 'did you really? That is interesting.'

His eyes swept over Lily Margrave in a quick comprehensive survey, taking in the details of her neat black suit, the touch of white at her throat and the smart little black hat. He saw the elegance of her, the pretty face with its slightly pointed chin, and the dark-blue, long-lashed eyes. Insensibly his attitude changed; he was interested now, not so much in the case as in the girl sitting opposite him.

'Lady Astwell is, I should imagine, Mademoiselle, just a trifle inclined to be unbalanced and hysterical?'

Lily Margrave nodded eagerly.

'That describes her exactly. She is, as I told you, very kind, but it is impossible to argue with her or to make her see things logically.'

'Possibly she suspects someone on her own account,' suggested Poirot, 'someone quite absurd.'

'That is exactly what she does do,' cried Lily. 'She has taken a great dislike to Sir Reuben's secretary, poor man. She says she *knows* he did it, and yet it has been proved quite conclusively that poor Owen Trefusis cannot possibly have done it.'

161

'And she has no reasons?'

'Of course not; it is all intuition with her.'

Lily Margrave's voice was very scornful.

'I perceive, Mademoiselle,' said Poirot, smiling, 'that you do not believe in intuition?'

'I think it is nonsense,' replied Lily.

Poirot leaned back in his chair.

'*Les femmes*,' he murmured, 'they like to think that it is a special weapon that the good God has given them, and for every once that it shows them the truth, at least nine times it leads them astray.'

'I know,' said Lily, 'but I have told you what Lady Astwell is like. You simply cannot argue with her.'

'So you, Mademoiselle, being wise and discreet, came along to me as you were bidden, and have managed to put me *au courant* of the situation.'

Something in the tone of his voice made the girl look up sharply.

'Of course, I know,' said Lily apologetically, 'how very valuable your time is.'

'You are too flattering, Mademoiselle,' said Poirot, 'but indeed – yes, it is true, at this present time I have many cases of moment on hand.'

'I was afraid that might be so,' said Lily, rising. 'I will tell Lady Astwell –'

But Poirot did not rise also. Instead he lay back in his chair and looked steadily up at the girl.

'You are in haste to be gone, Mademoiselle? Sit down one more little moment, I pray of you.'

He saw the colour flood into her face and ebb out again. She sat down once more slowly and unwillingly.

'Mademoiselle is quick and decisive,' said Poirot. 'She must make allowances for an old man like myself, who comes to his decisions slowly. You mistook me, Mademoiselle. I did not say that I would not go down to Lady Astwell.'

'You will come, then?'

The girl's tone was flat. She did not look at Poirot, but down at the ground, and so was unaware of the keen scrutiny with which he regarded her.

'Tell Lady Astwell, Mademoiselle, that I am entirely at her service. I will be at – Mon Repos, is it not? – this afternoon.'

He rose. The girl followed suit.

'I – I will tell her. It is very good of you to come, M. Poirot. I am afraid, though, you will find you have been brought on a wild goose chase.'

'Very likely, but – who knows?'

He saw her out with punctilious courtesy to the door. Then he returned to the sitting-room, frowning, deep in thought. Once or twice he nodded his head, then he opened the door and called to his valet.

'My good George, prepare me, I pray of you, a little valise. I go down to the country this afternoon.'

'Very good, sir,' said George.

He was an extremely English-looking person. Tall, cadaverous and unemotional.

'A young girl is a very interesting phenomenon, George,' said Poirot, as he dropped once more into his arm-chair and lighted a tiny cigarette. 'Especially, you understand, when she has brains. To ask someone to do a thing and at the same time to put them against doing it, that is a delicate operation. It requires finesse. She was very adroit – oh, very adroit – but Hercule Poirot, my good George, is of a cleverness quite exceptional.'

'I have heard you say so, sir.'

'It is not the secretary she has in mind,' mused Poirot. 'Lady Astwell's accusation of him she treats with contempt. Just the same she is anxious that no one should disturb the sleeping dogs. I, my good George, I go to disturb them, I go to make the dog fight! There is a drama there, at Mon Repos. A human drama, and it excites me. She was adroit, the little one, but not adroit enough. I wonder – I wonder what I shall find there?'

Into the dramatic pause which succeeded these words George's voice broke apologetically:

'Shall I pack dress clothes, sir?'

Poirot looked at him sadly.

'Always the concentration, the attention to your own job. You are very good for me, George.'

II

When the 4.55 drew up at Abbots Cross station, there descended from it M. Hercule Poirot, very neatly and foppishly attired, his moustaches waxed to a stiff point. He gave up his ticket, passed through the barrier, and was accosted by a tall chauffeur.

'M. Poirot?'

The little man beamed upon him.

'That is my name.'

'This way, sir, if you please.'

He held open the door of the big Rolls-Royce.

The house was a bare three minutes from the station. The chauffeur descended once more and opened the door of the car, and Poirot stepped out. The butler was already holding the front door open.

Poirot gave the outside of the house a swift appraising glance before passing through the open door. It was a big, solidly built red-brick mansion, with no pretensions to beauty, but with an air of solid comfort.

Poirot stepped into the hall. The butler relieved him

deftly of his hat and overcoat, then murmured with that deferential undertone only to be achieved by the best servants:

'Her ladyship is expecting you, sir.'

Poirot followed the butler up the soft-carpeted stairs. This, without doubt, was Parsons, a very well-trained servant, with a manner suitably devoid of emotion. At the top of the staircase he turned to the right along a corridor. He passed through a door into a little ante-room, from which two more doors led. He threw open the left-hand one of these, and announced:

'M. Poirot, m'lady.'

The room was not a very large one, and it was crowded with furniture and knick-knacks. A woman, dressed in black, got up from a sofa and came quickly towards Poirot.

'M. Poirot,' she said with outstretched hand. Her eye ran rapidly over the dandified figure. She paused a minute, ignoring the little man's bow over her hand, and his murmured 'Madame,' and then, releasing his hand after a sudden vigorous pressure, she exclaimed:

'I believe in small men! They are the clever ones.'

'Inspector Miller,' murmured Poirot, 'is, I think, a tall man?'

'He is a bumptious idiot,' said Lady Astwell. 'Sit down here by me, will you, M. Poirot?'

166

She indicated the sofa and went on:

'Lily did her best to put me off sending for you, but I have not come to my time of life without knowing my own mind.'

'A rare accomplishment,' said Poirot, as he followed her to the settee.

Lady Astwell settled herself comfortably among the cushions and turned so as to face him.

'Lily is a dear girl,' said Lady Astwell, 'but she thinks she knows everything, and as often as not in my experience those sort of people are wrong. I am not clever, M. Poirot, I never have been, but I am right where many a more stupid person is wrong. I believe in *guidance*. Now do you want me to tell you who is the murderer, or do you not? A woman knows, M. Poirot.'

'Does Miss Margrave know?'

'What did she tell you?' asked Lady Astwell sharply.

'She gave me the facts of the case.'

'The facts? Oh, of course they are dead against Charles, but I tell you, M. Poirot, he didn't do it. I *know* he didn't!' She bent upon him an earnestness that was almost disconcerting.

'You are very positive, Lady Astwell?'

'Trefusis killed my husband, M. Poirot. I am sure of it.'

167

'Why?'

'Why should he kill him, do you mean, or why am I sure? I tell you I *know* it! I am funny about those things. I make up my mind at once, and I stick to it.'

'Did Mr Trefusis benefit in any way by Sir Reuben's death?'

'Never left him a penny,' returned Lady Astwell promptly. 'Now that shows you dear Reuben couldn't have liked or trusted him.'

'Had he been with Sir Reuben long, then?'

'Close on nine years.'

'That is a long time,' said Poirot softly, 'a very long time to remain in the employment of one man. Yes, Mr Trefusis, he must have known his employer well.'

Lady Astwell stared at him.

'What are you driving at? I don't see what that has to do with it.'

'I was following out a little idea of my own,' said Poirot. 'A little idea, not interesting, perhaps, but original, on the effects of service.'

Lady Astwell still stared.

'You *are* very clever, aren't you?' she said in rather a doubtful tone. 'Everybody says so.'

Hercule Poirot laughed.

'Perhaps you shall pay me that compliment, too, Madame, one of these days. But let us return to the motive. Tell me now of your household, of the people who were here in the house on the day of the tragedy.'

'There was Charles, of course.'

'He was your husband's nephew, I understand, not yours.'

'Yes, Charles was the only son of Reuben's sister. She married a comparatively rich man, but one of those crashes came – they do, in the city – and he died, and his wife, too, and Charles came to live with us. He was twenty-three at the time, and going to be a barrister. But when the trouble came, Reuben took him into his office.'

'He was industrious, M. Charles?'

'I like a man who is quick on the uptake,' said Lady Astwell with a nod of approval. 'No, that's just the trouble, Charles was *not* industrious. He was always having rows with his uncle over some muddle or other that he had made. Not that poor Reuben was an easy man to get on with. Many's the time I've told him he had forgotten what it was to be young himself. He was very different in those days, M. Poirot.'

Lady Astwell heaved a sigh of reminiscence.

'Changes must come, Madame,' said Poirot. 'It is the law.'

'Still,' said Lady Astwell, 'he was never really rude to

me. At least if he was, he was always sorry afterwards – poor dear Reuben.'

'He was difficult, eh?' said Poirot.

'I could always manage him,' said Lady Astwell with the air of a successful lion tamer. 'But it was rather awkward sometimes when he would lose his temper with the servants. There are ways of doing that, and Reuben's was not the right way.'

'How exactly did Sir Reuben leave his money, Lady Astwell?'

'Half to me and half to Charles,' replied Lady Astwell promptly. 'The lawyers don't put it simply like that, but that's what it amounts to.'

Poirot nodded his head.

'I see – I see,' he murmured. 'Now, Lady Astwell, I will demand of you that you will describe to me the household. There was yourself, and Sir Reuben's nephew, Mr Charles Leverson, and the secretary, Mr Owen Trefusis, and there was Miss Lily Margrave. Perhaps you will tell me something of that young lady.'

'You want to know about Lily?'

'Yes, she had been with you long?'

'About a year. I have had a lot of secretary-companions you know, but somehow or other they all got on my nerves. Lily was different. She was tactful and full of common sense and besides she looks so nice. I do like to have a pretty face about me, M. Poirot. I am a funny kind of person; I take likes and dislikes straight away. As soon as I saw that girl, I said to myself: "She'll do."'

'Did she come to you through friends, Lady Astwell?'

'I think she answered an advertisement. Yes – that was it.'

'You know something of her people, of where she comes from?'

'Her father and mother are out in India, I believe. I don't really know much about them, but you can see at a glance that Lily is a lady, can't you, M. Poirot?'

'Oh, perfectly, perfectly.'

'Of course,' went on Lady Astwell, 'I am not a lady myself. I know it, and the servants know it, but there is nothing mean-spirited about me. I can appreciate the real thing when I see it, and no one could be nicer than Lily has been to me. I look upon that girl almost as a daughter M. Poirot, indeed I do.'

Poirot's right hand strayed out and straightened one or two of the objects lying on a table near him.

'Did Sir Reuben share this feeling?' he asked.

His eyes were on the knick-knacks, but doubtless he noted the pause before Lady Astwell's answer came.

'With a man it's different. Of course they – they got on very well.'

'Thank you, Madame,' said Poirot. He was smiling to himself.

'And these were the only people in the house that night?' he asked. 'Excepting, of course, the servants.'

'Oh, there was Victor.'

'Victor?'

'Yes, my husband's brother, you know, and his partner.'

'He lived with you?'

'No, he had just arrived on a visit. He has been out in West Africa for the past few years.'

'West Africa,' murmured Poirot.

He had learned that Lady Astwell could be trusted to develop a subject herself if sufficient time was given her.

'They say it's a wonderful country, but I think it's the kind of place that has a very bad effect upon a man. They drink too much, and they get uncontrolled. None of the Astwells has a good temper, and Victor's, since he came back from Africa, has been simply too shocking. He has frightened *me* once or twice.'

'Did he frighten Miss Margrave, I wonder?' murmured Poirot gently.

'Lily? Oh, I don't think he has seen much of Lily.'

Poirot made a note or two in a diminutive note-book; then he put the pencil back in its loop and returned the note-book to his pocket.

'I thank you, Lady Astwell. I will now, if I may, interview Parsons.'

'Will you have him up here?'

Lady Astwell's hand moved towards the bell. Poirot arrested the gesture quickly.

'No, no, a thousand times no. I will descend to him.'

'If you think it is better –'

Lady Astwell was clearly disappointed at not being able to participate in the forthcoming scene. Poirot adopted an air of secrecy.

'It is essential,' he said mysteriously, and left Lady Astwell duly impressed.

He found Parsons in the butler's pantry, polishing silver. Poirot opened the proceedings with one of his funny little bows.

'I must explain myself,' he said. 'I am a detective agent.'

'Yes, sir,' said Parsons, 'we gathered as much.'

His tone was respectful but aloof.

'Lady Astwell sent for me,' continued Poirot. 'She is not satisfied; no, she is not satisfied at all.'

'I have heard her ladyship say so on several occasions,' said Parsons.

'In fact,' said Poirot, 'I recount to you the things you already know? Eh? Let us then not waste time on these bagatelles. Take me, if you will be so good, to your bedroom and tell me exactly what it was you heard there on the night of the murder.'

The butler's room was on the ground floor, adjoining the servants' hall. It had barred windows, and the strong-room was in one corner of it. Parsons indicated the narrow bed.

'I had retired, sir, at eleven o'clock. Miss Margrave had gone to bed, and Lady Astwell was with Sir Reuben in the Tower room.'

'Lady Astwell was with Sir Reuben? Ah, proceed.'

'The Tower room, sir, is directly over this. If people are talking in it one can hear the murmur of voices, but naturally not anything that is said. I must have fallen asleep about half past eleven. It was just twelve o'clock when I was awakened by the sound of the front door being slammed to and knew Mr Leverson had returned. Presently I heard footsteps overhead, and a minute or two later Mr Leverson's voice talking to Sir Reuben.

'It was my fancy at the time, sir, that Mr Leverson was – I should not exactly like to say drunk, but inclined to be a little indiscreet and noisy. He was shouting at his uncle at the top of his voice. I caught a word or two here or there, but not enough to understand what it was all about, and then there was a sharp cry and a heavy thud.'

There was a pause, and Parsons repeated the last words.

'A heavy thud,' he said impressively.

'If I mistake not, it is a *dull* thud in most works of romance,' murmured Poirot.

'Maybe, sir,' said Parsons severely. 'It was a *heavy* thud I heard.'

'A thousand pardons,' said Poirot.

'Do not mention it, sir. After the thud, in the silence, I heard Mr Leverson's voice as plain as plain can be, raised high. "My God," he said, "my God," just like that, sir.'

Parsons, from his first reluctance to tell the tale, had now progressed to a thorough enjoyment of it. He fancied himself mightily as a narrator. Poirot played up to him.

'*Mon Dieu*,' he murmured. 'What emotion you must have experienced!'

'Yes, indeed, sir,' said Parsons, 'as you say, sir. Not that I thought very much of it at the time. But it *did* occur to me to wonder if anything was amiss, and whether I had better go up and see. I went to turn the electric light on, and was unfortunate enough to knock over a chair.

'I opened the door, and went through the servants'

175

hall, and opened the other door which gives on a passage. The back stairs lead up from there, and as I stood at the bottom of them, hesitating, I heard Mr Leverson's voice from up above, speaking hearty and cheery-like. "No harm done, luckily," he says. "Good night," and I heard him move off along the passage to his own room, whistling.

'Of course I went back to bed at once. Just something knocked over, that's all I thought it was. I ask you, sir, was I to think Sir Reuben was murdered, with Mr Leverson saying good night and all?'

'You are sure it was Mr Leverson's voice you heard?'

Parsons looked at the little Belgian pityingly, and Poirot saw clearly enough that, right or wrong, Parsons's mind was made up on this point.

'Is there anything further you would like to ask me, sir?'

'There is one thing,' said Poirot, 'do you like Mr Leverson?'

'I – I beg your pardon, sir?'

'It is a simple question. Do you like Mr Leverson?'

Parsons, from being startled at first, now seemed embarrassed.

'The general opinion in the servants' hall, sir,' he said, and paused.

'By all means,' said Poirot, 'put it that way if it pleases you.'

'The opinion is, sir, that Mr Leverson is an open-handed young gentleman, but not, if I may say so, particularly intelligent, sir.'

'Ah!' said Poirot. 'Do you know, Parsons, that without having seen him, that is also precisely my opinion of Mr Leverson.'

'Indeed, sir.'

'What is your opinion – I beg your pardon – the opinion of the servants' hall of the secretary?'

'He is a very quiet, patient gentleman, sir. Anxious to give no trouble.'

'*Vraiment*,' said Poirot.

The butler coughed.

'Her ladyship, sir,' he murmured, 'is apt to be a little hasty in her judgments.'

'Then, in the opinion of the servants' hall, Mr Leverson committed the crime?'

'We none of us wish to think it was Mr Leverson,' said Parsons. 'We – well, plainly, we didn't think he had it in him, sir.'

'But he has a somewhat violent temper, has he not?' asked Poirot.

Parsons came nearer to him.

'If you are asking me who had the most violent temper in the house –'

Poirot held up a hand.

'Ah! But that is not the question I should ask,' he

177

said softly. 'My question would be, who has the best temper?' Parsons stared at him open-mouthed.

III

Poirot wasted no further time on him. With an amiable little bow – he was always amiable – he left the room and wandered out into the big square hall of Mon Repos. There he stood a minute or two in thought, then, at a slight sound that came to him, cocked his head on one side in the manner of a perky robin, and finally, with noiseless steps, crossed to one of the doors that led out of the hall.

He stood in the doorway, looking into the room; a small room furnished as a library. At a big desk at the farther end of it sat a thin, pale young man busily writing. He had a receding chin, and wore pince-nez.

Poirot watched him for some minutes, and then he broke the silence by giving a completely artificial and theatrical cough.

'Ahem!' coughed M. Hercule Poirot.

The young man at the desk stopped writing and turned his head. He did not appear unduly startled, but an expression of perplexity gathered on his face as he eyed Poirot.

The latter came forward with a little bow.

'I have the honour of speaking to M. Trefusis, yes? Ah! My name is Poirot, Hercule Poirot. You may perhaps have heard of me.'

'Oh – er – yes, certainly,' said the young man.

Poirot eyed him attentively.

Owen Trefusis was about thirty-three years of age, and the detective saw at once why nobody was inclined to treat Lady Astwell's accusation seriously. Mr Owen Trefusis was a prim, proper young man, disarmingly meek, the type of man who can be, and is, systematically bullied. One could feel quite sure that he would never display resentment.

'Lady Astwell sent for you, of course,' said the secretary. 'She mentioned that she was going to do so. Is there any way in which I can help you?'

His manner was polite without being effusive. Poirot accepted a chair, and murmured gently:

'Has Lady Astwell said anything to you of her beliefs and suspicions?'

Owen Trefusis smiled a little.

'As far as that goes,' he said, 'I believe she suspects me. It is absurd, but there it is. She has hardly spoken a civil word to me since Sir Reuben's death, and she shrinks against the wall as I pass by.'

His manner was perfectly natural, and there was more amusement than resentment in his voice. Poirot nodded with an air of engaging frankness.

'Between ourselves,' he explained, 'she said the same thing to me. I did not argue with her – me, I have made it a rule never to argue with very positive ladies. You comprehend, it is a waste of time.'

'Oh, quite.'

'I say, yes, Madame – oh, perfectly, Madame – *précisément*, Madame. They mean nothing, those words, but they soothe all the same. I make my investigations, for though it seems almost impossible that anyone except M. Leverson could have committed the crime, yet – well, the impossible has happened before now.'

'I understand your position perfectly,' said the secretary. 'Please regard me as entirely at your service.'

'*Bon*,' said Poirot. 'We understand one another. Now recount to me the events of that evening. Better start with dinner.'

'Leverson was not at dinner, as you doubtless know,' said the secretary. 'He had a serious disagreement with his uncle, and went off to dine at the golf club. Sir Reuben was in a very bad temper in consequence.'

'Not too amiable, *ce Monsieur*, eh?' hinted Poirot delicately.

Trefusis laughed.

'Oh! He was a Tartar! I haven't worked with him for nine years without knowing most of his little ways. He was an extraordinarily difficult man, M. Poirot. He would get into childish fits of rage and abuse anybody who came near him.

'I was used to it by that time. I got into the habit of paying absolutely no attention to anything he said. He was not bad-hearted really, but he could be most foolish and exasperating in his manner. The great thing was never to answer him back.'

'Were other people as wise as you were in that respect?'

Trefusis shrugged his shoulders.

'Lady Astwell enjoyed a good row,' he said. 'She was not in the least afraid of Sir Reuben, and she always stood up to him and gave him as good as she got. They always made it up afterwards, and Sir Reuben was really devoted to her.'

'Did they quarrel that night?'

The secretary looked at him sideways, hesitated a minute, then he said:

'I believe so; what made you ask?'

'An idea, that is all.'

'I don't know, of course,' explained the secretary, 'but things looked as though they were working up that way.'

Poirot did not pursue the topic.

'Who else was at dinner?'

'Miss Margrave, Mr Victor Astwell, and myself.'

'And afterwards?'

181

'We went into the drawing-room. Sir Reuben did not accompany us. About ten minutes later he came in and hauled me over the coals for some trifling matter about a letter. I went up with him to the Tower room and set the thing straight; then Mr Victor Astwell came in and said he had something he wished to talk to his brother about, so I went downstairs and joined the two ladies.

'About a quarter of an hour later I heard Sir Reuben's bell ringing violently, and Parsons came to say I was to go up to Sir Reuben at once. As I entered the room, Mr Victor Astwell was coming out. He nearly knocked me over. Something had evidently happened to upset him. He has a very violent temper. I really believe he didn't see me.'

'Did Sir Reuben make any comment on the matter?'

'He said: "Victor is a lunatic; he will do for somebody some day when he is in one of these rages."'

'Ah!' said Poirot. 'Have you any idea what the trouble was about?'

'I couldn't say at all.'

Poirot turned his head very slowly and looked at the secretary. Those last words had been uttered too hastily. He formed the conviction that Trefusis could have said more had he wished to do so. But once again Poirot did not press the question.

'And then? Proceed, I pray of you.'

'I worked with Sir Reuben for about an hour and a half. At eleven o'clock Lady Astwell came in, and Sir Reuben told me I could go to bed.'

'And you went?'

'Yes.'

'Have you any idea how long she stayed with him?'

'None at all. Her room is on the first floor, and mine is on the second, so I would not hear her go to bed.'

'I see.'

Poirot nodded his head once or twice and sprang to his feet.

'And now, Monsieur, take me to the Tower room.'

He followed the secretary up the broad stairs to the first landing. Here Trefusis led him along the corridor, and through a baize door at the end of it, which gave on the servants' staircase and on a short passage that ended in a door. They passed through this door and found themselves on the scene of the crime.

It was a lofty room twice as high as any of the others, and was roughly about thirty feet square. Swords and assagais adorned the walls, and many native curios were arranged about on tables. At the far end, in the embrasure of the window, was a large writing-table. Poirot crossed straight to it.

'It was here Sir Reuben was found?'

Trefusis nodded.

'He was struck from behind, I understand?'

Again the secretary nodded.

'The crime was committed with one of these native clubs,' he explained. 'A tremendously heavy thing. Death must have been practically instantaneous.'

'That strengthens the conviction that the crime was not premeditated. A sharp quarrel, and a weapon snatched up almost unconsciously.'

'Yes, it does not look well for poor Leverson.'

'And the body was found fallen forward on the desk?'

'No, it had slipped sideways to the ground.'

'Ah,' said Poirot, 'that is curious.'

'Why curious?' asked the secretary.

'Because of this.'

Poirot pointed to a round irregular stain on the polished surface of the writing-table.

'That is a blood-stain, *mon ami.*'

'It may have spattered there,' suggested Trefusis, 'or it may have been made later, when they moved the body.'

'Very possibly, very possibly,' said the little man. 'There is only the one door to this room?'

'There is a staircase here.'

Trefusis pulled aside a velvet curtain in the corner of the room nearest the door, where a small spiral staircase lead upwards.

'This place was originally built by an astronomer. The stairs led up to the tower where the telescope was fixed. Sir Reuben had the place fitted up as a bedroom, and sometimes slept there if he was working very late.'

Poirot went nimbly up the stairs. The circular room upstairs was plainly furnished, with a camp-bed, a chair and dressing-table. Poirot satisfied himself that there was no other exit, and then came down again to where Trefusis stood waiting for him.

'Did you hear Mr Leverson come in?' he asked.

Trefusis shook his head.

'I was fast asleep by that time.'

Poirot nodded. He looked slowly round the room.

'*Eh bien!*' he said at last. 'I do not think there is anything further here, unless – perhaps you would be so kind as to draw the curtains.'

Obediently Trefusis pulled the heavy black curtains across the window at the far end of the room. Poirot switched on the light – which was masked by a big alabaster bowl hanging from the ceiling.

'There was a desk light?' he asked.

For reply the secretary clicked on a powerful green-shaded hand lamp, which stood on the writing-table. Poirot switched the other light off, then on, then off again.

'*C'est bien!* I have finished here.'

'Dinner is at half past seven,' murmured the secretary.

'I thank you, M. Trefusis, for your many amiabilities.'

'Not at all.'

Poirot went thoughtfully along the corridor to the room appointed for him. The inscrutable George was there laying out his master's things.

'My good George,' he said presently, 'I shall, I hope, meet at dinner a certain gentleman who begins to intrigue me greatly. A man who has come home from the tropics, George. With a tropical temper – so it is said. A man whom Parsons tries to tell me about, and whom Lily Margrave does not mention. The late Sir Reuben had a temper of his own, George. Supposing such a man to come into contact with a man whose temper was worse than his own – how do you say it? The fur would jump about, eh?'

'"Would fly" is the correct expression, sir, and it is not always the case, sir, not by a long way.'

'No?'

'No, sir. There was my Aunt Jemima, sir, a most shrewish tongue she had, bullied a poor sister of hers who lived with her, something shocking she did. Nearly worried the life out of her. But if anyone came along who stood up to her, well, it was a very different thing. It was meekness she couldn't bear.'

'Ha!' said Poirot, 'it is suggestive – that.'

George coughed apologetically.

'Is there anything I can do in any way,' he inquired delicately, 'to – er – assist you, sir?'

'Certainly,' said Poirot promptly. 'You can find out for me what colour evening dress Miss Lily Margrave wore that night, and which housemaid attends her.'

George received these commands with his usual stolidity.

'Very good, sir, I will have the information for you in the morning.'

Poirot rose from his seat and stood gazing into the fire.

'You are very useful to me, George,' he murmured. 'Do you know, I shall not forget your Aunt Jemima?'

IV

Poirot did not, after all, see Victor Astwell that night. A telephone message came from him that he was detained in London.

'He attends to the affairs of your late husband's business, eh?' asked Poirot of Lady Astwell.

'Victor is a partner,' she explained. 'He went out to Africa to look into some mining concessions for the firm. It *was* mining, wasn't it, Lily?'

Agatha Christie

'Yes, Lady Astwell.'

'Gold mines, I think, or was it copper or tin? You ought to know, Lily, you were always asking Reuben questions about it all. Oh, do be careful, dear, you will have that vase over!'

'It is dreadfully hot in here with the fire,' said the girl. 'Shall I – shall I open the window a little?'

'If you like, dear,' said Lady Astwell placidly.

Poirot watched while the girl went across to the window and opened it. She stood there a minute or two breathing in the cool night air. When she returned and sat down in her seat, Poirot said to her politely:

'So Mademoiselle is interested in mines?'

'Oh, not really,' said the girl indifferently. 'I listened to Sir Reuben, but I don't know anything about the subject.'

'You pretended very well, then,' said Lady Astwell. 'Poor Reuben actually thought you had some ulterior motive in asking all those questions.'

The little detective's eyes had not moved from the fire, into which he was steadily staring, but nevertheless, he did not miss the quick flush of vexation on Lily Margrave's face. Tactfully he changed the conversation. When the hour for good nights came, Poirot said to his hostess:

'May I have just two little words with you, Madame?'

Lily Margrave vanished discreetly. Lady Astwell looked inquiringly at the detective.

'You were the last person to see Sir Reuben alive that night?'

She nodded. Tears sprang into her eyes, and she hastily held a black-edged handkerchief to them.

'Ah, do not distress yourself, I beg of you do not distress yourself.'

'It's all very well, M. Poirot, but I can't help it.'

'I am a triple imbecile thus to vex you.'

'No, no, go on. What were you going to say?'

'It was about eleven o'clock, I fancy, when you went into the Tower room, and Sir Reuben dismissed Mr Trefusis. Is that right?'

'It must have been about then.'

'How long were you with him?'

'It was just a quarter to twelve when I got up to my room; I remember glancing at the clock.'

'Lady Astwell, will you tell me what your conversation with your husband was about?'

Lady Astwell sank down on the sofa and broke down completely. Her sobs were vigorous.

'We – qua – qua – quarrelled,' she moaned.

'What about?' Poirot's voice was coaxing, almost tender.

'L-l-lots of things. It b-b-began with L-Lily. Reuben

took a dislike to her – for no reason, and said he had caught her interfering with his papers. He wanted to send her away, and I said she was a dear girl, and I would not have it. And then he s-s-started shouting me down, and I wouldn't have that, so I just told him what I thought of him.

'Not that I really meant it, M. Poirot. He said he had taken me out of the gutter to marry me, and I said – ah, but what does it all matter now? I shall never forgive myself. You know how it is, M. Poirot, I always did say a good row clears the air, and how was I to know someone was going to murder him that very night? Poor old Reuben.'

Poirot had listened sympathetically to all this outburst.

'I have caused you suffering,' he said. 'I apologize. Let us now be very business-like – very practical, very exact. You still cling to your idea that Mr Trefusis murdered your husband?'

Lady Astwell drew herself up.

'A woman's instinct, M. Poirot,' she said solemnly, 'never lies.'

'Exactly, exactly,' said Poirot. 'But when did he do it?'

'When? After I left him, of course.'

'You left Sir Reuben at a quarter to twelve. At five minutes to twelve Mr Leverson came in. In that ten minutes you say the secretary came along from his bedroom and murdered him?'

'It is perfectly possible.'

'So many things are possible,' said Poirot. 'It could be done in ten minutes. Oh, yes! But was it?'

'Of course he *says* he was in bed and fast asleep,' said Lady Astwell, 'but who is to know if he was or not?'

'Nobody saw him about,' Poirot reminded her.

'Everybody was in bed and fast asleep,' said Lady Astwell triumphantly. 'Of course nobody saw him.'

'I wonder,' said Poirot to himself.

A short pause.

'*Eh bien*, Lady Astwell, I wish you good night.'

V

George deposited a tray of early-morning coffee by his master's bedside.

'Miss Margrave, sir, wore a dress of light green chiffon on the night in question.'

'Thank you, George, you are most reliable.'

'The third housemaid looks after Miss Margrave, sir. Her name is Gladys.'

'Thank you, George. You are invaluable.'

'Not at all, sir.'

'It is a fine morning,' said Poirot, looking out of the window, 'and no one is likely to be astir very early. I think, my good George, that we shall have the Tower room to ourselves if we proceed there to make a little experiment.'

'You need me, sir?'

'The experiment,' said Poirot, 'will not be painful.'

The curtains were still drawn in the Tower room when they arrived there. George was about to pull them, when Poirot restrained him.

'We will leave the room as it is. Just turn on the desk lamp.'

The valet obeyed.

'Now, my good George, sit down in that chair. Dispose yourself as though you were writing. *Très bien*. Me, I seize a club, I steal up behind you, so, and I hit you on the back of the head.'

'Yes, sir,' said George.

'Ah!' said Poirot, 'but when I hit you, do not continue to write. You comprehend I cannot be exact. I cannot hit you with the same force with which the assassin hit Sir Reuben. When it comes to that point, we must do the make-believe. I hit you on the head, and you collapse, so. The arms well relaxed, the body limp. Permit me to arrange you. But no, do not flex your muscles.'

He heaved a sigh of exasperation.

'You press admirably the trousers, George,' he said, 'but the imagination you possess it not. Get up and let me take your place.'

Poirot in his turn sat down at the writing-table.

'I write,' he declared, 'I write busily. You steal up behind me, you hit me on the head with the club. Crash! The pen slips from my fingers, I drop forward, but not very far forward, for the chair is low, and the desk is high, and, moreover, my arms support me. Have the goodness, George, to go back to the door, stand there, and tell me what you see.'

'Ahem!'

'Yes, George?' encouragingly.

'I see you, sir, sitting at the desk.

'*Sitting* at the desk?'

'It is a little difficult to see plainly, sir,' explained George, 'being such a long way away, sir, and the lamp being so heavily shaded. If I might turn on this light, sir?'

His hand reached out to the switch.

'Not at all,' said Poirot sharply. 'We shall do very well as we are. Here am I bending over the desk, there are you standing by the door. Advance now, George, advance, and put your hand on my shoulder.'

George obeyed.

'Lean on me a little, George, to steady yourself on your feet, as it were. Ah! *Voilà*.'

Hercule Poirot's limp body slid artistically sideways.

'I collapse – so!' he observed. 'Yes, it is very well imagined. There is now something most important that must be done.'

'Indeed, sir?' said the valet.

'Yes, it is necessary that I should breakfast well.'

The little man laughed heartily at his own joke.

'The stomach, George; it must not be ignored.'

George maintained a disapproving silence. Poirot went downstairs chuckling happily to himself. He was pleased at the way things were shaping. After breakfast he made the acquaintance of Gladys, the third housemaid. He was very interested in what she could tell him of the crime. She was sympathetic towards Charles, although she had no doubt of his guilt.

'Poor young gentleman, sir, it seems hard, it does, him not being quite himself at the time.'

'He and Miss Margrave should have got on well together,' suggested Poirot, 'as the only two young people in the house.'

Gladys shook her head.

'Very stand-offish Miss Lily was with him. She wouldn't have no carryings-on, and she made it plain.'

'He was fond of her, was he?'

'Oh, only in passing, so to speak; no harm in it,

sir. Mr Victor Astwell, now he *is* properly gone on Miss Lily.'

She giggled.

'Ah *vraiment*!'

Gladys giggled again.

'Sweet on her straight away he was. Miss Lily *is* just like a lily, isn't she, sir? So tall and such a lovely shade of gold hair.'

'She should wear a green evening frock,' mused Poirot. 'There is a certain shade of green –'

'She has one, sir,' said Gladys. 'Of course, she can't wear it now, being in mourning, but she had it on the very night Sir Reuben died.'

'It should be a light green, not a dark green,' said Poirot.

'It is a light green, sir. If you wait a minute I'll show it to you. Miss Lily has just gone out with the dogs.'

Poirot nodded. He knew that as well as Gladys did. In fact, it was only after seeing Lily safely off the premises that he had gone in search of the housemaid. Gladys hurried away, and returned a few minutes later with a green evening dress on a hanger.

'*Exquis*!' murmured Poirot, holding up hands of admiration. 'Permit me to take it to the light a minute.'

He took the dress from Gladys, turned his back on her and hurried to the window. He bent over it, then held it out at arm's length.

195

'It is perfect,' he declared. 'Perfectly ravishing. A thousand thanks for showing it to me.'

'Not at all, sir,' said Gladys. 'We all know that Frenchmen are interested in ladies' dresses.'

'You are too kind,' murmured Poirot.

He watched her hurry away again with the dress. Then he looked down at his two hands and smiled. In the right hand was a tiny pair of nail scissors, in the left was a neatly clipped fragment of green chiffon.

'And now,' he murmured, 'to be heroic.'

He returned to his own apartment and summoned George.

'On the dressing-table, my good George, you will perceive a gold scarf pin.'

'Yes, sir.'

'On the washstand is a solution of carbolic. Immerse, I pray you, the point of the pin in the carbolic.'

George did as he was bid. He had long ago ceased to wonder at the vagaries of his master.

'I have done that, sir.'

'*Très bien*! Now approach. I tender to you my first finger; insert the point of the pin in it.'

'Excuse me, sir, you want me to prick you, sir?'

'But yes, you have guessed correctly. You must draw blood, you understand, but not too much.'

George took hold of his master's finger. Poirot

shut his eyes and leaned back. The valet stabbed at the finger with the scarf pin, and Poirot uttered a shrill yell.

'*Je vous remercie*, George,' he said. 'What you have done is ample.'

Taking a small piece of green chiffon from his pocket, he dabbed his finger with it gingerly.

'The operation has succeeded to a miracle,' he remarked, gazing at the result. 'You have no curiosity, George? Now, that is admirable!'

The valet had just taken a discreet look out of the window.

'Excuse me, sir,' he murmured, 'a gentleman has driven up in a large car.'

'Ah! Ah!' said Poirot. He rose briskly to his feet. 'The elusive Mr Victor Astwell. I go down to make his acquaintance.'

Poirot was destined to hear Mr Victor Astwell some time before he saw him. A loud voice rang out from the hall.

'Mind what you are doing, you damned idiot! That case has got glass in it. Curse you, Parsons, get out of the way! Put it down, you fool!'

Poirot skipped nimbly down the stairs. Victor Astwell was a big man. Poirot bowed to him politely.

'Who the devil are you?' roared the big man.

Poirot bowed again.

'My name is Hercule Poirot.'

'Lord!' said Victor Astwell. 'So Nancy sent for you, after all, did she?'

He put a hand on Poirot's shoulder and steered him into the library.

'So you are the fellow they make such a fuss about,' he remarked, looking him up and down. 'Sorry for my language just now. That chauffeur of mine is a damned ass, and Parsons always does get on my nerves, blithering old idiot.

'I don't suffer fools gladly, you know,' he said, half-apologetically, 'but by all accounts you are not a fool, eh, M. Poirot?'

He laughed breezily.

'Those who have thought so have been sadly mistaken,' said Poirot placidly.

'Is that so? Well, so Nancy has carted you down here – got a bee in her bonnet about the secretary. There is nothing in that; Trefusis is as mild as milk – drinks milk, too, I believe. The fellow is a teetotaller. Rather a waste of your time isn't it?'

'If one has an opportunity to observe human nature, time is never wasted,' said Poirot quietly.

'Human nature, eh?'

Victor Astwell stared at him, then he flung himself down in a chair.

'Anything I can do for you?'

'Yes, you can tell me what your quarrel with your brother was about that evening.'

Victor Astwell shook his head.

'Nothing to do with the case,' he said decisively.

'One can never be sure,' said Poirot.

'It had nothing to do with Charles Leverson.'

'Lady Astwell thinks that Charles had nothing to do with the murder.'

'Oh, Nancy!'

'Parsons assumes that it was M. Charles Leverson who came in that night, but he didn't see him. Remember nobody saw him.'

'It's very simple. Reuben had been pitching into young Charles – not without good reason, I must say. Later on he tried to bully me. I told him a few home truths and, just to annoy him, I made up my mind to back the boy. I meant to see him that night, so as to tell him how the land lay. When I went up to my room I didn't go to bed. Instead, I left the door ajar and sat on a chair smoking. My room is on the second floor, M. Poirot, and Charles's room is next to it.'

'Pardon my interrupting you – Mr Trefusis, he, too, sleeps on that floor?'

Astwell nodded.

'Yes, his room is just beyond mine.'

'Nearer the stairs?'

'No, the other way.'

A curious light came into Poirot's face, but the other didn't notice it and went on:

'As I say, I waited up for Charles. I heard the front door slam, as I thought, about five minutes to twelve, but there was no sign of Charles for about ten minutes. When he did come up the stairs I saw that it was no good tackling him that night.'

He lifted his elbow significantly.

'I see,' murmured Poirot.

'Poor devil couldn't walk straight,' said Astwell. 'He was looking pretty ghastly, too. I put it down to his condition at the time. Of course, now, I realize that he had come straight from committing the crime.'

Poirot interposed a quick question.

'You heard nothing from the Tower room?'

'No, but you must remember that I was right at the other end of the building. The walls are thick, and I don't believe you would even hear a pistol shot fired from there.'

Poirot nodded.

'I asked if he would like some help getting to bed,' continued Astwell. 'But he said he was all right and went into his room and banged the door. I undressed and went to bed.'

Poirot was staring thoughtfully at the carpet.

'You realize, M. Astwell,' he said at last, 'that your evidence is very important?'

'I suppose so, at least – what do you mean?'

'Your evidence that ten minutes elapsed between the slamming of the front door and Leverson's appearance upstairs. He himself says, so I understand, that he came into the house and went straight up to bed. But there is more than that. Lady Astwell's accusation of the secretary is fantastic, I admit, yet up to now it has not been proved impossible. But your evidence creates an alibi.'

'How is that?'

'Lady Astwell says that she left her husband at a quarter to twelve, while the secretary had gone to bed at eleven o'clock. The only time he could have committed the crime was between a quarter to twelve and Charles Leverson's return. Now, if, as you say, you sat with your door open, he could not have come out of his room without your seeing him.'

'That is so,' agreed the other.

'There is no other staircase?'

'No, to get down to the Tower room he would have had to pass my door, and he didn't, I am quite sure of that. And, anyway, M. Poirot, as I said just now, the man is as meek as a parson, I assure you.'

'But yes, but yes,' said Poirot soothingly, 'I understand all that.' He paused. 'And you will not tell me the subject of your quarrel with Sir Reuben?'

The other's face turned a dark red.

'You'll get nothing out of me.'

Poirot looked at the ceiling.

'I can always be discreet,' he murmured, 'where a lady is concerned.'

Victor Astwell sprang to his feet.

'Damn you, how did you – what do you mean?'

'I was thinking,' said Poirot, 'of Miss Lily Margrave.'

Victor Astwell stood undecided for a minute or two, then his colour subsided, and he sat down again.

'You are too clever for me, M. Poirot. Yes, it was Lily we quarrelled about. Reuben had his knife into her; he had ferreted out something or other about the girl – false references, something of that kind. I don't believe a word of it myself.

'And then he went further than he had any right to go, talked about her stealing down at night and getting out of the house to meet some fellow or other. My God! I gave it to him; I told him that better men than he had been killed for saying less. That shut him up. Reuben was inclined to be a bit afraid of me when I got going.'

'I hardly wonder at it,' murmured Poirot politely.

'I think a lot of Lily Margrave,' said Victor in another tone. 'A nice girl through and through.'

Poirot did not answer. He was staring in front of him, seemingly lost in abstraction. He came out of his brown study with a jerk.

'I must, I think, promenade myself a little. There is a hotel here, yes?'

'Two,' said Victor Astwell, 'the Golf Hotel up by the links and the Mitre down by the station.'

'I thank you,' said Poirot. 'Yes, certainly I must promenade myself a little.'

The Golf Hotel, as befits its name, stands on the golf links almost adjoining the club house. It was to this hostelry that Poirot repaired first in the course of that 'promenade' which he had advertised himself as being about to take. The little man had his own way of doing things. Three minutes after he had entered the Golf Hotel he was in private consultation with Miss Langdon, the manageress.

'I regret to incommode you in any way, Mademoiselle,' said Poirot, 'but you see I am a detective.'

Simplicity always appealed to him. In this case the method proved efficacious at once.

'A detective!' exclaimed Miss Langdon, looking at him doubtfully.

'Not from Scotland Yard,' Poirot assured her. 'In fact – you may have noticed it? I am not an Englishman. No, I make the private inquiries into the death of Sir Reuben Astwell.'

'You don't say, now!' Miss Langdon goggled at him expectantly.

'Precisely,' said Poirot, beaming. 'Only to someone

of discretion like yourself would I reveal the fact. I think, Mademoiselle, you may be able to aid me. Can you tell me of any gentleman staying here on the night of the murder who was absent from the hotel that evening and returned to it about twelve or half past?'

Miss Langdon's eyes opened wider than ever.

'You don't think –?' she breathed.

'That you had the murderer here? No, but I have reason to believe that a guest staying here promenaded himself in the direction of Mon Repos that night, and if so he may have seen something which, though conveying no meaning to him, might be very useful to me.'

The manageress nodded her head sapiently, with an air of one thoroughly well up in the annals of detective logic.

'I understand perfectly. Now, let me see; who did we have staying here?'

She frowned, evidently running over the names in her mind, and helping her memory by occasionally checking them off on her fingertips.

'Captain Swann, Mr Elkins, Major Blyunt, old Mr Benson. No, really, sir, I don't believe anyone went out that evening.'

'You would have noticed if they had done so, eh?'

'Oh, yes, sir, it is not very usual, you see. I mean

gentlemen go out to dinner and all that, but they don't go out after dinner, because – well, there is nowhere to go to, is there?'

The attractions of Abbots Cross were golf and nothing but golf.

'That is so,' agreed Poirot. 'Then, as far as you remember, Mademoiselle, nobody from here was out that night?'

'Captain England and his wife were out to dinner.'

Poirot shook his head.

'That is not the kind of thing I mean. I will try the other hotel; the Mitre, is it not?'

'Oh, the Mitre,' said Miss Langdon. 'Of course, anyone might have gone out walking from *there*.'

The disparagement of her tone, though vague, was evident, and Poirot beat a tactful retreat.

VI

Ten minutes later he was repeating the scene, this time with Miss Cole, the brusque manageress of the Mitre, a less pretentious hotel with lower prices, situated close to the station.

'There was one gentleman out late that night, came in about half past twelve, as far as I can remember. Quite a habit of his it was, to go out for a walk at that time of the evening. He had done it once or twice before. Let me see now, what was his name? Just for the moment I can't remember it.'

She pulled a large ledger towards her and began turning over the pages.

'Nineteenth, twentieth, twenty-first, twenty-second. Ah, here we are. Naylor, Captain Humphrey Naylor.'

'He had stayed here before? You know him well?'

'Once before,' said Miss Cole, 'about a fortnight earlier. He went out then in the evening, I remember.'

'He came to play golf, eh?'

'I suppose so,' said Miss Cole, 'that's what most of the gentlemen come for.'

'Very true,' said Poirot. 'Well, Mademoiselle, I thank you infinitely, and I wish you good day.'

He went back to Mon Repos with a very thoughtful face. Once or twice he drew something from his pocket and looked at it.

'It must be done,' he murmured to himself, 'and soon, as soon as I can make the opportunity.'

His first proceeding on re-entering the house was to ask Parsons where Miss Margrave might be found. He was told that she was in the small study dealing with Lady Astwell's correspondence, and the information seemed to afford Poirot satisfaction.

He found the little study without difficulty. Lily

Margrave was seated at a desk by the window, writing.
But for her the room was empty. Poirot carefully shut
the door behind him and came towards the girl.

'I may have a little minute of your time, Mademoiselle, you will be so kind?'

'Certainly.'

Lily Margrave put the papers aside and turned
towards him.

'What can I do for you?'

'On the evening of the tragedy, Mademoiselle, I
understand that when Lady Astwell went to her husband you went straight up to bed. Is that so?'

Lily Margrave nodded.

'You did not come down again, by any chance?'

The girl shook her head.

'I think you said, Mademoiselle, that you had
not at any time that evening been in the Tower
room?'

'I don't remember saying so, but as a matter of fact
that is quite true. I was not in the Tower room that
evening.'

Poirot raised his eyebrows.

'Curious,' he murmured.

'What do you mean?'

'Very curious,' murmured Hercule Poirot again.
'How do you account, then, for this?'

He drew from his pocket a little scrap of stained

green chiffon and held it up for the girl's inspection.

Her expression did not change, but he felt rather than heard the sharp intake of breath.

'I don't understand, M. Poirot.'

'You wore, I understand, a green chiffon dress that evening, Mademoiselle. This –' he tapped the scrap in his fingers – 'was torn from it.'

'And you found it in the Tower room?' asked the girl sharply. 'Whereabouts?'

Hercule Poirot looked at the ceiling.

'For the moment shall we just say – in the Tower room?'

For the first time, a look of fear sprang into the girl's eyes. She began to speak, then checked herself. Poirot watched her small white hands clenching themselves on the edge of the desk.

'I wonder if I did go into the Tower room that evening?' she mused. 'Before dinner, I mean. I don't think so. I am almost sure I didn't. If that scrap has been in the Tower room all this time, it seems to me a very extraordinary thing the police did not find it right away.'

'The police,' said the little man, 'do not think of things that Hercule Poirot thinks of.'

'I may have run in there for a minute just before dinner,' mused Lily Margrave, 'or it may have been the night before. I wore the same dress then. Yes, I am almost sure it was the night before.'

'I think not,' said Poirot evenly.

'Why?'

He only shook his head slowly from side to side.

'What do you mean?' whispered the girl.

She was leaning forward, staring at him, all the colour ebbing out of her face.

'You do not notice, Mademoiselle, that this fragment is stained? There is no doubt about it, that stain is human blood.'

'You mean –'

'I mean, Mademoiselle, that you were in the Tower room *after* the crime was committed, not before. I think you will do well to tell me the whole truth, lest worse should befall you.'

He stood up now, a stern little figure of a man, his forefinger pointed accusingly at the girl.

'How did you find out?' gasped Lily.

'No matter, Mademoiselle. I tell you Hercule Poirot *knows*. I know all about Captain Humphrey Naylor, and that you went down to meet him that night.'

Lily suddenly put her head down on her arms and burst into tears. Immediately Poirot relinquished his accusing attitude.

'There, there, my little one,' he said, patting the girl on the shoulder. 'Do not distress yourself. Impossible to deceive Hercule Poirot; once realize that and all your troubles will be at an end. And now you will tell me the whole story, will you not? You will tell old Papa Poirot?'

'It is not what you think, it isn't, indeed. Humphrey – my brother – never touched a hair of his head.'

'Your brother, eh?' said Poirot. 'So that is how the land lies. Well, if you wish to save him from suspicion, you must tell me the whole story now, without reservation.'

Lily sat up again, pushing back the hair from her forehead. After a minute or two, she began to speak in a low, clear voice.

'I will tell you the truth, M. Poirot. I can see now that it would be absurd to do anything else. My real name is Lily Naylor, and Humphrey is my only brother. Some years ago, when he was out in Africa, he discovered a gold mine, or rather, I should say, discovered the presence of gold. I can't tell you this part of it properly, because I don't understand the technical details, but what it amounted to was this:

'The thing seemed likely to be a very big undertaking, and Humphrey came home with letters to Sir Reuben Astwell in the hopes of getting him interested in the matter. I don't understand the rights of it even now, but I gather that Sir Reuben sent out an expert to report, and that he subsequently told my brother that the expert's report was unfavourable and that he, Humphrey, had made a great mistake. My brother went back to Africa on an expedition into the interior and was lost sight of. It was assumed that he and the expedition had perished.

'It was soon after that that a company was formed to exploit the Mpala Gold Fields. When my brother got back to England he at once jumped to the conclusion that these gold fields were identical with those he had discovered. Sir Reuben Astwell had apparently nothing to do with this company, and they had seemingly discovered the place on their own. But my brother was not satisfied; he was convinced that Sir Reuben had deliberately swindled him.

'He became more and more violent and unhappy about the matter. We two are alone in the world, M. Poirot, and as it was necessary then for me to go out and earn my own living, I conceived the idea of taking a post in this household and trying to find out if any connection existed between Sir Reuben and the Mpala Gold Fields. For obvious reasons I concealed my real name, and I'll admit frankly that I used a forged reference.

'There were many applicants for the post, most of them with better qualifications than mine, so – well, M. Poirot, I wrote a beautiful letter from the Duchess of Perthshire, who I knew had gone to America. I thought a duchess would have a great effect upon Lady Astwell, and I was quite right. She engaged me on the spot.

'Since then I have been that hateful thing, a spy, and until lately with no success. Sir Reuben is not a man to give away his business secrets, but when Victor Astwell came back from Africa he was less guarded in his talk, and I began to believe that, after all, Humphrey had not been mistaken. My brother came down here about a fortnight before the murder, and I crept out of the house to meet him secretly at night. I told him the things Victor Astwell had said, and he became very excited and assured me I was definitely on the right track.

'But after that things began to go wrong; someone must have seen me stealing out of the house and have reported the matter to Sir Reuben. He became suspicious and hunted up my references, and soon discovered the fact that they were forged. The crisis came on the day of the murder. I think he thought I was after his wife's jewels. Whatever his suspicions were, he had no intention of allowing me to remain any longer at Mon Repos, though he agreed not to prosecute me on account of the references. Lady Astwell took my part throughout and stood up valiantly to Sir Reuben.'

She paused. Poirot's face was very grave.

'And now, Mademoiselle,' he said, 'we come to the night of the murder.'

Lily swallowed hard and nodded her head.

'To begin with, M. Poirot, I must tell you that my brother had come down again, and that I had arranged to creep out and meet him once more. I went up to my room, as I have said, but I did not go to bed. Instead, I waited till I thought everyone was asleep, and then stole downstairs again and out by the side door. I met Humphrey and acquainted him in a few hurried words with what had occurred. I told him that I believed the papers he wanted were in Sir Reuben's safe in the Tower room, and we agreed as a last desperate adventure to try and get hold of them that night.

'I was to go in first and see that the way was clear. I heard the church clock strike twelve as I went in by the side door. I was half-way up the stairs leading to the Tower room, when I heard a thud of something falling, and a voice cried out, "My God!" A minute or two afterwards the door of the Tower room opened, and Charles Leverson came out. I could see his face quite clearly in the moonlight, but I was crouching some way below him on the stairs where it was dark, and he did not see me at all.

'He stood there a moment swaying on his feet and looking ghastly. He seemed to be listening; then with an effort he seemed to pull himself together and, opening the door into the Tower room, called out something about there being no harm done. His voice was quite jaunty and debonair, but his face gave the lie to it. He waited a minute more, and then slowly went on upstairs and out of sight.

'When he had gone I waited a minute or two and then crept to the Tower room door. I had a feeling that something tragic had happened. The main light was out, but the desk lamp was on, and by its light I saw Sir Reuben lying on the floor by the desk. I don't know how I managed it, but I nerved myself at last to go over and kneel down by him. I saw at once that he was dead, struck down from behind, and also that he couldn't have been dead long; I touched his hand and it was still quite warm. It was just horrible, M. Poirot. Horrible!'

She shuddered again at the remembrance.

'And then?' said Poirot, looking at her keenly.

Lily Margrave nodded.

'Yes, M. Poirot, I know what you are thinking. Why didn't I give the alarm and raise the house? I should have done so, I know, but it came over me in a flash, as I knelt there, that my quarrel with Sir Reuben, my stealing out to meet Humphrey, the fact that I was being sent away on the morrow, made a fatal sequence. They would say that I had let Humphrey in, and that Humphrey had killed Sir Reuben out of revenge. If I said that I had seen Charles Leverson leaving the room, no one would believe me.

'It was terrible, M. Poirot! I knelt there, and thought and thought, and the more I thought the more my nerve failed me. Presently I noticed Sir Reuben's keys which had dropped from his pocket as he fell. Among them was the key of the safe, the combination word I already knew, since Lady Astwell had mentioned it once in my hearing. I went over to that safe, M. Poirot, unlocked it and rummaged through the papers I found there.

'In the end I found what I was looking for. Humphrey had been perfectly right. Sir Reuben was behind the Mpala Gold Fields, and he had deliberately swindled Humphrey. That made it all the worse. It gave a perfectly definite motive for Humphrey having committed the crime. I put the papers back in the safe, left the key in the door of it, and went straight upstairs to my room. In the morning I pretended to be surprised and horror-stricken, like everyone else, when the housemaid discovered the body.'

She stopped and looked piteously across at Poirot.

'You do believe me, M. Poirot. Oh, do say you believe me!'

'I believe you, Mademoiselle,' said Poirot; 'you have explained many things that puzzled me. Your absolute certainty, for one thing, that Charles Leverson had committed the crime, and at the same time your persistent efforts to keep me from coming down here.'

Lily nodded.

'I was afraid of you,' she admitted frankly. 'Lady Astwell could not know, as I did, that Charles was guilty, and I couldn't say anything. I hoped against hope that you would refuse to take the case.'

'But for that obvious anxiety on your part, I might have done so,' said Poirot drily.

Lily looked at him swiftly, her lips trembled a little.

'And now, M. Poirot, what – what are you going to do?'

'As far as you are concerned, Mademoiselle, nothing. I believe your story, and I accept it. The next step is to go to London and see Inspector Miller.'

'And then?' asked Lily.

'And then,' said Poirot, 'we shall see.'

Outside the door of the study he looked once more at the little square of stained green chiffon which he held in his hand.

'Amazing,' he murmured to himself complacently, 'the ingenuity of Hercule Poirot.'

VII

Detective-Inspector Miller was not particularly fond of M. Hercule Poirot. He did not belong to that small band of inspectors at the Yard who welcomed the little Belgian's co-operation. He was wont to say that Hercule Poirot was much over-rated. In this case he felt pretty sure of himself, and greeted Poirot with high good humour in consequence.

'Acting for Lady Astwell, are you? Well, you have taken up a mare's nest in that case.'

'There is, then, no possible doubt about the matter?'

Miller winked. 'Never was a clearer case, short of catching a murderer absolutely red-handed.'

'M. Leverson has made a statement, I understand?'

'He had better have kept his mouth shut,' said the detective. 'He repeats over and over again that he went straight up to his room and never went near his uncle. That's a fool story on the face of it.'

'It is certainly against the weight of evidence,' murmured Poirot. 'How does he strike you, this young M. Leverson?'

'Darned young fool.'

'A weak character, eh?'

The inspector nodded.

217

'One would hardly think a young man of that type would have the – how do you say it – the bowels to commit such a crime.'

'On the face of it, no,' agreed the inspector. 'But, bless you, I have come across the same thing many times. Get a weak, dissipated young man into a corner, fill him up with a drop too much to drink, and for a limited amount of time you can turn him into a fire-eater. A weak man in a corner is more dangerous than a strong man.'

'That is true; yes; that is true what you say.'

Miller unbent a little further.

'Of course, it is all right for you, M. Poirot,' he said. 'You get your fees just the same, and naturally you have to make a pretence of examining the evidence to satisfy her ladyship. I can understand all that.'

'You understand such interesting things,' murmured Poirot, and took his leave.

His next call was upon the solicitor representing Charles Leverson. Mr Mayhew was a thin, dry, cautious gentleman. He received Poirot with reserve. Poirot, however, had his own ways of inducing confidence. In ten minutes' time the two were talking together amicably.

'You will understand,' said Poirot, 'I am acting in this case solely on behalf of Mr Leverson. That is Lady Astwell's wish. She is convinced that he is not guilty.'

'Yes, yes, quite so,' said Mr Mayhew without enthusiasm.

Poirot's eyes twinkled. 'You do not perhaps attach much importance to the opinions of Lady Astwell?' he suggested.

'She might be just as sure of his guilt tomorrow,' said the lawyer drily.

'Her intuitions are not evidence certainly,' agreed Poirot, 'and on the face of it the case looks very black against this poor young man.'

'It is a pity he said what he did to the police,' said the lawyer; 'it will be no good his sticking to that story.'

'Has he stuck to it with you?' inquired Poirot.

Mayhew nodded. 'It never varies an iota. He repeats it like a parrot.'

'And that is what destroys your faith in him,' mused the other. 'Ah, don't deny it,' he added quickly, holding up an arresting hand. 'I see it only too plainly. In your heart you believe him guilty. But listen now to me, to me, Hercule Poirot. I present to you a case.

'This young man comes home, he has drunk the cocktail, the cocktail, and again the cocktail, also without doubt the English whisky and soda many times. He is full of, what you call it? the courage Dutch, and in that mood he let himself into the house with his latch-key, and he goes with unsteady steps up to the Tower room. He looks in at the door and sees in the dim light his uncle, apparently bending over the desk.

'M. Leverson is full, as we have said, of the courage Dutch. He lets himself go, he tells his uncle just what he thinks of him. He defies him, he insults him, and the more his uncle does not answer back, the more he is encouraged to go on, to repeat himself, to say the same thing over and over again, and each time more loudly. But at last the continued silence of his uncle awakens an apprehension. He goes nearer to him, he lays his hand on his uncle's shoulder, and his uncle's figure crumples under his touch and sinks in a heap to the ground.

'He is sobered then, this M. Leverson. The chair falls with a crash, and he bends over Sir Reuben. He realizes what has happened, he looks at his hand covered with something warm and red. He is in a panic then, he would give anything on earth to recall the cry which has just sprung from his lips, echoing through the house. Mechanically he picks up the chair, then he hastens out through the door and listens. He fancies he hears a sound, and immediately, automatically, he pretends to be speaking to his uncle through the open door.

'The sound is not repeated. He is convinced he has

been mistaken in thinking he heard one. Now all is silence, he creeps up to his room, and at once it occurs to him how much better it will be if he pretends never to have been near his uncle that night. So he tells his story. Parsons at that time, remember, has said nothing of what he heard. When he does do so, it is too late for M. Leverson to change. He is stupid, and he is obstinate, he sticks to his story. Tell me, Monsieur, is that not possible?'

'Yes,' said the lawyer, 'I suppose in the way you put it that it is possible.'

Poirot rose to his feet.

'You have the privilege of seeing M. Leverson,' he said. 'Put to him the story I have told you, and ask him if it is not true.'

Outside the lawyer's office, Poirot hailed a taxi.

'Three-four-eight Harley Street,' he murmured to the driver.

VIII

Poirot's departure for London had taken Lady Astwell by surprise, for the little man had not made any mention of what he proposed doing. On his return, after an absence of twenty-four hours, he was informed by Parsons that Lady Astwell would like to see him as soon as possible. Poirot found the lady in her own boudoir. She was lying down on the divan, her head propped up by cushions, and she looked startlingly ill and haggard; far more so than she had done on the day Poirot arrived.

'So you have come back, M. Poirot?'

'I have returned, Madame.'

'You went to London?'

Poirot nodded.

'You didn't tell me you were going,' said Lady Astwell sharply.

'A thousand apologies, Madame, I am in error, I should have done so. *La prochaine fois* –'

'You will do exactly the same,' interrupted Lady Astwell with a shrewd touch of humour. 'Do things first and tell people afterwards, that is your motto right enough.'

'Perhaps it has also been Madame's motto?' His eyes twinkled.

'Now and then, perhaps,' admitted the other. 'What did you go up to London for, M. Poirot? You can tell me now, I suppose?'

'I had an interview with the good Inspector Miller, and also with the excellent Mr Mayhew.'

Lady Astwell's eyes searched his face.

'And you think, now –?' she said slowly.

Poirot's eyes were fixed on her steadily.

'That there is a possibility of Charles Leverson's innocence,' he said gravely.

'Ah!' Lady Astwell half-sprung up, sending two cushions rolling to the ground. 'I was right, then, I was right!'

'I said a possibility, Madame, that is all.'

Something in his tone seemed to strike her. She raised herself on one elbow and regarded him piercingly.

'Can I do anything?' she asked.

'Yes,' he nodded his head, 'you can tell me, Lady Astwell, why you suspect Owen Trefusis.'

'I have told you I *know* – that's all.'

'Unfortunately, that is not enough,' said Poirot drily. 'Cast your mind back to the fatal evening, Madame. Remember each detail, each tiny happening. What did you notice or observe about the secretary? I, Hercule Poirot, tell you there must have been *something*.'

Lady Astwell shook her head.

'I hardly noticed him at all that evening,' she said, 'and I certainly was not thinking of him.'

'Your mind was taken up by something else?'

'Yes.'

'With your husband's animus against Miss Lily Margrave?'

'That's right,' said Lady Astwell, nodding her head; 'you seem to know all about it, M. Poirot.'

223

'Me, I know everything,' declared the little man with an absurdly grandiose air.

'I am fond of Lily, M. Poirot; you have seen that for yourself. Reuben began kicking up a rumpus about some reference or other of hers. Mind you, I don't say she hadn't cheated about it. She had. But, bless you, I have done many worse things than that in the old days. You have got to be up to all sorts of tricks to get round theatrical managers. There is nothing I wouldn't have written, or said, or done, in my time.

'Lily wanted this job, and she put in a lot of slick work that was not quite – well, quite the thing, you know. Men are so stupid about that sort of thing; Lily really might have been a bank clerk absconding with millions for the fuss he made about it. I was terribly worried all the evening, because, although I could usually get round Reuben in the end, he was terribly pig-headed at times, poor darling. So of course I hadn't time to go noticing secretaries, not that one does notice Mr Trefusis much, anyway. He is just there and that's all there is to it.'

'I have noticed that fact about M. Trefusis,' said Poirot. 'His is not a personality that stands forth, that shines, that hits you cr-r-rack.'

'No,' said Lady Astwell, 'he is not like Victor.'

'M. Victor Astwell is, I should say, explosive.'

'That is a splendid word for him,' said Lady Astwell.

'He explodes all over the house, like one of those thingamajig firework things.'

'A somewhat quick temper, I should imagine?' suggested Poirot.

'Oh, he's a perfect devil when roused,' said Lady Astwell, 'but bless you, *I'm* not afraid of him. All bark and no bite to Victor.'

Poirot looked at the ceiling.

'And you can tell me nothing about the secretary that evening?' he murmured gently.

'I tell you, M. Poirot, I *know*. It's intuition. A woman's intuition –'

'Will not hang a man,' said Poirot, 'and what is more to the point, it will not save a man from being hanged. Lady Astwell, if you sincerely believe that M. Leverson is innocent, and that your suspicions of the secretary are well-founded, will you consent to a little experiment?'

'What kind of an experiment?' demanded Lady Astwell suspiciously.

'Will you permit yourself to be put into a condition of hypnosis?'

'Whatever for?'

Poirot leaned forward.

'If I were to tell you, Madame, that your intuition is based on certain facts recorded subconsciously, you would probably be sceptical. I will only say, then, that this experiment I propose may be of great importance to that unfortunate young man, Charles Leverson. You will not refuse?'

'Who is going to put me into a trance?' demanded Lady Astwell suspiciously. 'You?'

'A friend of mine, Lady Astwell, arrives, if I mistake not, at this very minute. I hear the wheels of the car outside.'

'Who is he?'

'A Dr Cazalet of Harley Street.'

'Is he – all right?' asked Lady Astwell apprehensively.

'He is not a quack, Madame, if that is what you mean. You can trust yourself in his hands quite safely.'

'Well,' said Lady Astwell with a sigh, 'I think it is all bunkum, but you can try if you like. Nobody is going to say that I stood in your way.'

'A thousand thanks, Madame.'

Poirot hurried from the room. In a few minutes he returned ushering in a cheerful, round-faced little man, with spectacles, who was very upsetting to Lady Astwell's conception of what a hypnotist should look like. Poirot introduced them.

'Well,' said Lady Astwell good-humouredly, 'how do we start this tomfoolery?'

'Quite simple, Lady Astwell, quite simple,' said the

little doctor. 'Just lean back, so – that's right, that's right. No need to be uneasy.'

'I am not in the least uneasy,' said Lady Astwell. 'I should like to see anyone hypnotizing me against my will.'

Dr Cazalet smiled broadly.

'Yes, but if you consent, it won't be against your will, will it?' he said cheerfully. 'That's right. Turn off that other light, will you, M. Poirot? Just let yourself go to sleep, Lady Astwell.'

He shifted his position a little.

'It's getting late. You are sleepy – very sleepy. Your eyelids are heavy, they are closing – closing – closing. Soon you will be asleep . . .'

His voice droned on, low, soothing, and monotonous. Presently he leaned forward and gently lifted Lady Astwell's right eyelid. Then he turned to Poirot, nodding in a satisfied manner.

'That's all right,' he said in a low voice. 'Shall I go ahead?'

'If you please.'

The doctor spoke out sharply and authoritatively: 'You are asleep, Lady Astwell, but you hear me, and you can answer my questions.'

Without stirring or raising an eyelid, the motionless figure on the sofa replied in a low, monotonous voice:

'I hear you. I can answer your questions.'

'Lady Astwell, I want you to go back to the evening on which your husband was murdered. You remember that evening?'

'Yes.'

'You are at the dinner table. Describe to me what you saw and felt.'

The prone figure stirred a little restlessly.

'I am in great distress. I am worried about Lily.'

'We know that; tell us what you saw.'

'Victor is eating all the salted almonds; he is greedy. Tomorrow I shall tell Parsons not to put the dish on that side of the table.'

'Go on, Lady Astwell.'

'Reuben is in a bad humour tonight. I don't think it is altogether about Lily. It is something to do with business. Victor looks at him in a queer way.'

'Tell us about Mr Trefusis, Lady Astwell.'

'His left shirt cuff is frayed. He puts a lot of grease on his hair. I wish men didn't, it ruins the covers in the drawing-room.'

Cazalet looked at Poirot; the other made a motion with his head.

'It is after dinner, Lady Astwell, you are having coffee. Describe the scene to me.'

'The coffee is good tonight. It varies. Cook is very unreliable over her coffee. Lily keeps looking out of the window, I don't know why. Now Reuben comes into the room; he is in one of his worst moods tonight, and bursts out with a perfect flood of abuse to poor Mr Trefusis. Mr Trefusis has his hand round the paper knife, the big one with the sharp blade like a knife. How hard he is grasping it; his knuckles are quite white. Look, he has dug it so hard in the table that the point snaps. He holds it just as you would hold a dagger you were going to stick into someone. There, they have gone out together now. Lily has got her green evening dress on; she looks so pretty in green, just like a lily. I must have the covers cleaned next week.'

'Just a minute, Lady Astwell.'

The doctor leaned across to Poirot.

'We have got it, I think,' he murmured; 'that action with the paper knife, that's what convinced her that the secretary did the thing.'

'Let us go on to the Tower room now.'

The doctor nodded, and began once more to question Lady Astwell in his high, decisive voice.

'It is later in the evening; you are in the Tower room with your husband. You and he have had a terrible scene together, have you not?'

Again the figure stirred uneasily.

'Yes – terrible – terrible. We said dreadful things – both of us.'

'Never mind that now. You can see the room clearly, the curtains were drawn, the lights were on.'

'Not the middle light, only the desk light.'

'You are leaving your husband now, you are saying good night to him.'

'No, I was too angry.'

'It is the last time you will see him; very soon he will be murdered. Do you know who murdered him, Lady Astwell?'

'Yes. Mr Trefusis.'

'Why do you say that?'

'Because of the bulge – the bulge in the curtain.'

'There was a bulge in the curtain?'

'Yes.'

'You saw it?'

'Yes. I almost touched it.'

'Was there a man concealed there – Mr Trefusis?'

'Yes.'

'How do you know?'

For the first time the monotonous answering voice hesitated and lost confidence.

'I – I – because of the paper knife.'

Poirot and the doctor again interchanged swift glances.

'I don't understand you, Lady Astwell. There was a bulge in the curtain, you say? Someone concealed there? You didn't see that person?'

'No.'

'You thought it was Mr Trefusis because of the way he held the paper knife earlier?'

'Yes.'

'But Mr Trefusis had gone to bed, had he not?'

'Yes – yes, that's right, he had gone away to his room.'

'So he couldn't have been behind the curtain in the window?'

'No – no, of course not, he wasn't there.'

'He had said good night to your husband some time before, hadn't he?'

'Yes.'

'And you didn't see him again?'

'No.'

She was stirring now, throwing herself about, moaning faintly.

'She is coming out,' said the doctor. 'Well, I think we have got all we can, eh?'

Poirot nodded. The doctor leaned over Lady Astwell.

'You are waking,' he murmured softly. 'You are waking now. In another minute you will open your eyes.'

The two men waited, and presently Lady Astwell sat upright and stared at them both.

'Have I been having a nap?'

'That's it, Lady Astwell, just a little sleep,' said the doctor.

She looked at him.

'Some of your hocus-pocus, eh?'

'You don't feel any the worse, I hope,' he asked.

Lady Astwell yawned.

'I feel rather tired and done up.'

The doctor rose.

'I will ask them to send you up some coffee,' he said, 'and we will leave you for the present.'

'Did I – say anything?' Lady Astwell called after them as they reached the door.

Poirot smiled back at her.

'Nothing of great importance, Madame. You informed us that the drawing-room covers needed cleaning.'

'So they do,' said Lady Astwell. 'You needn't have put me into a trance to get me to tell you that.' She laughed good-humouredly. 'Anything more?'

'Do you remember M. Trefusis picking up a paper knife in the drawing-room that night?' asked Poirot.

'I don't know, I'm sure,' said Lady Astwell. 'He may have done so.'

'Does a bulge in the curtain convey anything to you?'

Lady Astwell frowned.

'I seem to remember,' she said slowly. 'No – it's gone, and yet –'

'Do not distress yourself, Lady Astwell,' said Poirot

quickly; 'it is of no importance – of no importance whatever.'

The doctor went with Poirot to the latter's room.

'Well,' said Cazalet, 'I think this explains things pretty clearly. No doubt when Sir Reuben was dressing down the secretary, the latter grabbed tight hold on a paper knife, and had to exercise a good deal of self-control to prevent himself answering back. Lady Astwell's conscious mind was wholly taken up with the problem of Lily Margrave, but her subconscious mind noticed and misconstrued the action.

'It implanted in her the firm conviction that Trefusis murdered Sir Reuben. Now we come to the bulge in the curtain. That is interesting. I take it from what you have told me of the Tower room that the desk was right in the window. There are curtains across that window, of course?'

'Yes, *mon ami*, black velvet curtains.'

'And there is room in the embrasure of the window for anyone to remain concealed behind them?'

'There would be just room, I think.'

'Then there seems at least a possibility,' said the doctor slowly, 'that someone was concealed in the room, but if so it could not be the secretary, since they both saw him leave the room. It could not be Victor Astwell, for Trefusis met him going out, and it could not be Lily Margrave. Whoever it was must have been concealed there *before* Sir Reuben entered the room that evening. You have told me pretty well how the land lies. Now what about Captain Naylor? Could it have been he who was concealed there?'

'It is always possible,' admitted Poirot. 'He certainly dined at the hotel, but how soon he went out afterwards is difficult to fix exactly. He returned about half past twelve.'

'Then it might have been he,' said the doctor, 'and if so, he committed the crime. He had the motive, and there was a weapon near at hand. You don't seem satisfied with the idea, though?'

'Me, I have other ideas,' confessed Poirot. 'Tell me now, *M. le Docteur*, supposing for one minute that Lady Astwell herself had committed this crime, would she necessarily betray the fact in the hypnotic state?'

The doctor whistled.

'So that's what you are getting at? Lady Astwell is the criminal, eh? Of course – it is possible; I never thought of it till this minute. She was the last to be with him, and no one saw him alive afterwards. As to your question, I should be inclined to say – no. Lady Astwell would go into the hypnotic state with a strong mental reservation to say nothing of her own part in the crime. She would answer my questions truthfully, but she would be dumb on that one point. Yet I should hardly have expected her to be so insistent on Mr Trefusis's guilt.'

'I comprehend,' said Poirot. 'But I have not said that I believe Lady Astwell to be the criminal. It is a suggestion, that is all.'

'It is an interesting case,' said the doctor after a minute or two. 'Granting Charles Leverson is innocent, there are so many possibilities: Humphrey Naylor, Lady Astwell, and even Lily Margrave.'

'There is another you have not mentioned,' said Poirot quietly, 'Victor Astwell. According to his own story, he sat in his room with the door open waiting for Charles Leverson's return, but we have only his own words for it, you comprehend?'

'He is the bad-tempered fellow, isn't he?' asked the doctor. 'The one you told me about?'

'That is so,' agreed Poirot.

The doctor rose to his feet.

'Well, I must be getting back to town. You will let me know how things shape, won't you?'

After the doctor had left, Poirot pulled the bell for George.

'A cup of tisane, George. My nerves are much disturbed.'

'Certainly, sir,' said George. 'I will prepare it immediately.'

Ten minutes later he brought a steaming cup to

his master. Poirot inhaled the noxious fumes with pleasure. As he sipped it, he soliloquized aloud.

'The chase is different all over the world. To catch the fox you ride hard with the dogs. You shout, you run, it is a matter of speed. I have not shot the stag myself, but I understand that to do so you crawl for many long, long hours upon your stomach. My friend Hastings has recounted the affair to me. Our method here, my good George, must be neither of these. Let us reflect upon the household cat. For many long, weary hours, he watches the mousehole, he makes no movement, he betrays no energy, but – he does not go away.'

He sighed and put the empty cup down on its saucer.

'I told you to pack for a few days. Tomorrow, my good George, you will go to London and bring down what is necessary for a fortnight.'

'Very good, sir,' said George. As usual he displayed no emotion.

IX

The apparently permanent presence of Hercule Poirot at Mon Repos was disquieting to many people. Victor Astwell remonstrated with his sister-in-law about it.

'It's all very well, Nancy. You don't know what fellows of that kind are like. He has found jolly comfortable quarters here, and he is evidently going to settle down comfortably for about a month, charging you several guineas a day all the while.'

Lady Astwell's reply was to the effect that she could manage her own affairs without interference.

Lily Margrave tried earnestly to conceal her perturbation. At the time, she had felt sure that Poirot believed her story. Now she was not so certain.

Poirot did not play an entirely quiescent game. On the fifth day of his sojourn he brought down a small thumbograph album to dinner. As a method of getting the thumbprints of the household, it seemed a rather clumsy device, yet not perhaps so clumsy as it seemed, since no one could afford to refuse their thumbprints. Only after the little man had retired to bed did Victor Astwell state his views.

'You see what it means, Nancy. He is out after one of us.'

'Don't be absurd, Victor.'

'Well, what other meaning could that blinking little book of his have?'

'M. Poirot knows what he is doing,' said Lady Astwell complacently, and looked with some meaning at Owen Trefusis.

On another occasion, Poirot introduced the game of

237

tracing footprints on a sheet of paper. The following morning, going with his soft cat-like tread into the library, the detective startled Owen Trefusis, who leaped from his chair as though he had been shot.

'You must really excuse me, M. Poirot,' he said primly, 'but you have us on the jump.'

'Indeed, how is that?' demanded the little man innocently.

'I will admit,' said the secretary, 'that I thought the case against Charles Leverson utterly overwhelming. You apparently do not find it so.'

Poirot was standing looking out of the window. He turned suddenly to the other.

'I shall tell you something, M. Trefusis – in confidence.'

'Yes?'

Poirot seemed in no hurry to begin. He waited a minute, hesitating. When he did speak, the opening words were coincident with the opening and shutting of the front door. For a man saying something in confidence, he spoke rather loudly, his voice drowning the sound of a footstep in the hall outside.

'I shall tell you this in confidence, Mr Trefusis. There is new evidence. It goes to prove that when Charles Leverson entered the Tower room that night, Sir Reuben was already dead.'

The secretary stared at him.

'But what evidence? Why have we not heard of it?'

'You *will* hear,' said the little man mysteriously. 'In the meantime, you and I alone know the secret.'

He skipped nimbly out of the room, and almost collided with Victor Astwell in the hall outside.

'You have just come in, eh, Monsieur?'

Astwell nodded.

'Beastly day outside,' he said, breathing hard, 'cold and blowy.'

'Ah,' said Poirot, 'I shall not promenade myself today – me, I am like a cat, I sit by the fire and keep myself warm.'

'*Ça marche*, George,' he said that evening to the faithful valet, rubbing his hands as he spoke, 'they are on the tenterhooks – the jump! It is hard, George, to play the game of the cat, the waiting game, but it answers, yes, it answers wonderfully. Tomorrow we make a further effect.'

On the following day, Trefusis was obliged to go up to town. He went up by the same train as Victor Astwell. No sooner had they left the house than Poirot was galvanized into a fever of activity.

'Come, George, let us hurry to work. If the housemaid should approach these rooms, you must delay her. Speak to her sweet nothings, George, and keep her in the corridor.'

He went first to the secretary's room, and began a thorough search. Not a drawer or a shelf was left uninspected. Then he replaced everything hurriedly, and declared his quest finished. George, on guard in the doorway, gave way to a deferential cough.

'If you will excuse me, sir?'

'Yes, my good George?'

'The shoes, sir. The two pairs of brown shoes were on the second shelf, and the patent leather ones were on the shelf underneath. In replacing them you have reversed the order.'

'Marvellous!' cried Poirot, holding up his hands. 'But let us not distress ourselves over that. It is of no importance, I assure you, George. Never will M. Trefusis notice such a trifling matter.'

'As you think, sir,' said George.

'It is your business to notice such things,' said Poirot encouragingly as he clapped the other on the shoulder. 'It reflects credit upon you.'

The valet did not reply, and when, later in the day, the proceeding was repeated in the room of Victor Astwell, he made no comment on the fact that Mr Astwell's underclothing was not returned to its drawers strictly according to plan. Yet, in the second case at least, events proved the valet to be right and Poirot wrong. Victor Astwell came storming into the drawing-room that evening.

'Now, look here, you blasted little Belgian jacka-napes, what do you mean by searching my room? What the devil do you think you are going to find there? I won't have it, do you hear? That's what comes of having a ferreting little spy in the house.'

Poirot's hands spread themselves out eloquently as his words tumbled one over the other. He offered a hundred apologies, a thousand, a million. He had been maladroit, officious, he was confused. He had taken an unwarranted liberty. In the end the infuriated gentleman was forced to subside, still growling.

And again that evening, sipping his tisane, Poirot murmured to George:

'It marches, my good George, yes – it marches.'

X

'Friday,' observed Hercule Poirot thoughtfully, 'is my lucky day.'

'Indeed, sir.'

'You are not superstitious, perhaps, my good George?'

'I prefer not to sit down thirteen at table, sir, and I am adverse to passing under ladders. I have no superstitions about a Friday, sir.'

'That is well,' said Poirot, 'for, see you, today we make our Waterloo.'

Agatha Christie

'Really, sir.'

'You have such enthusiasm, my good George, you do not even ask what I propose to do.'

'And what is that, sir?'

'Today, George, I make a final thorough search of the Tower room.'

True enough, after breakfast, Poirot, with the permission of Lady Astwell, went to the scene of the crime. There, at various times of the morning, members of the household saw him crawling about on all fours, examining minutely the black velvet curtains and standing on high chairs to examine the picture frames on the wall. Lady Astwell for the first time displayed uneasiness.

'I have to admit it,' she said. 'He is getting on my nerves at last. He has something up his sleeve, and I don't know what it is. And the way he is crawling about on the floor up there like a dog makes me downright shivery. What is he looking for, I'd like to know? Lily, my dear, I wish you would go up and see what he is up to now. No, on the whole, I'd rather you stayed with me.'

'Shall I go, Lady Astwell?' asked the secretary, rising from the desk.

'If you would, Mr Trefusis.'

Owen Trefusis left the room and mounted the stairs to the Tower room. At first glance, he thought the room was empty, there was certainly no sign of Hercule Poirot there. He was just returning to go down again when a sound caught his ears; he then saw the little man half-way down the spiral staircase that led to the bedroom above.

He was on his hands and knees; in his left hand was a little pocket lens, and through this he was examining minutely something on the woodwork beside the stair carpet.

As the secretary watched him, he uttered a sudden grunt, and slipped the lens into his pocket. He then rose to his feet, holding something between his finger and thumb. At that moment he became aware of the secretary's presence.

'Ah, hah! M. Trefusis, I didn't hear you enter.'

He was in that moment a different man. Triumph and exultation beamed all over his face. Trefusis stared at him in surprise.

'What is the matter, M. Poirot? You look very pleased.'

The little man puffed out his chest.

'Yes, indeed. See you I have at last found that which I have been looking for from the beginning. I have here between my finger and thumb the one thing necessary to convict the criminal.'

'Then,' the secretary raised his eyebrows, 'it was not Charles Leverson?'

'It was not Charles Leverson,' said Poirot. 'Until this moment, though I know the criminal, I am not sure of his name, but at last all is clear.'

He stepped down the stairs and tapped the secretary on the shoulder.

'I am obliged to go to London immediately. Speak to Lady Astwell for me. Will you request of her that everyone should be assembled in the Tower room this evening at nine o'clock? I shall be there then, and I shall reveal the truth. Ah, me, but I am well content.'

And, breaking into a fantastic little dance, he skipped from the Tower room. Trefusis was left staring after him.

A few minutes later Poirot appeared in the library, demanding if anyone could supply him with a little cardboard box.

'Unfortunately, I have not such a thing with me,' he explained, 'and there is something of great value that it is necessary for me to put inside.'

From one of the drawers in the desk Trefusis produced a small box, and Poirot professed himself highly delighted with it.

He hurried upstairs with his treasure-trove; meeting George on the landing, he handed the box to him.

'There is something of great importance inside,' he explained. 'Place it, my good George, in the second drawer of my dressing-table, beside the jewel case that contains my pearl studs.'

'Very good, sir,' said George.

'Do not break it,' said Poirot. 'Be very careful. Inside that box is something that will hang a criminal.'

'You don't say, sir,' said George.

Poirot hurried down the stairs again and, seizing his hat, departed from the house at a brisk run.

XI

His return was more unostentatious. The faithful George, according to orders, admitted him by the side door.

'They are all in the Tower room?' inquired Poirot.

'Yes, sir.'

There was a murmured interchange of a few words, and then Poirot mounted with the triumphant step of the victor to that room where the murder had taken place less than a month ago. His eyes swept around the room. They were all there: Lady Astwell, Victor Astwell, Lily Margrave, the secretary, and Parsons, the butler. The latter was hovering by the door uncertainly.

'George, sir, said I should be needed here,' said

245

Parsons as Poirot made his appearance. 'I don't know if that is right, sir?'

'Quite right,' said Poirot. 'Remain, I pray of you.'

He advanced to the middle of the room.

'This has been a case of great interest,' he said in a slow, reflective voice. 'It is interesting because anyone might have murdered Sir Reuben Astwell. Who inherits his money? Charles Leverson and Lady Astwell. Who was with him last that night? Lady Astwell. Who quarrelled with him violently? Again Lady Astwell.'

'What are you talking about?' cried Lady Astwell. 'I don't understand, I –'

'But someone else quarrelled with Sir Reuben,' continued Poirot in a pensive voice. 'Someone else left him that night white with rage. Supposing Lady Astwell left her husband alive at a quarter to twelve that night, there would be ten minutes before Mr Charles Leverson returned, ten minutes in which it would be possible for someone from the second floor to steal down and do the deed, and then return to his room again.'

Victor Astwell sprang up with a cry.

'What the hell –?' He stopped, choking with rage.

'In a rage, Mr Astwell, you once killed a man in West Africa.'

'I don't believe it,' cried Lily Margrave.

She came forward, her hands clenched, two bright spots of colour in her cheeks.

'I don't believe it,' repeated the girl. She came close to Victor Astwell's side.

'It's true, Lily,' said Astwell, 'but there are things this man doesn't know. The fellow I killed was a witchdoctor who had just massacred fifteen children. I consider that I was justified.'

Lily came up to Poirot.

'M. Poirot,' she said earnestly, 'you are wrong. Because a man has a sharp temper, because he breaks out and says all kinds of things, that is not any reason why he should do a murder. I know – I *know*, I tell you – that Mr Astwell is incapable of such a thing.'

Poirot looked at her, a very curious smile on his face. Then he took her hand in his and patted it gently.

'You see, Mademoiselle,' he said gently, 'you also have your intuitions. So you believe in Mr Astwell, do you?'

Lily spoke quietly.

'Mr Astwell is a good man,' she said, 'and he is honest. He had nothing to do with the inside work of the Mpala Gold Fields. He is good through and through, and – I have promised to marry him.'

Victor Astwell came to her side and took her other hand.

Agatha Christie

'Before God, M. Poirot,' he said, 'I didn't kill my brother.'

'I know you did not,' said Poirot.

His eyes swept around the room.

'Listen, my friends. In a hypnotic trance, Lady Astwell mentioned having seen a bulge in the curtain that night.'

Everyone's eyes swept to the window.

'You mean there was a burglar concealed there?' exclaimed Victor Astwell. 'What a splendid solution!'

'Ah,' said Poirot gently. 'But it was not *that* curtain.'

He wheeled around and pointed to the curtain that masked the little staircase.

'Sir Reuben used the bedroom the night prior to the crime. He breakfasted in bed, and he had Mr Trefusis up there to give him instructions. I don't know what it was that Mr Trefusis left in that bedroom, but there was something. When he said good night to Sir Reuben and Lady Astwell, he remembered this thing and ran up the stairs to fetch it. I don't think either the husband or wife noticed him, for they had already begun a violent discussion. They were in the middle of this quarrel when Mr Trefusis came down the stairs again.

'The things they were saying to each other were of so intimate and personal a nature that Mr Trefusis was placed in a very awkward position. It was clear to him that they imagined he had left the room some time ago. Fearing to arouse Sir Reuben's anger against himself, he decided to remain where he was and slip out later. He stayed there behind the curtain, and as Lady Astwell left the room she subconsciously noticed the outline of his form there.

'When Lady Astwell had left the room, Trefusis tried to steal out unobserved, but Sir Reuben happened to turn his head, and became aware of the secretary's presence. Already in a bad temper, Sir Reuben hurled abuse at his secretary, and accused him of deliberately eavesdropping and spying.

'Messieurs and Mesdames, I am a student of psychology. All through this case I have looked, not for the bad-tempered man or woman, for bad temper is its own safety valve. He who can bark does not bite. No, I have looked for the good-tempered man, for the man who is patient and self-controlled, for the man who for nine years has played the part of the under dog. There is no strain so great as that which has endured for years, there is no resentment like that which accumulates slowly.

'For nine years Sir Reuben has bullied and browbeaten his secretary, and for nine years that man has endured in silence. But there comes a day when at last the strain reaches its breaking point. *Something snaps!* It was so that night. Sir Reuben sat down at his desk again, but the secretary, instead of turning humbly and meekly to the door, picks up the heavy wooden club, and strikes down the man who had bullied him once too often.'

He turned to Trefusis, who was staring at him as though turned to stone.

'It was so simple, your alibi. Mr Astwell thought you were in your room, but *no one saw you go there.* You were just stealing out after striking down Sir Reuben when you heard a sound, and you hastened back to cover, behind the curtain. You were behind there when Charles Leverson entered the room, you were there when Lily Margrave came. It was not till long after that that you crept up through a silent house to your bedroom. Do you deny it?'

Trefusis began to stammer.

'I – I never –'

'Ah! Let us finish this. For two weeks now I have played the comedy. I have showed you the net closing slowly around you. The fingerprints, footprints, the search of your room with the things artistically replaced. I have struck terror into you with all of this; you have lain awake at night fearing and wondering; did you leave a fingerprint in the room or a footprint somewhere?

'Again and again you have gone over the events of that night wondering what you have done or left undone, and so I brought you to the state where you made a slip. I saw the fear leap into your eyes today when I picked up something from the stairs where you had stood hidden that night. Then I made a great parade, the little box, the entrusting of it to George, and I go out.'

Poirot turned towards the door.

'George?'

'I am here, sir.'

The valet came forward.

'Will you tell these ladies and gentlemen what my instructions were?'

'I was to remain concealed in the wardrobe in your room, sir, having placed the cardboard box where you told me to. At half past three this afternoon, sir, Mr Trefusis entered the room; he went to the drawer and took out the box in question.'

'And in that box,' continued Poirot, 'was a common pin. Me, I speak always the truth. I did pick up something on the stairs this morning. That is your English saying, is it not? "See a pin and pick it up, all the day you'll have good luck." Me, I have had good luck, I have found the murderer.'

He turned to the secretary.

'You see?' he said gently. '*You betrayed yourself.*'

Suddenly Trefusis broke down. He sank into a chair sobbing, his face buried in his hands.

'I was mad,' he groaned. 'I was mad. But, oh, my God, he badgered and bullied me beyond bearing. For years I had hated and loathed him.'

'I knew!' cried Lady Astwell.

She sprang forward, her face irradiated with savage triumph.

'I *knew* that man had done it.'

She stood there, savage and triumphant.

'And you were right,' said Poirot. 'One may call things by different names, but the fact remains. Your "intuition", Lady Astwell, proved correct. I felicitate you.'

Four-and-Twenty
Blackbirds

I

Hercule Poirot was dining with his friend, Henry Bonnington at the Gallant Endeavour in the King's Road, Chelsea.

Mr Bonnington was fond of the Gallant Endeavour. He liked the leisurely atmosphere, he liked the food which was 'plain' and 'English' and 'not a lot of made up messes'. He liked to tell people who dined with him there just exactly where Augustus John had been wont to sit and draw their attention to the famous artists' names in the visitors' book. Mr Bonnington was himself the least artistic of men – but he took a certain pride in the artistic activities of others.

Molly, the sympathetic waitress, greeted Mr Bonnington as an old friend. She prided herself on remembering her customers' likes and dislikes in the way of food.

'Good evening, sir,' she said, as the two men took

their seats at a corner table. 'You're in luck today –
turkey stuffed with chestnuts – that's your favourite,
isn't it? And ever such a nice Stilton we've got! Will
you have soup first or fish?'

Mr Bonnington deliberated the point. He said to
Poirot warningly as the latter studied the menu:

'None of your French kickshaws now. Good well-
cooked English food.'

'My friend,' Hercule Poirot waved his hand, 'I
ask no better! I put myself in your hands unre-
servedly.'

'Ah – hruup – er – hm,' replied Mr Bonnington and
gave careful attention to the matter.

These weighty matters, and the question of wine,
settled, Mr Bonnington leaned back with a sigh and
unfolded his napkin as Molly sped away.

'Good girl, that,' he said approvingly. 'Was quite
a beauty once – artists used to paint her. She knows
about food, too – and that's a great deal more important. Women are very unsound on food as a rule.
There's many a woman if she goes out with a fellow
she fancies – won't even notice what she eats. She'll
just order the first thing she sees.'

Hercule Poirot shook his head.

'C'est terrible.'

'Men aren't like that, thank God!' said Mr Bonnington
complacently.

'Never?' There was a twinkle in Hercule Poirot's eye.

'Well, perhaps when they're very young,' conceded Mr Bonnington. 'Young puppies! Young fellows nowadays are all the same – no guts – no stamina. I've no use for the young – and they,' he added with strict impartiality, 'have no use for me. Perhaps they're right! But to hear some of these young fellows talk you'd think no man had a right to be *alive* after sixty! From the way they go on, you'd wonder more of them didn't help their elderly relations out of the world.'

'It is possible,' said Hercule Poirot, 'that they do.'

'Nice mind you've got, Poirot, I must say. All this police work saps your ideals.'

Hercule Poirot smiled.

'*Tout de même,*' he said. 'It would be interesting to make a table of accidental deaths over the age of sixty. I assure you it would raise some curious speculations in your mind.'

'The trouble with you is that you've started going to look for crime – instead of waiting for crime to come to you.'

'I apologize,' said Poirot. 'I talk what you call "the shop". Tell me, my friend, of your own affairs. How does the world go with you?'

'Mess!' said Mr Bonnington. 'That's what's the matter with the world nowadays. Too much mess.

257

Agatha Christie

And too much fine language. The fine language helps to conceal the mess. Like a highly-flavoured sauce concealing the fact that the fish underneath it is none of the best! Give me an honest fillet of sole and no messy sauce over it.'

It was given him at that moment by Molly and he grunted approval.

'You know just what I like, my girl,' he said.

'Well, you come here pretty regular, don't you, sir? I ought to know what you like.'

Hercule Poirot said:

'Do people then always like the same things? Do not they like a change sometimes?'

'Not gentlemen, sir. Ladies like variety – gentlemen always like the same thing.'

'What did I tell you?' grunted Bonnington. 'Women are fundamentally unsound where food is concerned!'

He looked round the restaurant.

'The world's a funny place. See that odd-looking old fellow with a beard in the corner? Molly'll tell you he's always here Tuesdays and Thursday nights. He has come here for close on ten years now – he's a kind of landmark in the place. Yet nobody here knows his name or where he lives or what his business is. It's odd when you come to think of it.'

When the waitress brought the portions of turkey he said:

'I see you've still got Old Father Time over there?'

'That's right, sir. Tuesdays and Thursdays, his days are. Not but what he came in here on a *Monday* last week! It quite upset me! I felt I'd got my dates wrong and that it must be Tuesday without my knowing it! But he came in the next night as well – so the Monday was just a kind of extra, so to speak.'

'An interesting deviation from habit,' murmured Poirot. 'I wonder what the reason was?'

'Well, sir, if you ask me, I think he'd had some kind of upset or worry.'

'Why did you think that? His manner?'

'No, sir – not his manner exactly. He was very quiet as he always is. Never says much except good evening when he comes and goes. No, it was his *order.*'

'His order?'

'I dare say you gentlemen will laugh at me,' Molly flushed up, 'but when a gentleman has been here for ten years, you get to know his likes and dislikes. He never could bear suet pudding or blackberries and I've never known him take thick soup – but on that Monday night he ordered thick tomato soup, beefsteak and kidney pudding and blackberry tart! Seemed as though he just didn't notice *what* he ordered!'

259

Agatha Christie

'Do you know,' said Hercule Poirot, 'I find that extraordinarily interesting.'

Molly looked gratified and departed.

'Well, Poirot,' said Henry Bonnington with a chuckle. 'Let's have a few deductions from you. All in your best manner.'

'I would prefer to hear yours first.'

'Want me to be Watson, eh? Well, old fellow went to a doctor and the doctor changed his diet.'

'To thick tomato soup, steak and kidney pudding and blackberry tart? I cannot imagine any doctor doing that.'

'Don't believe it, old boy. Doctors will put you on to anything.'

'That is the only solution that occurs to you?'

Henry Bonnington said:

'Well, seriously, I suppose there's only one explanation possible. Our unknown friend was in the grip of some powerful mental emotion. He was so perturbed by it that he literally did not notice what he was ordering or eating.'

He paused a minute and then said:

'You'll be telling me next that you know just *what* was on his mind. You'll say perhaps that he was making up his mind to commit a murder.'

He laughed at his own suggestion.

Hercule Poirot did not laugh.

He has admitted that at that moment he was seriously worried. He claims that he ought then to have had some inkling of what was likely to occur.

His friends assure him that such an idea is quite fantastic.

It was some three weeks later that Hercule Poirot and Bonnington met again – this time their meeting was in the Tube.

They nodded to each other, swaying about, hanging on to adjacent straps. Then at Piccadilly Circus there was a general exodus and they found seats right at the forward end of the car – a peaceful spot since nobody passed in or out that way.

'That's better,' said Mr Bonnington. 'Selfish lot, the human race, they won't pass up the car however much you ask 'em to!'

Hercule Poirot shrugged his shoulders.

'What will you?' he said. 'Life is too uncertain.'

'That's it. Here today, gone tomorrow,' said Mr Bonnington with a kind of gloomy relish. 'And talking of that, d'you remember that old boy we noticed at the Gallant Endeavour? I shouldn't wonder if *he'd* hopped it to a better world. He's not been there for a whole week. Molly's quite upset about it.'

Hercule Poirot sat up. His green eyes flashed.

'Indeed?' he said. 'Indeed?'

Bonnington said:

'D'you remember I suggested he'd been to a doctor and been put on a diet? Diet's nonsense of course – but I shouldn't wonder if he had consulted a doctor about his health and what the doctor said gave him a bit of a jolt. That would account for him ordering things off the menu without noticing what he was doing. Quite likely the jolt he got hurried him out of the world sooner than he would have gone otherwise. Doctors ought to be careful what they tell a chap.'

'They usually are,' said Hercule Poirot.

'This is my station,' said Mr Bonnington. 'Bye, bye. Don't suppose we shall ever know now who the old boy was – not even his name. Funny world!'

He hurried out of the carriage.

Hercule Poirot, sitting frowning, looked as though he did not think it was such a funny world.

He went home and gave certain instructions to his faithful valet, George.

II

Hercule Poirot ran his finger down a list of names. It was a record of deaths within a certain area.

Poirot's finger stopped.

'Henry Gascoigne. Sixty-nine. I might try him first.'

Later in the day, Hercule Poirot was sitting in Dr MacAndrew's surgery just off the King's Road. MacAndrew was a tall red-haired Scotsman with an intelligent face.

'Gascoigne?' he said. 'Yes, that's right. Eccentric old bird. Lived alone in one of those derelict old houses that are being cleared away in order to build a block of modern flats. I hadn't attended him before, but I'd seen him about and I knew who he was. It was the dairy people got the wind up first. The milk bottles began to pile up outside. In the end the people next door sent word to the police and they broke the door in and found him. He'd pitched down the stairs and broken his neck. Had on an old dressing-gown with a ragged cord – might easily have tripped himself up with it.'

'I see,' said Hercule Poirot. 'It was quite simple – an accident.'

'That's right.'

'Had he any relations?'

'There's a nephew. Used to come along and see his uncle about once a month. Lorrimer, his name is, George Lorrimer. He's a medico himself. Lives at Wimbledon.'

'Was he upset at the old man's death?'

'I don't know that I'd say he was upset. I mean, he had an affection for the old man, but he didn't really know him very well.'

Agatha Christie

'How long had Mr Gascoigne been dead when you saw him?'

'Ah!' said Dr MacAndrew. 'This is where we get official. Not less than forty-eight hours and not more than seventy-two hours. He was found on the morning of the sixth. Actually, we got closer than that. He'd got a letter in the pocket of his dressing-gown – written on the third – posted in Wimbledon that afternoon – would have been delivered somewhere around nine-twenty p.m. That puts the time of death at after nine-twenty on the evening of the third. That agrees with the contents of the stomach and the processes of digestion. He had had a meal about two hours before death. I examined him on the morning of the sixth and his condition was quite consistent with death having occurred about sixty hours previously – round about ten p.m. on the third.'

'It all seems very consistent. Tell me, when was he last seen alive?'

'He was seen in the King's Road about seven o'clock that same evening, Thursday the third, and he dined at the Gallant Endeavour restaurant at seven-thirty. It seems he always dined there on Thursdays. He was by way of being an artist, you know. An extremely bad one.'

'He had no other relations? Only this nephew?'

'There was a twin brother. The whole story is rather

curious. They hadn't seen each other for years. It seems the other brother, Anthony Gascoigne, married a very rich woman and gave up art – and the brothers quarrelled over it. Hadn't seen each other since, I believe. But oddly enough, *they died on the same day.* The elder twin passed away at three o'clock on the afternoon of the third. Once before I've known a case of twins dying on the same day – in different parts of the world! Probably just a coincidence – but there it is.'

'Is the other brother's wife alive?'

'No, she died some years ago.'

'Where did Anthony Gascoigne live?'

'He had a house on Kingston Hill. He was, I believe, from what Dr Lorrimer tells me, very much of a recluse.'

Hercule Poirot nodded thoughtfully.

The Scotsman looked at him keenly.

'What exactly have you got in your mind, M. Poirot?' he asked bluntly. 'I've answered your questions – as was my duty seeing the credentials you brought. But I'm in the dark as to what it's all about.'

Poirot said slowly:

'A simple case of accidental death, that's what you said. What I have in mind is equally simple – a simple push.'

Dr MacAndrew looked startled.

'In other words, murder! Have you any grounds for that belief?'

'No,' said Poirot. 'It is a mere supposition.'

'There must be something –' persisted the other.

Poirot did not speak. MacAndrew said:

'If it's the nephew, Lorrimer, you suspect, I don't mind telling you here and now that you are barking up the wrong tree. Lorrimer was playing bridge in Wimbledon from eight-thirty till midnight. That came out at the inquest.'

Poirot murmured:

'And presumably it was verified. The police are careful.'

The doctor said:

'Perhaps you know something against him?'

'I didn't know that there was such a person until you mentioned him.'

'Then you suspect somebody else?'

'No, no. It is not that at all. It's a case of the routine habits of the human animal. That is very important. And the dead M. Gascoigne does not fit in. It is all wrong, you see.'

'I really don't understand.'

Hercule Poirot murmured:

'The trouble is, there is too much sauce over the bad fish.'

'My dear sir?'

Hercule Poirot smiled.

'You will be having me locked up as a lunatic soon, *Monsieur le Docteur*. But I am not really a mental case – just a man who has a liking for order and method and who is worried when he comes across a fact *that does not fit in*. I must ask you to forgive me for having given you so much trouble.'

He rose and the doctor rose also.

'You know,' said MacAndrew, 'honestly I can't see anything the least bit suspicious about the death of Henry Gascoigne. I say he fell – you say somebody pushed him. It's all – well – in the air.'

Hercule Poirot sighed.

'Yes,' he said. 'It is workmanlike. Somebody has made the good job of it!'

'You still think –'

The little man spread out his hands.

'I'm an obstinate man – a man with a little idea – and nothing to support it! By the way, did Henry Gascoigne have false teeth?'

'No, his own teeth were in excellent preservation. Very creditable indeed at his age.'

'He looked after them well – they were white and well brushed?'

'Yes, I noticed them particularly. Teeth tend to grow a little yellow as one grows older, but they were in good condition.'

267

'Not discoloured in any way?'

'No. I don't think he was a smoker if that is what you mean.'

'I did not mean that precisely – it was just a long shot – which probably will not come off! Goodbye, Dr MacAndrew, and thank you for your kindness.'

He shook the doctor's hand and departed.

'And now,' he said, 'for the long shot.'

III

At the Gallant Endeavour, he sat down at the same table which he had shared with Bonnington. The girl who served him was not Molly. Molly, the girl told him, was away on a holiday.

It was only just seven and Hercule Poirot found no difficulty in entering into conversation with the girl on the subject of old Mr Gascoigne.

'Yes,' she said. 'He'd been here for years and years. But none of us girls ever knew his name. We saw about the inquest in the paper, and there was a picture of him. "There," I said to Molly. "If that isn't our 'Old Father Time'" as we used to call him.'

'He dined here on the evening of his death, did he not?'

'That's right, Thursday, the third. He was always

here on a Thursday. Tuesdays and Thursdays – punctual as a clock.'

'You don't remember, I suppose, what he had for dinner?'

'Now let me see, it was mulligatawny soup, that's right, and beefsteak pudding or was it the mutton? – no pudding, that's right, and blackberry and apple pie and cheese. And then to think of him going home and falling down those stairs that very same evening. A frayed dressing-gown cord they said it was as caused it. Of course, his clothes were always something awful – old-fashioned and put on anyhow, and all tattered, and yet he *had* a kind of air, all the same, as though he was *somebody*! Oh, we get all sorts of interesting customers here.'

She moved off.

Hercule Poirot ate his filleted sole. His eyes showed a green light.

'It is odd,' he said to himself, 'how the cleverest people slip over details. Bonnington will be interested.'

But the time had not yet come for leisurely discussion with Bonnington.

Agatha Christie

IV

Armed with introductions from a certain influential quarter, Hercule Poirot found no difficulty at all in dealing with the coroner for the district.

'A curious figure, the deceased man Gascoigne,' he observed. 'A lonely, eccentric old fellow. But his decease seems to arouse an unusual amount of attention?'

He looked with some curiosity at his visitor as he spoke.

Hercule Poirot chose his words carefully.

'There are circumstances connected with it, Monsieur, which make investigation desirable.'

'Well, how can I help you?'

'It is, I believe, within your province to order documents produced in your court to be destroyed, or to be impounded – as you think fit. A certain letter was found in the pocket of Henry Gascoigne's dressing-gown, was it not?'

'That is so.'

'A letter from his nephew, Dr George Lorrimer?'

'Quite correct. The letter was produced at the inquest as helping to fix the time of death.'

'Which was corroborated by the medical evidence?'

'Exactly.'

'Is that letter still available?'

Hercule Poirot waited rather anxiously for the reply.

When he heard that the letter was still available for examination he drew a sigh of relief.

When it was finally produced he studied it with some care. It was written in a slightly cramped hand-writing with a stylographic pen.

It ran as follows:

Dear Uncle Henry,

I am sorry to tell you that I have had no success as regards Uncle Anthony. He showed no enthusiasm for a visit from you and would give me no reply to your request that he would let bygones be bygones. He is, of course, extremely ill, and his mind is inclined to wander. I should fancy that the end is very near. He seemed hardly to remember who you were.

I am sorry to have failed you, but I can assure you that I did my best.

Your affectionate nephew,

George Lorrimer

The letter itself was dated 3rd November. Poirot glanced at the envelope's postmark – 4.30 p.m. 3 Nov.

He murmured:

'It is beautifully in order, is it not?'

V

Kingston Hill was his next objective. After a little trouble, with the exercise of good-humoured pertinacity, he obtained an interview with Amelia Hill, cook-housekeeper to the late Anthony Gascoigne.

Mrs Hill was inclined to be stiff and suspicious at first, but the charming geniality of this strange-looking foreigner would have had its effect on a stone. Mrs Amelia Hill began to unbend.

She found herself, as had so many other women before her, pouring out her troubles to a really sympathetic listener.

For fourteen years she had had charge of Mr Gascoigne's household – *not* an easy job! No, indeed! Many a woman would have quailed under the burdens *she* had had to bear! Eccentric the poor gentleman was and no denying it. Remarkably close with his money – a kind of mania with him it was – and he as rich a gentleman as might be! But Mrs Hill had served him faithfully, and put up with his ways, and naturally she'd expected at any rate a *remembrance*. But no – nothing at all! Just an old will that left all his money to his wife and if she predeceased him then everything to his brother, Henry. A will made years ago. It didn't seem fair!

Gradually Hercule Poirot detached her from her main theme of unsatisfied cupidity. It was indeed a heartless injustice! Mrs Hill could not be blamed for feeling hurt and surprised. It was well known that Mr Gascoigne was tight-fisted about money. It had even been said that the dead man had refused his only brother assistance. Mrs Hill probably knew all about that.

'Was it that that Dr Lorrimer came to see him about?' asked Mrs Hill. 'I knew it was something about his brother, but I thought it was just that his brother wanted to be reconciled. They'd quarrelled years ago.'

'I understand,' said Poirot, 'that Mr Gascoigne refused absolutely?'

'That's right enough,' said Mrs Hill with a nod. '"*Henry*?" he says, rather weak like. "*What's this about Henry? Haven't seen him for years and don't want to. Quarrelsome fellow, Henry.*" Just that.'

The conversation then reverted to Mrs Hill's own special grievances, and the unfeeling attitude of the late Mr Gascoigne's solicitor.

With some difficulty Hercule Poirot took his leave without breaking off the conversation too abruptly.

And so, just after the dinner hour, he came to Elmcrest, Dorset Road, Wimbledon, the residence of Dr George Lorrimer.

Agatha Christie

The doctor was in. Hercule Poirot was shown into the surgery and there presently Dr George Lorrimer came to him, obviously just risen from the dinner table.

'I'm not a patient, Doctor,' said Hercule Poirot. 'And my coming here is, perhaps, somewhat of an impertinence – but I'm an old man and I believe in plain and direct dealing. I do not care for lawyers and their long-winded roundabout methods.'

He had certainly aroused Lorrimer's interest. The doctor was a clean-shaven man of middle height. His hair was brown but his eyelashes were almost white which gave his eyes a pale, boiled appearance. His manner was brisk and not without humour.

'Lawyers?' he said, raising his eyebrows. 'Hate the fellows! You rouse my curiosity, my dear sir. Pray sit down.'

Poirot did so and then produced one of his professional cards which he handed to the doctor.

George Lorrimer's white eyelashes blinked.

Poirot leaned forward confidentially. 'A good many of my clients are women,' he said.

'Naturally,' said Dr George Lorrimer, with a slight twinkle.

'As you say, naturally,' agreed Poirot. 'Women distrust the official police. They prefer private investigations. They do not want to have their troubles made public. An elderly woman came to consult me a few days ago. She was unhappy about a husband she'd quarrelled with many years before. This husband of hers was your uncle, the late Mr Gascoigne.' George Lorrimer's face went purple.

'My uncle? Nonsense! His wife died many years ago.'

'Not your uncle, Mr *Anthony* Gascoigne. Your uncle, Mr *Henry* Gascoigne.'

'Uncle Henry? But *he* wasn't married!'

'Oh yes, he was,' said Hercule Poirot, lying unblushingly. 'Not a doubt of it. The lady even brought along her marriage certificate.'

'It's a lie!' cried George Lorrimer. His face was now as purple as a plum. 'I don't believe it. You're an impudent liar.'

'It is too bad, is it not?' said Poirot. 'You have committed murder for nothing.'

'Murder?' Lorrimer's voice quavered. His pale eyes bulged with terror.

'By the way,' said Poirot, 'I see you have been eating blackberry tart again. An unwise habit. Blackberries are said to be full of vitamins, but they may be deadly in other ways. On this occasion I rather fancy they have helped to put a rope round a man's neck – your neck, Dr Lorrimer.'

Agatha Christie

VI

'You see, *mon ami*, where you went wrong was over your fundamental assumption.' Hercule Poirot, beaming placidly across the table at his friend, waved an expository hand. 'A man under severe mental stress doesn't choose that time to do something that he's never done before. His reflexes just follow the track of least resistance. A man who is upset about something *might* conceivably come down to dinner dressed in his pyjamas – but they will be his *own* pyjamas – not somebody else's.

'A man who dislikes thick soup, suet pudding and blackberries suddenly orders all three one evening. *You* say, because he is thinking of something else. But *I* say *that a man who has got something on his mind will order automatically the dish he has ordered most often before.*

'*Eh bien*, then, what other explanation could there be? I simply could not think of a reasonable explanation. And I was worried! The incident was all wrong. It did not fit! I have an orderly mind and I like things to fit. Mr Gascoigne's dinner order worried me.

'Then you told me that the man had disappeared. He had missed a Tuesday and a Thursday the first time for years. I liked that even less. A queer hypothesis sprang up in my mind. If I were right about it *the man was dead*. I made inquiries. The man *was* dead. And he was very neatly and tidily dead. In other words the bad fish was covered up with the sauce!

'He had been seen in the King's Road at seven o'clock. He had had dinner here at seven-thirty – two hours before he died. It all fitted in – the evidence of the stomach contents, the evidence of the letter. Much too much sauce! You couldn't see the fish at all!

'Devoted nephew wrote the letter, devoted nephew had beautiful alibi for time of death. Death very simple – a fall down the stairs. Simple accident? Simple murder? Everyone says the former.

'Devoted nephew only surviving relative. Devoted nephew will inherit – but is there anything *to* inherit? Uncle notoriously poor.

'But there is a brother. And brother in his time had married a rich wife. And brother lives in a big rich house on Kingston Hill, so it would seem that rich wife must have left him all her money. You see the sequence – rich wife leaves money to Anthony, Anthony leaves money to Henry, Henry's money goes to George – a complete chain.'

'All very pretty in theory,' said Bonnington. 'But what did you do?'

'Once you *know* – you can usually get hold of what

you want. Henry had died two hours after a *meal* – that is all the inquest really bothered about. But supposing the meal was not dinner, but *lunch*. Put yourself in George's place. George wants money – badly. Anthony Gascoigne is dying – but his death is no good to George. His money goes to Henry, and Henry Gascoigne may live for years. So Henry must die too – and the sooner the better – but his death must take place *after* Anthony's, and at the same time George must have an alibi. Henry's habit of dining regularly at a restaurant on two evenings of the week suggests an alibi to George. Being a cautious fellow, he tries his plan out first. *He impersonates his uncle on Monday evening at the restaurant in question.* It goes without a hitch. Everyone there accepts him as his uncle. He is satisfied. He has only to wait till Uncle Anthony shows definite signs of pegging out. The time comes. He writes a letter to his uncle on the afternoon of the second November but dates it the third. He comes up to town on the afternoon of the third, calls on his uncle, and carries his scheme into action. A sharp shove and down the stairs goes Uncle Henry. George hunts about for the letter he has written, and shoves it in the pocket of his uncle's dressing-gown. At seven-thirty he is at the Gallant Endeavour, beard, bushy eyebrows all complete. Undoubtedly Mr Henry Gascoigne is alive at seven-thirty. Then a rapid metamorphosis in a lavatory and back full speed in his car to Wimbledon and an evening of bridge. The perfect alibi.'

Mr Bonnington looked at him.

'But the postmark on the letter?'

'Oh, that was very simple. The postmark was smudgy. Why? It had been altered with lamp black from second November to third November. You would not notice it *unless you were looking for it*. And finally there were the blackbirds.'

'Blackbirds?'

'Four-and-twenty blackbirds baked in a pie! Or blackberries if you prefer to be literal! George, you comprehend, was after all not quite a good enough actor. Do you remember the fellow who blacked himself all over to play Othello? That is the kind of actor you have got to be in crime. George *looked* like his uncle and *walked* like his uncle and *spoke* like his uncle and had his uncles' beard and eyebrows, but he forgot to *eat* like his uncle. He ordered the dishes that he himself liked. Blackberries discolour the teeth – the corpse's teeth were not discoloured, and yet Henry Gascoigne ate blackberries at the Gallant Endeavour that night. But there were no blackberries in the stomach. I asked this morning. And George had been fool enough to keep the beard and the rest of the make-up. Oh! plenty of evidence once you look for it. I called on George and rattled him. That finished it!

279

He had been eating blackberries again, by the way. A greedy fellow – cared a lot about his food. *Eh bien*, greed will hang him all right unless I am very much mistaken.'

A waitress brought them two portions of blackberry and apple tart.

'Take it away,' said Mr Bonnington. 'One can't be too careful. Bring me a small helping of sago pudding.'

The Dream

I

Hercule Poirot gave the house a steady appraising glance. His eyes wandered a moment to its surroundings, the shops, the big factory building on the right, the blocks of cheap mansion flats opposite.

Then once more his eyes returned to Northway House, relic of an earlier age – an age of space and leisure, when green fields had surrounded its well-bred arrogance. Now it was an anachronism, submerged and forgotten in the hectic sea of modern London, and not one man in fifty could have told you where it stood.

Furthermore, very few people could have told you to whom it belonged, though its owner's name would have been recognized as one of the world's richest men. But money can quench publicity as well as flaunt it. Benedict Farley, that eccentric millionaire, chose not to advertise his choice of residence. He himself was rarely seen, seldom making a public appearance. From time to time, he appeared at board meetings, his lean figure, beaked nose, and rasping voice easily dominating the assembled directors. Apart from that, he was just a well-known figure of legend. There were his strange meannesses, his incredible generosities, as well as more personal details – his famous patchwork dressing-gown, now reputed to be twenty-eight years old, his invariable diet of cabbage soup and caviare, his hatred of cats. All these things the public knew.

Hercule Poirot knew them also. It was all he did know of the man he was about to visit. The letter which was in his coat pocket told him little more.

After surveying this melancholy landmark of a past age for a minute or two in silence, he walked up the steps to the front door and pressed the bell, glancing as he did so at the neat wrist-watch which had at last replaced an old favourite – the large turnip-faced watch of earlier days. Yes, it was exactly nine-thirty. As ever, Hercule Poirot was exact to the minute.

The door opened after just the right interval. A perfect specimen of the genus butler stood outlined against the lighted hall.

'Mr Benedict Farley?' asked Hercule Poirot.

The impersonal glance surveyed him from head to

foot, inoffensively but effectively.

En gros et en détail, thought Hercule Poirot to himself with appreciation.

'You have an appointment, sir?' asked the suave voice.

'Yes.'

'Your name, sir?'

'Monsieur Hercule Poirot.'

The butler bowed and drew back. Hercule Poirot entered the house. The butler closed the door behind him.

But there was yet one more formality before the deft hands took hat and stick from the visitor.

'You will excuse me, sir. I was to ask for a letter.'

With deliberation Poirot took from his pocket the folded letter and handed it to the butler. The latter gave it a mere glance, then returned it with a bow. Hercule Poirot returned it to his pocket. Its contents were simple.

Northway House, W.8

M. Hercule Poirot
Dear Sir,

　　Mr Benedict Farley would like to have the benefit of your advice. If convenient to yourself he would be glad if you would call upon him at the above address at 9.30 tomorrow (Thursday) evening.

Agatha Christie

Yours truly,
Hugo Cornworthy
(Secretary)
P.S. Please bring this letter with you.

Deftly the butler relieved Poirot of hat, stick and overcoat. He said:

'Will you please come up to Mr Cornworthy's room?'

He led the way up the broad staircase. Poirot followed him, looking with appreciation at such *objets d'art* as were of an opulent and florid nature! His taste in art was always somewhat bourgeois.

On the first floor the butler knocked on a door.

Hercule Poirot's eyebrows rose very slightly. It was the first jarring note. For the best butlers do not knock at doors – and yet indubitably this was a first-class butler!

It was, so to speak, the first intimation of contact with the eccentricity of a millionaire.

A voice from within called out something. The butler threw open the door. He announced (and again Poirot sensed the deliberate departure from orthodoxy):

'The gentleman you are expecting, sir.'

Poirot passed into the room. It was a fair-sized room, very plainly furnished in a workmanlike fashion.

Filing cabinets, books of reference, a couple of easy-chairs, and a large and imposing desk covered with neatly docketed papers. The corners of the room were dim, for the only light came from a big green-shaded reading lamp which stood on a small table by the arm of one of the easy-chairs. It was placed so as to cast its full light on anyone approaching from the door. Hercule Poirot blinked a little, realizing that the lamp bulb was at least 150 watts. In the arm-chair sat a thin figure in a patchwork dressing-gown – Benedict Farley. His head was stuck forward in a characteristic attitude, his beaked nose projecting like that of a bird. A crest of white hair like that of a cockatoo rose above his forehead. His eyes glittered behind thick lenses as he peered suspiciously at his visitor.

'Hey,' he said at last – and his voice was shrill and harsh, with a rasping note in it. 'So you're Hercule Poirot, hey?'

'At your service,' said Poirot politely and bowed, one hand on the back of the chair.

'Sit down – sit down,' said the old man testily.

Hercule Poirot sat down – in the full glare of the lamp. From behind it the old man seemed to be studying him attentively.

'How do I know you're Hercule Poirot – hey?' he demanded fretfully. 'Tell me that – hey?'

Agatha Christie

Once more Poirot drew the letter from his pocket and handed it to Farley.

'Yes,' admitted the millionaire grudgingly. 'That's it. That's what I got Cornworthy to write.' He folded it up and tossed it back. 'So you're the fellow, are you?'

With a little wave of his hand Poirot said:

'I assure you there is no deception!'

Benedict Farley chuckled suddenly.

'That's what the conjurer says before he takes the goldfish out of the hat! Saying that is part of the trick, you know!'

Poirot did not reply. Farley said suddenly:

'Think I'm a suspicious old man, hey? So I am. Don't trust anybody! That's my motto. Can't trust anybody when you're rich. No, no, it doesn't do.'

'You wished,' Poirot hinted gently, 'to consult me?'

The old man nodded.

'Go to the expert and don't count the cost. You'll notice, M. Poirot, I haven't asked you your fee. I'm not going to! Send me in the bill later – *I* shan't cut up rough over it. Damned fools at the dairy thought they could charge me two and nine for eggs when two and seven's the market price – lot of swindlers! I won't be swindled. But the man at the top's different. He's worth the money. I'm at the top myself – I know.'

Hercule Poirot made no reply. He listened attentively, his head poised a little on one side.

Behind his impassive exterior he was conscious of a feeling of disappointment. He could not exactly put his finger on it. So far Benedict Farley had run true to type – that is, he had conformed to the popular idea of himself; and yet – Poirot was disappointed.

'The man,' he said disgustedly to himself, 'is a mountebank – nothing but a mountebank!'

He had known other millionaires, eccentric men too, but in nearly every case he had been conscious of a certain force, an inner energy that had commanded his respect. If they had worn a patchwork dressing-gown, it would have been because they liked wearing such a dressing-gown. But the dressing-gown of Benedict Farley, or so it seemed to Poirot, was essentially a stage property. And the man himself was essentially stagy. Every word he spoke was uttered, so Poirot felt assured, sheerly for effect.

He repeated again unemotionally, 'You wished to consult me, Mr Farley?'

Abruptly the millionaire's manner changed.

He leaned forward. His voice dropped to a croak.

'Yes. Yes . . . I want to hear what you've got to say – what you think . . . Go to the top! That's my way! The best doctor – the best detective – it's between the two of them.'

'As yet, Monsieur, I do not understand.'

'Naturally,' snapped Farley. 'I haven't begun to tell you.'

He leaned forward once more and shot out an abrupt question.

'What do you know, M. Poirot, about dreams?'

The little man's eyebrows rose. Whatever he had expected, it was not this.

'For that, M. Farley, I should recommend Napoleon's *Book of Dreams* – or the latest practising psychologist from Harley Street.'

Benedict Farley said soberly, 'I've tried both . . .'

There was a pause, then the millionaire spoke, at first almost in a whisper, then with a voice growing higher and higher.

'It's the same dream – night after night. And I'm afraid, I tell you – I'm afraid . . . It's always the same. I'm sitting in my room next door to this. Sitting at my desk, writing. There's a clock there and I glance at it and see the time – exactly twenty-eight minutes past three. Always the same time, you understand.

'*And when I see the time, M. Poirot, I know I've got to do it*. I don't want to do it – I loathe doing it – but I've got to . . .'

His voice had risen shrilly.

Unperturbed, Poirot said, 'And what is it that you have to do?'

'At twenty-eight minutes past three,' Benedict Farley said hoarsely, 'I open the second drawer down on the right of my desk, take out the revolver that I keep there, load it and walk over to the window. And then – and then –'

'Yes?'

Benedict Farley said in a whisper:

'Then I shoot myself . . .'

There was silence.

Then Poirot said, 'That is your dream?'

'Yes.'

'The same every night?'

'Yes.'

'What happens after you shoot yourself?'

'I wake up.'

Poirot nodded his head slowly and thoughtfully. 'As a matter of interest, do you keep a revolver in that particular drawer?'

'Yes.'

'Why?'

'I have always done so. It is as well to be prepared.'

'Prepared for what?'

Farley said irritably, 'A man in my position has to be on his guard. All rich men have enemies.'

Poirot did not pursue the subject. He remained silent for a moment or two, then he said:

'Why exactly did you send for me?'

'I will tell you. First of all I consulted a doctor – three doctors to be exact.'

'Yes?'

'The first told me it was all a question of diet. He was an elderly man. The second was a young man of the modern school. He assured me that it all hinged on a certain event that took place in infancy at that particular time of day – three twenty-eight. I am so determined, he says, not to remember the event, that I symbolize it by destroying myself. That is his explanation.'

'And the third doctor?' asked Poirot.

Benedict Farley's voice rose in shrill anger.

'He's a young man too. He has a preposterous theory! He asserts that I, myself, am tired of life, that my life is so unbearable to me that I deliberately want to end it! But since to acknowledge that fact would be to acknowledge that essentially I am a failure, I refuse in my waking moments to face the truth. But when I am asleep, all inhibitions are removed, and I proceed to do that *which I really wish to do*. I put an end to myself.'

'His view is that you really wish, unknown to yourself, to commit suicide?' said Poirot.

Benedict Farley cried shrilly:

'And that's impossible – impossible! I'm perfectly

happy! I've got everything I want – everything money can buy! It's fantastic – unbelievable even to suggest a thing like that!'

Poirot looked at him with interest. Perhaps something in the shaking hands, the trembling shrillness of the voice, warned him that the denial was *too* vehement, that its very insistence was in itself suspect. He contented himself with saying:

'And where do I come in, Monsieur?'

Benedict Farley calmed down suddenly. He tapped with an emphatic finger on the table beside him.

'There's another possibility. And if it's right, you're the man to know about it! You're famous, you've had hundreds of cases – fantastic, improbable cases! You'd know if anyone does.'

'Know what?'

Farley's voice dropped to a whisper.

'Supposing someone wants to kill me . . . Could they do it this way? Could they make me dream that dream night after night?'

'Hypnotism, you mean?'

'Yes.'

Hercule Poirot considered the question.

'It would be possible, I suppose,' he said at last. 'It is more a question for a doctor.'

'You don't know of such a case in your experience?'

'Not precisely on those lines, no.'

'You see what I'm driving at? I'm made to dream the same dream, night after night, night after night – and then – one day the suggestion is too much for me – *and I act upon it*. I do what I've dreamed of so often – kill myself!'

Slowly Hercule Poirot shook his head.

'You don't think that is possible?' asked Farley.

'*Possible?*' Poirot shook his head. 'That is not a word I care to meddle with.'

'But you think it improbable?'

'Most improbable.'

Benedict Farley murmured. 'The doctor said so too . . .' Then his voice rising shrilly again, he cried out, 'But why do I have this dream? Why? Why?'

Hercule Poirot shook his head. Benedict Farley said abruptly, 'You're sure you've never come across anything like this in your experience?'

'Never.'

'That's what I wanted to know.'

Delicately, Poirot cleared his throat.

'You permit,' he said, 'a question?'

'What is it? What is it? Say what you like.'

'Who is it you suspect of wanting to kill you?'

Farley snapped out, 'Nobody. Nobody at all.'

'But the idea presented itself to your mind?' Poirot persisted.

'I wanted to know – if it was a possibility.'

'Speaking from my own experience, I should say No. Have you ever been hypnotized, by the way?'

'Of course not. D'you think I'd lend myself to such tomfoolery?'

'Then I think one can say that your theory is definitely improbable.'

'But the dream, you fool, the dream.'

'The dream is certainly remarkable,' said Poirot thoughtfully. He paused and then went on. 'I should like to see the scene of this drama – the table, the clock, and the revolver.'

'Of course, I'll take you next door.'

Wrapping the folds of his dressing-gown round him, the old man half-rose from his chair. Then suddenly, as though a thought had struck him, he resumed his seat.

'No,' he said. 'There's nothing to see there. I've told you all there is to tell.'

'But I should like to see for myself –'

'There's no need,' Farley snapped. 'You've given me your opinion. That's the end.'

Poirot shrugged his shoulders. 'As you please.' He rose to his feet. 'I am sorry, Mr Farley, that I have not been able to be of assistance to you.'

Benedict Farley was staring straight ahead of him.

'Don't want a lot of hanky-pankying around,' he

growled out. 'I've told you the facts – you can't make anything of them. That closes the matter. You can send me a bill for the consultation fee.'

'I shall not fail to do so,' said the detective drily. He walked towards the door.

'Stop a minute.' The millionaire called him back. 'That letter – I want it.'

'The letter from your secretary?'

'Yes.'

Poirot's eyebrows rose. He put his hand into his pocket, drew out a folded sheet, and handed it to the old man. The latter scrutinized it, then put it down on the table beside him with a nod.

Once more Hercule Poirot walked to the door. He was puzzled. His busy mind was going over and over the story he had been told. Yet in the midst of his mental preoccupation, a nagging sense of something wrong obtruded itself. And that something had to do with himself – not with Benedict Farley.

With his hand on the door knob, his mind cleared. He, Hercule Poirot, had been guilty of an error! He turned back into the room once more.

'A thousand pardons! In the interest of your problem I have committed a folly! That letter I handed to you – by mischance I put my hand into my right-hand pocket instead of the left –'

'What's all this? What's all this?'

'The letter that I handed you just now – an apology from my laundress concerning the treatment of my collars.' Poirot was smiling, apologetic. He dipped into his left-hand pocket. 'This is *your* letter.'

Benedict Farley snatched at it – grunted: 'Why the devil can't you mind what you're doing?'

Poirot retrieved his laundress's communication, apologized gracefully once more, and left the room.

He paused for a moment outside on the landing. It was a spacious one. Directly facing him was a big old oak settle with a refectory table in front of it. On the table were magazines. There were also two arm-chairs and a table with flowers. It reminded him a little of a dentist's waiting-room.

The butler was in the hall below waiting to let him out.

'Can I get you a taxi, sir?'

'No, I thank you. The night is fine. I will walk.'

Hercule Poirot paused a moment on the pavement waiting for a lull in the traffic before crossing the busy street.

A frown creased his forehead.

'No,' he said to himself. 'I do not understand at all. Nothing makes sense. Regrettable to have to admit it, but I, Hercule Poirot, am completely baffled.'

That was what might be termed the first act of the drama. The second act followed a week later. It opened with a telephone call from one John Stillingfleet, MD.

He said with a remarkable lack of medical decorum:

'That you, Poirot, old horse? Stillingfleet here.'

'Yes, my friend. What is it?'

'I'm speaking from Northway House – Benedict Farley's.'

'Ah, yes?' Poirot's voice quickened with interest. 'What of – Mr Farley?'

'Farley's dead. Shot himself this afternoon.'

There was a pause, then Poirot said:

'Yes . . .'

'I notice you're not overcome with surprise. Know something about it, old horse?'

'Why should you think that?'

'Well, it isn't brilliant deduction or telepathy or anything like that. We found a note from Farley to you making an appointment about a week ago.'

'I see.'

'We've got a tame police inspector here – got to be careful, you know, when one of these millionaire blokes bumps himself off. Wondered whether you could throw any light on the case. If so, perhaps you'd come round?'

'I will come immediately.'

'Good for you, old boy. Some dirty work at the crossroads – eh?'

Poirot merely repeated that he would set forth immediately.

'Don't want to spill the beans over the telephone? Quite right. So long.'

A quarter of an hour later Poirot was sitting in the library, a low long room at the back of Northway House on the ground floor. There were five other persons in the room: Inspector Barnett, Dr Stillingfleet, Mrs Farley, the widow of the millionaire, Joanna Farley, his only daughter, and Hugo Cornworthy, his private secretary.

Of these, Inspector Barnett was a discreet soldierly-looking man. Dr Stillingfleet, whose professional manner was entirely different from his telephonic style, was a tall, long-faced young man of thirty. Mrs Farley was obviously very much younger than her husband. She was a handsome dark-haired woman. Her mouth was hard and her black eyes gave absolutely no clue to her emotions. She appeared perfectly self-possessed. Joanna Farley had fair hair and a freckled face. The prominence of her nose and chin was clearly inherited from her father. Her eyes were intelligent and shrewd. Hugo Cornworthy was a good-looking young fellow, very correctly dressed. He seemed intelligent and efficient.

After greetings and introductions, Poirot narrated simply and clearly the circumstances of his visit and the story told him by Benedict Farley. He could not complain of any lack of interest.

'Most extraordinary story I've ever heard!' said the inspector. 'A dream, eh? Did you know anything about this, Mrs Farley?'

She bowed her head.

'My husband mentioned it to me. It upset him very much. I – I told him it was indigestion – his diet, you know, was very peculiar – and suggested his calling in Dr Stillingfleet.'

The young man shook his head.

'He didn't consult me. From M. Poirot's story, I gather he went to Harley Street.'

'I would like your advice on that point, Doctor,' said Poirot. 'Mr Farley told me that he consulted three specialists. What do you think of the theories they advanced?'

Stillingfleet frowned.

'It's difficult to say. You've got to take into account that what he passed on to you wasn't exactly what had been said to him. It was a layman's interpretation.'

'You mean he had got the phraseology wrong?'

'Not exactly. I mean they would put a thing to him in professional terms, he'd get the meaning a little distorted, and then recast it in his own language.'

'So that what he told me was not really what the doctors said.'

'That's what it amounts to. He's just got it all a little wrong, if you know what I mean.'

Poirot nodded thoughtfully. 'Is it known whom he consulted?' he asked.

Mrs Farley shook her head, and Joanna Farley remarked:

'None of us had any idea he had consulted any-one.'

'Did he speak to *you* about his dream?' asked Poirot.

The girl shook her head.

'And you, Mr Cornworthy?'

'No, he said nothing at all. I took down a letter to you at his dictation, but I had no idea why he wished to consult you. I thought it might possibly have something to do with some business irregularity.'

Poirot asked: 'And now as to the actual facts of Mr Farley's death?'

Inspector Barnett looked interrogatively at Mrs Farley and at Dr Stillingfleet, and then took upon himself the role of spokesman.

'Mr Farley was in the habit of working in his own room on the first floor every afternoon. I understand that there was a big amalgamation of business in prospect –'

He looked at Hugo Cornworthy who said, 'Consoli-dated Coachlines.'

'In connection with that,' continued Inspector Barnett,

'Mr Farley had agreed to give an interview to two members of the Press. He very seldom did anything of the kind – only about once in five years, I understand. Accordingly two reporters, one from the Associated Newsgroups, and one from Amalgamated Press-sheets, arrived at a quarter past three by appointment. They waited on the first floor outside Mr Farley's door – which was the customary place for people to wait who had an appointment with Mr Farley. At twenty past three a messenger arrived from the office of Consolidated Coachlines with some urgent papers. He was shown into Mr Farley's room where he handed over the documents. Mr Farley accompanied him to the door, and from there spoke to the two members of the Press. He said:

'"I'm sorry, gentlemen, to have to keep you waiting, but I have some urgent business to attend to. I will be as quick as I can."

'The two gentlemen, Mr Adams and Mr Stoddart, assured Mr Farley that they would await his convenience. He went back into his room, shut the door – and was never seen alive again!'

'Continue,' said Poirot.

'At a little after four o'clock,' went on the inspector, 'Mr Cornworthy here came out of his room which is next door to Mr Farley's and was surprised to see the two reporters still waiting. He wanted Mr

Farley's signature to some letters and thought he had also better remind him that these two gentlemen were waiting. He accordingly went into Mr Farley's room. To his surprise he could not at first see Mr Farley and thought the room was empty. Then he caught sight of a boot sticking out behind the desk (which is placed in front of the window). He went quickly across and discovered Mr Farley lying there dead, with a revolver beside him.

'Mr Cornworthy hurried out of the room and directed the butler to ring up Dr Stillingfleet. By the latter's advice, Mr Cornworthy also informed the police.'

'Was the shot heard?' asked Poirot.

'No. The traffic is very noisy here, the landing window was open. What with lorries and motor horns it would be most unlikely if it had been noticed.'

Poirot nodded thoughtfully. 'What time is it supposed he died?' he asked.

Stillingfleet said:

'I examined the body as soon as I got here – that is, at thirty-two minutes past four. Mr Farley had been dead at least an hour.'

Poirot's face was very grave.

'So then, it seems possible that his death could have occurred at the time he mentioned to me – that is, at twenty-eight minutes past three.'

'Exactly,' said Stillingfleet.

'Any fingermarks on the revolver?'

'Yes, his own.'

'And the revolver itself?'

The inspector took up the tale.

'Was one which he kept in the second right-hand drawer of his desk, just as he told you. Mrs Farley has identified it positively. Moreover, you understand, there is only one entrance to the room, the door giving on to the landing. The two reporters were sitting exactly opposite that door and they swear that no one entered the room from the time Mr Farley spoke to them, until Mr Cornworthy entered it at a little after four o'clock.'

'So that there is every reason to suppose that Mr Farley committed suicide.'

Inspector Barnett smiled a little.

'There would have been no doubt at all but for one point.'

'And that?'

'The letter written to you.'

Poirot smiled too.

'I see! Where Hercule Poirot is concerned – immediately the suspicion of murder arises!'

'Precisely,' said the inspector drily. 'However, after your clearing up of the situation –'

Poirot interrupted him. 'One little minute.' He turned

to Mrs Farley. 'Had your husband ever been hypnotized?'

'Never.'

'Had he studied the question of hypnotism? Was he interested in the subject?'

She shook her head. 'I don't think so.'

Suddenly her self-control seemed to break down. 'That horrible dream! It's uncanny! That he should have dreamed that – night after night – and then – it's as though he were – *hounded* to death!'

Poirot remembered Benedict Farley saying – '*I proceed to do that which I really wish to do. I put an end to myself.*'

He said, 'Had it ever occurred to you that your husband might be tempted to do away with himself?'

'No – at least – sometimes he was very queer . . .'

Joanna Farley's voice broke in clear and scornful. 'Father would never have killed himself. He was far too careful of himself.'

Dr Stillingfleet said, 'It isn't the people who threaten to commit suicide who usually do it, you know, Miss Farley. That's why suicides sometimes seem unaccountable.'

Poirot rose to his feet. 'Is it permitted,' he asked, 'that I see the room where the tragedy occurred?'

'Certainly. Dr Stillingfleet –'

The doctor accompanied Poirot upstairs.

Agatha Christie

Benedict Farley's room was a much larger one than the secretary's next door. It was luxuriously furnished with deep leather-covered arm-chairs, a thick pile carpet, and a superb outsize writing-desk.

Poirot passed behind the latter to where a dark stain on the carpet showed just before the window. He remembered the millionaire saying, '*At twenty-eight minutes past three I open the second drawer on the right of my desk, take out the revolver that I keep there, load it, and walk over to the window. And then – and then I shoot myself.*'

He nodded slowly. Then he said:

'The window was open like this?'

'Yes. But nobody could have got in that way.'

Poirot put his head out. There was no sill or parapet and no pipes near. Not even a cat could have gained access that way. Opposite rose the blank wall of the factory, a dead wall with no windows in it.

Stillingfleet said, 'Funny room for a rich man to choose as his own sanctum, with that outlook. It's like looking out on to a prison wall.'

'Yes,' said Poirot. He drew his head in and stared at the expanse of solid brick. 'I think,' he said, 'that that wall is important.'

Stillingfleet looked at him curiously. 'You mean – psychologically?'

Poirot had moved to the desk. Idly, or so it seemed

he picked up a pair of what are usually called lazy-tongs. He pressed the handles; the tongs shot out to their full length. Delicately, Poirot picked up a burnt match stump with them from beside a chair some feet away and conveyed it carefully to the waste-paper basket.

'When you've finished playing with those things . . .' said Stillingfleet irritably.

Hercule Poirot murmured, 'An ingenious invention,' and replaced the tongs neatly on the writing-table. Then he asked:

'Where were Mrs Farley and Miss Farley at the time of the – death?'

'Mrs Farley was resting in her room on the floor above this. Miss Farley was painting in her studio at the top of the house.'

Hercule Poirot drummed idly with his fingers on the table for a minute or two. Then he said:

'I should like to see Miss Farley. Do you think you could ask her to come here for a minute or two?'

'If you like.'

Stillingfleet glanced at him curiously, then left the room. In another minute or two the door opened and Joanna Farley came in.

'You do not mind, Mademoiselle, if I ask you a few questions?'

She returned his glance coolly. 'Please ask anything you choose.'

'Did you know that your father kept a revolver in his desk?'

'No.'

'Where were you and your mother – that is to say your stepmother – that is right?'

'Yes, Louise is my father's second wife. She is only eight years older than I am. You were about to say –?'

'Where were you and she on Thursday of last week? That is to say, on Thursday night.'

She reflected for a minute or two.

'Thursday? Let me see. Oh, yes, we had gone to the theatre. To see *Little Dog Laughed*.'

'Your father did not suggest accompanying you?'

'He never went out to theatres.'

'What did he usually do in the evenings?'

'He sat in here and read.'

'He was not a very sociable man?'

The girl looked at him directly. 'My father,' she said, 'had a singularly unpleasant personality. No one who lived in close association with him could possibly be fond of him.'

'That, Mademoiselle, is a very candid statement.'

'I am saving you time, M. Poirot. I realize quite well what you are getting at. My stepmother married my father for his money. I live here because I have no money to live elsewhere. There is a man I wish to marry – a poor man; my father saw to it that he lost his job. He wanted me, you see, to marry well – an easy matter since I was to be his heiress!'

'Your father's fortune passes to you?'

'Yes. That is, he left Louise, my stepmother, a quarter of a million free of tax, and there are other legacies, but the residue goes to me.' She smiled suddenly. 'So you see, M. Poirot, I had every reason to desire my father's death!'

'I see, Mademoiselle, that you have inherited your father's intelligence.'

She said thoughtfully, 'Father was clever . . . One felt that with him – that he had force – driving power – but it had all turned sour – bitter – there was no humanity left . . .'

Hercule Poirot said softly, '*Grand Dieu*, but what an imbecile I am . . .'

Joanna Farley turned towards the door. 'Is there anything more?'

'Two little questions. These tongs here,' he picked up the lazy-tongs, 'were they always on the table?'

'Yes. Father used them for picking up things. He didn't like stooping.'

'One other question. Was your father's eyesight good?'

She stared at him.

'Oh, no – he couldn't see at all – I mean he couldn't see without his glasses. His sight had always been bad from a boy.'

'But with his glasses?'

'Oh, he could see all right then, of course.'

'He could read newspapers and fine print?'

'Oh, yes.'

'That is all, Mademoiselle.'

She went out of the room.

Poirot murmured, 'I was stupid. It was there, all the time, under my nose. And because it was so near I could not see it.'

He leaned out of the window once more. Down below, in the narrow way between the house and the factory, he saw a small dark object.

Hercule Poirot nodded, satisfied, and went downstairs again.

The others were still in the library. Poirot addressed himself to the secretary:

'I want you, Mr Cornworthy, to recount to me in detail the exact circumstances of Mr Farley's summons to me. When, for instance, did Mr Farley dictate that letter?'

'On Wednesday afternoon – at five-thirty, as far as I can remember.'

'Were there any special directions about posting it?'

'He told me to post it myself.'

'And you did so?'

'Yes.'

'Did he give any special instructions to the butler about admitting me?'

'Yes. He told me to tell Holmes (Holmes is the butler) that a gentleman would be calling at nine-thirty. He was to ask the gentleman's name. He was also to ask to see the letter.'

'Rather peculiar precaution to take, don't you think?'

Cornworthy shrugged his shoulders.

'Mr Farley,' he said carefully, 'was rather a peculiar man.'

'Any other instructions?'

'Yes. He told me to take the evening off.'

'Did you do so?'

'Yes, immediately after dinner I went to the cinema.'

'When did you return?'

'I let myself in about a quarter past eleven.'

'Did you see Mr Farley again that evening?'

'No.'

'And he did not mention the matter the next morning?'

'No.'

Poirot paused a moment, then resumed, 'When I arrived I was not shown into Mr Farley's own room.'

'No. He told me that I was to tell Holmes to show you into my room.'

'Why was that? Do you know?'

Cornworthy shook his head. 'I never questioned any of Mr Farley's orders,' he said drily. 'He would have resented it if I had.'

'Did he usually receive visitors in his own room?'

'Usually, but not always. Sometimes he saw them in my room.'

'Was there any reason for that?'

Hugo Cornworthy considered.

'No – I hardly think so – I've never really thought about it.'

Turning to Mrs Farley, Poirot asked:

'You permit that I ring for your butler?'

'Certainly, M. Poirot.'

Very correct, very urbane, Holmes answered the bell.

'You rang, madam?'

Mrs Farley indicated Poirot with a gesture. Holmes turned politely. 'Yes, sir?'

'What were your instructions, Holmes, on the Thursday night when I came here?'

Holmes cleared his throat, then said:

'After dinner Mr Cornworthy told me that Mr Farley expected a Mr Hercule Poirot at nine-thirty. I was to ascertain the gentleman's name, and I was to verify the information by glancing at a letter. Then I was to show him up to Mr Cornworthy's room.'

'Were you also told to knock on the door?'

An expression of distaste crossed the butler's countenance.

'That was one of Mr Farley's orders. I was always to knock when introducing visitors – business visitors, that is,' he added.

'Ah, that puzzled me! Were you given any other instructions concerning me?'

'No, sir. When Mr Cornworthy had told me what I have just repeated to you he went out.'

'What time was that?'

'Ten minutes to nine, sir.'

'Did you see Mr Farley after that?'

'Yes, sir, I took him up a glass of hot water as usual at nine o'clock.'

'Was he then in his own room or in Mr Cornworthy's?'

'He was in his own room, sir.'

'You noticed nothing unusual about that room?'

'Unusual? No, sir.'

'Where were Mrs Farley and Miss Farley?'

'They had gone to the theatre, sir.'

'Thank you, Holmes, that will do.'

Holmes bowed and left the room. Poirot turned to the millionaire's widow.

'One more question, Mrs Farley. Had your husband good sight?'

'No. Not without his glasses.'

'He was very short-sighted?'

'Oh, yes, he was quite helpless without his spectacles.'

'He had several pairs of glasses?'

'Yes.'

'Ah,' said Poirot. He leaned back. 'I think that that concludes the case . . .'

There was silence in the room. They were all looking at the little man who sat there complacently stroking his moustache. On the inspector's face was perplexity, Dr Stillingfleet was frowning, Cornworthy merely stared uncomprehendingly, Mrs Farley gazed in blank astonishment, Joanna Farley looked eager.

Mrs Farley broke the silence.

'I don't understand, M. Poirot.' Her voice was fretful. 'The dream –'

'Yes,' said Poirot. 'That dream was very important.'

Mrs Farley shivered. She said:

'I've never believed in anything supernatural before – but now – to dream it night after night beforehand –'

'It's extraordinary,' said Stillingfleet. 'Extraordinary! If we hadn't got your word for it, Poirot, and if you hadn't had it straight from the horse's mouth –' he coughed in embarrassment, and readopting his professional manner, 'I beg your pardon, Mrs Farley. If Mr Farley himself had not told that story –'

'Exactly,' said Poirot. His eyes, which had been half-closed, opened suddenly. They were very green. '*If Benedict Farley hadn't told me –*'

He paused a minute, looking round at a circle of blank faces.

'There are certain things, you comprehend, that happened that evening which I was quite at a loss to explain. First, why make such a point of my bringing that letter with me?'

'Identification,' suggested Cornworthy.

'No, no, my dear young man. Really that idea is too ridiculous. There must be some much more valid reason. For not only did Mr Farley require to see that letter produced, but he definitely demanded that I should leave it behind me. And moreover even then he did not destroy it! It was found among his papers this afternoon. *Why did he keep it?*'

Joanna Farley's voice broke in. 'He wanted, in case anything happened to him, that the facts of his strange dream should be made known.'

Poirot nodded approvingly.

'You are astute, Mademoiselle. That must be – that can only be – the point of the keeping of the letter. When Mr Farley was dead, the story of that strange dream was to be told! That dream was very important. That dream, Mademoiselle, was *vital*!

'I will come now,' he went on, 'to the second point.

315

After hearing his story I ask Mr Farley to show me the desk and the revolver. He seems about to get up to do so, then suddenly refuses. Why did he refuse?'

This time no one advanced an answer.

'I will put that question differently. *What was there in that next room that Mr Farley did not want me to see?*'

There was still silence.

'Yes,' said Poirot, 'it is difficult, that. And yet there was some reason – some *urgent* reason why Mr Farley received me in his secretary's room and refused point blank to take me into his own room. *There was something in that room he could not afford to have me see.*

'And now I come to the third inexplicable thing that happened on that evening. Mr Farley, just as I was leaving, requested me to hand him the letter I had received. By inadvertence I handed him a communication from my laundress. He glanced at it and laid it down beside him. Just before I left the room I discovered my error – and rectified it! After that I left the house and – I admit it – I was completely at sea! The whole affair and especially that last incident seemed to me quite inexplicable.'

He looked round from one to the other.

'You do not see?'

Stillingfleet said, 'I don't really see how your laundress comes into it, Poirot.'

'My laundress,' said Poirot, 'was very important. That miserable woman who ruins my collars, was, for the first time in her life, useful to somebody. Surely you see – it is so obvious. Mr Farley glanced at that communication – *one glance* would have told him that it was the wrong letter – and yet he knew nothing. Why? *Because he could not see it properly!*'

Inspector Barnett said sharply, 'Didn't he have his glasses on?'

Hercule Poirot smiled. 'Yes,' he said. 'He had his glasses on. That is what makes it so very interesting.'

He leaned forward.

'Mr Farley's dream was very important. He dreamed, you see, that he committed suicide. And a little later on, he did commit suicide. That is to say he was alone in a room and was found there with a revolver by him, and no one entered or left the room at the time that he was shot. What does that mean? It means, does it not, that it *must* be suicide!'

'Yes,' said Stillingfleet.

Hercule Poirot shook his head.

'On the contrary,' he said. 'It was murder. An unusual and a very cleverly planned murder.'

Again he leaned forward, tapping the table, his eyes green and shining.

'Why did Mr Farley not allow me to go into his own room that evening? What was there in there that I must not be allowed to see? I think, my friends, that there was – Benedict Farley himself!'

He smiled at the blank faces.

'Yes, yes, it is not nonsense what I say. Why could the Mr Farley to whom I had been talking not realize the difference between two totally dissimilar letters? Because, *mes amis*, he was a man of *normal sight* wearing a pair of very powerful glasses. Those glasses would render a man of normal eyesight practically blind. Isn't that so, Doctor?'

Stillingfleet murmured, 'That's so – of course.'

'Why did I feel that in talking to Mr Farley I was talking to a *mountebank*, to an actor playing a part! Consider the setting. The dim room, the green-shaded light turned blindingly away from the figure in the chair. What did I see – the famous patchwork dressing-gown, the beaked nose (faked with that useful substance, nose putty) the white crest of hair, the powerful lenses concealing the eyes. What evidence is there that Mr Farley ever had a dream? Only the story I was told and the evidence of *Mrs Farley*. What evidence is there that Benedict Farley kept a revolver in his desk? Again only the story told me and the word of Mrs Farley. Two people carried this fraud through – Mrs Farley and Hugo Cornworthy. Cornworthy wrote the letter to me, gave instructions to the butler, went out ostensibly to the cinema, but let himself in again immediately with a key, went to his room, made himself up, and played the part of Benedict Farley.

'And so we come to this afternoon. The opportunity for which Mr Cornworthy has been waiting arrives. There are two witnesses on the landing to swear that no one goes in or out of Benedict Farley's room. Cornworthy waits until a particularly heavy batch of traffic is about to pass. Then he leans out of his window, and with the lazy-tongs which he has purloined from the desk next door he holds an object against the window of that room. Benedict Farley comes to the window. Cornworthy snatches back the tongs and as Farley leans out, and the lorries are passing outside, Cornworthy shoots him with the revolver that he has ready. There is a blank wall opposite, remember. There can be no witness of the crime. Cornworthy waits for over half an hour, then gathers up some papers, conceals the lazy-tongs and the revolver between them and goes out on to the landing and into the next room. He replaces the tongs on the desk, lays down the revolver after pressing the dead man's fingers on it, and hurries out with the news of Mr Farley's "suicide".

'He arranges that the letter to me shall be found and that I shall arrive with my story – the story I heard *from Mr Farley's own lips* – of his extraordinary "dream" –

the strange compulsion he felt to kill himself! A few credulous people will discuss the hypnotism theory – but the main result will be to confirm without a doubt that the actual hand that held the revolver was Benedict Farley's own.'

Hercule Poirot's eyes went to the widow's face – he noted with satisfaction the dismay – the ashy pallor – the blind fear . . .

'And in due course,' he finished gently, 'the happy ending would have been achieved. A quarter of a million and two hearts that beat as one . . .'

II

John Stillingfleet, MD, and Hercule Poirot walked along the side of Northway House. On their right was the towering wall of the factory. Above them, on their left, were the windows of Benedict Farley's and Hugo Cornworthy's rooms. Hercule Poirot stopped and picked up a small object – a black stuffed cat.

'*Voilà*,' he said. 'That is what Cornworthy held in the lazy-tongs against Farley's window. You remember, he hated cats? Naturally he rushed to the window.'

'Why on earth didn't Cornworthy come out and pick it up after he'd dropped it?'

'How could he? To do so would have been definitely suspicious. After all, if this object were found what would anyone think – that some child had wandered round here and dropped it.'

'Yes,' said Stillingfleet with a sigh. 'That's probably what the ordinary person *would* have thought. But not good old Hercule! D'you know, old horse, up to the very last minute I thought you were leading up to some subtle theory of high-falutin' psychological "suggested" murder? I bet those two thought so too! Nasty bit of goods, the Farley. Goodness, how she cracked! Cornworthy might have got away with it if she hadn't had hysterics and tried to spoil your beauty by going for you with her nails. I only got her off you just in time.'

He paused a minute and then said:

'I rather like the girl. Grit, you know, and brains. I suppose I'd be thought to be a fortune hunter if I had a shot at her . . . ?'

'You are too late, my friend. There is already someone *sur le tapis*. Her father's death has opened the way to happiness.'

'Take it all round, *she* had a pretty good motive for bumping off the unpleasant parent.'

'Motive and opportunity are not enough,' said Poirot. 'There must also be the criminal temperament!'

'I wonder if you'll ever commit a crime, Poirot?'

said Stillingfleet. 'I bet you could get away with it all right. As a matter of fact, it would be *too* easy for you – I mean the thing would be off as definitely too unsporting.'

'That,' said Poirot, 'is a typical English idea.'

Greenshaw's Folly

I

The two men rounded the corner of the shrubbery.

'Well, there you are,' said Raymond West. 'That's it.'

Horace Bindler took a deep, appreciative breath.

'But my dear,' he cried, 'how wonderful.' His voice rose in a high screech of æsthetic delight, then deepened in reverent awe. 'It's unbelievable. Out of this world! A period piece of the best.'

'I thought you'd like it,' said Raymond West, complacently.

'Like it? My dear –' Words failed Horace. He unbuckled the strap of his camera and got busy. 'This will be one of the gems of my collection,' he said happily. 'I do think, don't you, that it's rather amusing to have a collection of monstrosities? The idea came to me one night seven years ago in my bath. My last real gem was in the Campo Santo at Genoa, but I really think this beats it. What's it called?'

'I haven't the least idea,' said Raymond.

'I suppose it's got a name?'

'It must have. But the fact is that it's never referred to round here as anything but Greenshaw's Folly.'

'Greenshaw being the man who built it?'

'Yes. In eighteen-sixty or seventy or thereabouts. The local success story of the time. Barefoot boy who had risen to immense prosperity. Local opinion is divided as to why he built this house, whether it was sheer exuberance of wealth or whether it was done to impress his creditors. If the latter, it didn't impress them. He either went bankrupt or the next thing to it. Hence the name, Greenshaw's Folly.'

Horace's camera clicked. 'There,' he said in a satisfied voice. 'Remind me to show you No. 310 in my collection. A really incredible marble mantelpiece in the Italian manner.' He added, looking at the house, 'I can't conceive of how Mr Greenshaw thought of it all.'

'Rather obvious in some ways,' said Raymond. 'He had visited the châteaux of the Loire, don't you think? Those turrets. And then, rather unfortunately, he seems to have travelled in the Orient. The influence of the Taj Mahal is unmistakable. I rather like the Moorish wing,' he added, 'and the traces of a Venetian palace.'

'One wonders how he ever got hold of an architect to carry out these ideas.'

Raymond shrugged his shoulders.

'No difficulty about that, I expect,' he said. 'Probably the architect retired with a good income for life while poor old Greenshaw went bankrupt.'

'Could we look at it from the other side?' asked Horace, 'or are we trespassing!'

'We're trespassing all right,' said Raymond, 'but I don't think it will matter.'

He turned towards the corner of the house and Horace skipped after him.

'But who lives here, my dear? Orphans or holiday visitors? It can't be a school. No playing-fields or brisk efficiency.'

'Oh, a Greenshaw lives here still,' said Raymond over his shoulder. 'The house itself didn't go in the crash. Old Greenshaw's son inherited it. He was a bit of a miser and lived here in a corner of it. Never spent a penny. Probably never had a penny to spend. His daughter lives here now. Old lady – very eccentric.'

As he spoke Raymond was congratulating himself on having thought of Greenshaw's Folly as a means of entertaining his guest. These literary critics always professed themselves as longing for a week-end in the country, and were wont to find the country extremely boring when they got there. Tomorrow there would be

Agatha Christie

the Sunday papers, and for today Raymond West congratulated himself on suggesting a visit to Greenshaw's Folly to enrich Horace Bindler's well-known collection of monstrosities.

They turned the corner of the house and came out on a neglected lawn. In one corner of it was a large artificial rockery, and bending over it was a figure at sight of which Horace clutched Raymond delightedly by the arm.

'My dear,' he exclaimed, 'do you see what she's got on? A sprigged print dress. Just like a housemaid – when there were housemaids. One of my most cherished memories is staying at a house in the country when I was quite a boy where a real housemaid called you in the morning, all crackling in a print dress and a cap. Yes, my boy, really – a cap. Muslin with streamers. No, perhaps it was the parlour-maid who had the streamers. But anyway she was a real housemaid and she brought in an enormous brass can of hot water. What an exciting day we're having.'

The figure in the print dress had straightened up and had turned towards them, trowel in hand. She was a sufficiently startling figure. Unkempt locks of iron-grey fell wispily on her shoulders, a straw hat rather like the hats that horses wear in Italy was crammed down on her head. The coloured prin dress she wore fell nearly to her ankles. Out of a weatherbeaten, not too clean face, shrewd eyes surveyed them appraisingly.

'I must apologize for trespassing, Miss Greenshaw,' said Raymond West, as he advanced towards her, 'but Mr Horace Bindler who is staying with me –'

Horace bowed and removed his hat.

'– is most interested in – er – ancient history and – er – fine buildings.'

Raymond West spoke with the ease of a well-known author who knows that he is a celebrity, that he can venture where other people may not.

Miss Greenshaw looked up at the sprawling exuberance behind her.

'It *is* a fine house,' she said appreciatively. 'My grandfather built it – before my time, of course. He is reported as having said that he wished to astonish the natives.'

'I'll say he did that, ma'am,' said Horace Bindler.

'Mr Bindler is the well-known literary critic,' said Raymond West.

Miss Greenshaw had clearly no reverence for literary critics. She remained unimpressed.

'I consider it,' said Miss Greenshaw, referring to the house, 'as a monument to my grandfather's genius. Silly fools come here, and ask me why I don't sell it and go and live in a flat. What would *I* do in a flat?

Agatha Christie

It's my home and I live in it,' said Miss Greenshaw.
'Always have lived here.' She considered, brooding
over the past. 'There were three of us. Laura married
the curate. Papa wouldn't give her any money, said
clergymen ought to be unworldly. She died, having
a baby. Baby died too. Nettie ran away with the
riding master. Papa cut her out of his will, of course.
Handsome fellow, Harry Fletcher, but no good. Don't
think Nettie was happy with him. Anyway, she didn't
live long. They had a son. He writes to me sometimes,
but of course he isn't a Greenshaw. *I*'m the last of the
Greenshaws.' She drew up her bent shoulders with a
certain pride, and readjusted the rakish angle of the
straw hat. Then, turning, she said sharply,

'Yes, Mrs Cresswell, what is it?'

Approaching them from the house was a figure that
seen side by side with Miss Greenshaw, seemed ludi-
crously dissimilar. Mrs Cresswell had a marvellously
dressed head of well-blued hair towering upwards in
meticulously arranged curls and rolls. It was as though
she had dressed her head to go as a French marquise
to a fancy dress party. The rest of her middle-aged
person was dressed in what ought to have been rustling
black silk but was actually one of the shinier varieties of
black rayon. Although she was not a large woman, she
had a well-developed and sumptuous bust. Her voice
when she spoke, was unexpectedly deep. She spoke

330

with exquisite diction, only a slight hesitation over words beginning with 'h' and the final pronunciation of them with an exaggerated aspirate gave rise to a suspicion that at some remote period in her youth she might have had trouble over dropping her h's.

'The fish, madam,' said Mrs Cresswell, 'the slice of cod. It has not arrived. I have asked Alfred to go down for it and he refuses to do so.'

Rather unexpectedly, Miss Greenshaw gave a cackle of laughter.

'Refuses, does he?'

'Alfred, madam, has been most disobliging.'

Miss Greenshaw raised two earth-stained fingers to her lips, suddenly produced an ear-splitting whistle and at the same time yelled:

'Alfred. Alfred, come here.'

Round the corner of the house a young man appeared in answer to the summons, carrying a spade in his hand. He had a bold, handsome face and as he drew near he cast an unmistakably malevolent glance towards Mrs Cresswell.

'You wanted me, miss?' he said.

'Yes, Alfred. I hear you've refused to go down for the fish. What about it, eh?'

Alfred spoke in a surly voice.

'I'll go down for it if you wants it, miss. You've only got to say.'

'I do want it. I want it for my supper.'

'Right you are, miss. I'll go right away.'

He threw an insolent glance at Mrs Cresswell, who flushed and murmured below her breath:

'Really! It's unsupportable.'

'Now that I think of it,' said Miss Greenshaw, 'a couple of strange visitors are just what we need aren't they, Mrs Cresswell?'

Mrs Cresswell looked puzzled.

'I'm sorry, madam –'

'For you-know-what,' said Miss Greenshaw, nodding her head. 'Beneficiary to a will mustn't witness it. That's right, isn't it?' She appealed to Raymond West.

'Quite correct,' said Raymond.

'I know enough law to know that,' said Miss Greenshaw. 'And you two are men of standing.'

She flung down her trowel on her weeding-basket.

'Would you mind coming up to the library with me?'

'Delighted,' said Horace eagerly.

She led the way through french windows and through a vast yellow and gold drawing-room with faded brocade on the walls and dust covers arranged over the furniture, then through a large dim hall, up a staircase and into a room on the first floor.

'My grandfather's library,' she announced.

Horace looked round the room with acute pleasure. It was a room, from his point of view, quite full of monstrosities. The heads of sphinxes appeared on the most unlikely pieces of furniture, there was a colossal bronze representing, he thought, Paul and Virginia, and a vast bronze clock with classical motifs of which he longed to take a photograph.

'A fine lot of books,' said Miss Greenshaw.

Raymond was already looking at the books. From what he could see from a cursory glance there was no book here of any real interest or, indeed, any book which appeared to have been read. They were all superbly bound sets of the classics as supplied ninety years ago for furnishing a gentleman's library. Some novels of a bygone period were included. But they too showed little signs of having been read.

Miss Greenshaw was fumbling in the drawers of a vast desk. Finally she pulled out a parchment document.

'My will,' she explained. 'Got to leave your money to someone – or so they say. If I died without a will I suppose that son of a horse-coper would get it. Handsome fellow, Harry Fletcher, but a rogue if there ever was one. Don't see why *his* son should inherit this place. No,' she went on, as though answering some unspoken objection, 'I've made up my mind. I'm leaving it to Cresswell.'

'Your housekeeper?'

'Yes. I've explained it to her. I make a will leaving her all I've got and then I don't need to pay her any wages. Saves me a lot in current expenses, and it keeps her up to the mark. No giving me notice and walking off at any minute. Very la-di-dah and all that, isn't she? But her father was a working plumber in a very small way. *She's* nothing to give herself airs about.'

She had by now unfolded the parchment. Picking up a pen she dipped it in the inkstand and wrote her signature, Katherine Dorothy Greenshaw.

'That's right,' she said. 'You've seen me sign it, and then you two sign it, and that makes it legal.'

She handed the pen to Raymond West. He hesitated a moment, feeling an unexpected repulsion to what he was asked to do. Then he quickly scrawled the well-known signature, for which his morning's mail usually brought at least six demands a day.

Horace took the pen from him and added his own minute signature.

'That's done,' said Miss Greenshaw.

She moved across to the bookcase and stood looking at them uncertainly, then she opened a glass door, took out a book and slipped the folded parchment inside.

'I've my own places for keeping things,' she said.

'*Lady Audley's Secret*,' Raymond West remarked, catching sight of the title as she replaced the book.

Miss Greenshaw gave another cackle of laughter.

'Best-seller in its day,' she remarked. 'Not like your books, eh?'

She gave Raymond a sudden friendly nudge in the ribs. Raymond was rather surprised that she even knew he wrote books. Although Raymond West was quite a name in literature, he could hardly be described as a best-seller. Though softening a little with the advent of middle-age, his books dealt bleakly with the sordid side of life.

'I wonder,' Horace demanded breathlessly, 'if I might just take a photograph of the clock?'

'By all means,' said Miss Greenshaw. 'It came, I believe, from the Paris exhibition.'

'Very probably,' said Horace. He took his picture.

'This room's not been used much since my grandfather's time,' said Miss Greenshaw. 'This desk's full of old diaries of his. Interesting, I should think. I haven't the eyesight to read them myself. I'd like to get them published, but I suppose one would have to work on them a good deal.'

'You could engage someone to do that,' said Raymond West.

'Could I really? It's an idea, you know. I'll think about it.'

Raymond West glanced at his watch.

'We mustn't trespass on your kindness any longer,' he said.

'Pleased to have seen you,' said Miss Greenshaw graciously. 'Thought you were the policeman when I heard you coming round the corner of the house.'

'Why a policeman?' demanded Horace, who never minded asking questions.

Miss Greenshaw responded unexpectedly.

'If you want to know the time, ask a policeman,' she carolled, and with this example of Victorian wit, nudged Horace in the ribs and roared with laughter.

'It's been a wonderful afternoon,' sighed Horace as they walked home. 'Really, that place has everything. The only thing the library needs is a body. Those old-fashioned detective stories about murder in the library – that's just the kind of library I'm sure the authors had in mind.'

'If you want to discuss murder,' said Raymond, 'you must talk to my Aunt Jane.'

'Your Aunt Jane? Do you mean Miss Marple?' He felt a little at a loss.

The charming old-world lady to whom he had been introduced the night before seemed the last person to be mentioned in connection with murder.

'Oh, yes,' said Raymond. 'Murder is a speciality of hers.'

'But my dear, how intriguing. What do you really mean?'

'I mean just that,' said Raymond. He paraphrased: 'Some commit murder, some get mixed up in murders, others have murder thrust upon them. My Aunt Jane comes into the third category.'

'You are joking.'

'Not in the least. I can refer you to the former Commissioner of Scotland Yard, several Chief Constables and one or two hard-working inspectors of the CID.'

Horace said happily that wonders would never cease. Over the tea table they gave Joan West, Raymond's wife, Lou Oxley her niece, and old Miss Marple, a résumé of the afternoon's happenings, recounting in detail everything that Miss Greenshaw had said to them.

'But I do think,' said Horace, 'that there is something a little *sinister* about the whole set-up. That duchess-like creature, the housekeeper – arsenic, perhaps, in the teapot, now that she knows her mistress has made the will in her favour?'

'Tell us, Aunt Jane,' said Raymond. 'Will there be murder or won't there? What do *you* think?'

'I think,' said Miss Marple, winding up her wool with a rather severe air, 'that you shouldn't joke about these things as much as you do, Raymond. Arsenic is, of course, *quite* a possibility. So easy to obtain.

Probably present in the toolshed already in the form of weed killer.'

'Oh, really, darling,' said Joan West, affectionately. 'Wouldn't that be rather too obvious?'

'It's all very well to make a will,' said Raymond, 'I don't suppose really the poor old thing has anything to leave except that awful white elephant of a house, and who would want that?'

'A film company possibly,' said Horace, 'or a hotel or an institution?'

'They'd expect to buy it for a song,' said Raymond, but Miss Marple was shaking her head.

'You know, dear Raymond, I cannot agree with you there. About the money, I mean. The grandfather was evidently one of those lavish spenders who make money easily, but can't keep it. He may have gone broke, as you say, but hardly bankrupt or else his son would not have had the house. Now the son, as is so often the case, was an entirely different character to his father. A miser. A man who saved every penny. I should say that in the course of his lifetime he probably put by a very good sum. This Miss Greenshaw appears to have taken after him, to dislike spending money that is. Yes, I should think it quite likely that she had quite a good sum tucked away.'

'In that case,' said Joan West, 'I wonder now – what about Lou?'

They looked at Lou as she sat, silent, by the fire.

Lou was Joan West's niece. Her marriage had recently, as she herself put it, come unstuck, leaving her with two young children and a bare sufficiency of money to keep them on.

'I mean,' said Joan, 'if this Miss Greenshaw really wants someone to go through diaries and get a book ready for publication . . .'

'It's an idea,' said Raymond.

Lou said in a low voice:

'It's work I could do – and I'd enjoy it.'

'I'll write to her,' said Raymond.

'I wonder,' said Miss Marple thoughtfully, 'what the old lady meant by that remark about a policeman?'

'Oh, it was just a joke.'

'It reminded me,' said Miss Marple, nodding her head vigorously, 'yes, it reminded me very much of Mr Naysmith.'

'Who was Mr Naysmith?' asked Raymond, curiously.

'He kept bees,' said Miss Marple, 'and was very good at doing the acrostics in the Sunday papers. And he liked giving people false impressions just for fun. But sometimes it led to trouble.'

Everybody was silent for a moment, considering Mr Naysmith, but as there did not seem to be any points of resemblance between him and Miss Greenshaw, they

339

decided that dear Aunt Jane was perhaps getting a *little* bit disconnected in her old age.

II

Horace Bindler went back to London without having collected any more monstrosities and Raymond West wrote a letter to Miss Greenshaw telling her that he knew of a Mrs Louisa Oxley who would be competent to undertake work on the diaries. After a lapse of some days, a letter arrived, written in spidery old-fashioned handwriting, in which Miss Greenshaw declared herself anxious to avail herself of the services of Mrs Oxley, and making an appointment for Mrs Oxley to come and see her.

Lou duly kept the appointment, generous terms were arranged and she started work on the following day.

'I'm awfully grateful to you,' she said to Raymond. 'It will fit in beautifully. I can take the children to school, go on to Greenshaw's Folly and pick them up on my way back. How fantastic the whole set-up is! That old woman has to be seen to be believed.'

On the evening of her first day at work she returned and described her day.

'I've hardly seen the housekeeper,' she said. 'She

came in with coffee and biscuits at half past eleven with her mouth pursed up very prunes and prisms, and would hardly speak to me. I think she disapproves deeply of my having been engaged.' She went on, 'It seems there's quite a feud between her and the gardener, Alfred. He's a local boy and fairly lazy, I should imagine, and he and the housekeeper won't speak to each other. Miss Greenshaw said in her rather grand way, "There have always been feuds as far as I can remember between the garden and the house staff. It was so in my grandfather's time. There were three men and a boy in the garden then, and eight maids in the house, but there was always friction."'

On the following day Lou returned with another piece of news.

'Just fancy,' she said, 'I was asked to ring up the nephew this morning.'

'Miss Greenshaw's nephew?'

'Yes. It seems he's an actor playing in the company that's doing a summer season at Boreham on Sea. I rang up the theatre and left a message asking him to lunch tomorrow. Rather fun, really. The old girl didn't want the housekeeper to know. I think Mrs Cresswell has done something that's annoyed her.'

'Tomorrow another instalment of this thrilling serial,' murmured Raymond.

'It's exactly like a serial, isn't it? Reconciliation with

the nephew, blood is thicker than water – another will
to be made and the old will destroyed.'

'Aunt Jane, you're looking very serious.'

'Was I, my dear? Have you heard any more about
the policeman?'

Lou looked bewildered. 'I don't know anything
about a policeman.'

'That remark of hers, my dear,' said Miss Marple,
'must have meant *something*.'

Lou arrived at her work the next day in a cheerful
mood. She passed through the open front door –
the doors and windows of the house were always
open. Miss Greenshaw appeared to have no fear of
burglars, and was probably justified, as most things
in the house weighed several tons and were of no
marketable value.

Lou had passed Alfred in the drive. When she first
caught sight of him he had been leaning against
a tree smoking a cigarette, but as soon as he had
caught sight of her he had seized a broom and begun
diligently to sweep leaves. An idle young man, she
thought, but good looking. His features reminded her
of someone. As she passed through the hall on her
way upstairs to the library she glanced at the large
picture of Nathaniel Greenshaw which presided over
the mantelpiece, showing him in the acme of Victorian prosperity, leaning back in a large arm-chair, his

hands resting on the gold albert across his capacious stomach. As her glance swept up from the stomach to the face with its heavy jowls, its bushy eyebrows and its flourishing black moustache, the thought occurred to her that Nathaniel Greenshaw must have been handsome as a young man. He had looked, perhaps, a little like Alfred . . .

She went into the library, shut the door behind her, opened her typewriter and got out the diaries from the drawer at the side of the desk. Through the open window she caught a glimpse of Miss Greenshaw in a puce-coloured sprigged print, bending over the rockery, weeding assiduously. They had had two wet days, of which the weeds had taken full advantage.

Lou, a town bred girl, decided that if she ever had a garden it would never contain a rockery which needed hand weeding. Then she settled down to her work.

When Mrs Cresswell entered the library with the coffee tray at half past eleven, she was clearly in a very bad temper. She banged the tray down on the table, and observed to the universe:

'Company for lunch – and nothing in the house! What am *I* supposed to do, I should like to know? And no sign of Alfred.'

'He was sweeping in the drive when I got here,' Lou offered.

'I dare say. A nice soft job.'

343

Mrs Cresswell swept out of the room and banged the door behind her. Lou grinned to herself. She wondered what 'the nephew' would be like.

She finished her coffee and settled down to her work again. It was so absorbing that time passed quickly. Nathaniel Greenshaw, when he started to keep a diary, had succumbed to the pleasure of frankness. Trying out a passage relating to the personal charm of a barmaid in the neighbouring town, Lou reflected that a good deal of editing would be necessary.

As she was thinking this, she was startled by a scream from the garden. Jumping up, she ran to the open window. Miss Greenshaw was staggering away from the rockery towards the house. Her hands were clasped to her breast and between them there protruded a feathered shaft that Lou recognized with stupefaction to be the shaft of an arrow.

Miss Greenshaw's head, in its battered straw hat, fell forward on her breast. She called up to Lou in a failing voice: '. . . shot . . . he shot me . . . with an arrow . . . get help . . .'

Lou rushed to the door. She turned the handle, but the door would not open. It took her a moment or two of futile endeavour to realize that she was locked in. She rushed back to the window.

'I'm locked in.'

Miss Greenshaw, her back towards Lou, and swaying

a little on her feet was calling up to the housekeeper at a window farther along.

'Ring police . . . telephone . . .'

Then, lurching from side to side like a drunkard, she disappeared from Lou's view through the window below into the drawing-room. A moment later Lou heard a crash of broken china, a heavy fall, and then silence. Her imagination reconstructed the scene. Miss Greenshaw must have staggered blindly into a small table with a Sèvres teaset on it.

Desperately Lou pounded on the door, calling and shouting. There was no creeper or drain-pipe outside the window that could help her to get out that way.

Tired at last of beating on the door, she returned to the window. From the window of her sitting-room farther along, the housekeeper's head appeared.

'Come and let me out, Mrs Oxley. I'm locked in.'

'So am I.'

'Oh dear, isn't it awful? I've telephoned the police. There's an extension in this room, but what I can't understand, Mrs Oxley, is our being locked in. *I* never heard a key turn, did you?'

'No. I didn't hear anything at all. Oh dear, what shall we do? Perhaps Alfred might hear us.' Lou shouted at the top of her voice, 'Alfred, Alfred.'

'Gone to his dinner as likely as not. What time is it?'

Lou glanced at her watch.

'Twenty-five past twelve.'

'He's not supposed to go until half past, but he sneaks off earlier whenever he can.'

'Do you think – do you think –'

Lou meant to ask 'Do you think she's dead?' but the words stuck in her throat.

There was nothing to do but wait. She sat down on the window-sill. It seemed an eternity before the stolid helmeted figure of a police constable came round the corner of the house. She leant out of the window and he looked up at her, shading his eyes with his hand. When he spoke his voice held reproof.

'What's going on here?' he asked disapprovingly.

From their respective windows, Lou and Mrs Cresswell poured a flood of excited information down on him.

The constable produced a note-book and pencil. 'You ladies ran upstairs and locked yourselves in? Can I have your names, please?'

'No. Somebody else locked us in. Come and let us out.'

The constable said reprovingly, 'All in good time,' and disappeared through the window below.

Once again time seemed infinite. Lou heard the sound of a car arriving, and, after what seemed an hour but was actually three minutes, first Mrs Cresswell and then Lou were released by a police sergeant more alert than the original constable.

'Miss Greenshaw?' Lou's voice faltered. 'What – what's happened?'

The sergeant cleared his throat.

'I'm sorry to have to tell you, madam,' he said, 'what I've already told Mrs Cresswell here. Miss Greenshaw is dead.'

'Murdered,' said Mrs Cresswell. 'That's what it is – murder.'

The sergeant said dubiously:

'Could have been an accident – some country lads shooting with bows and arrows.'

Again there was the sound of a car arriving. The sergeant said:

'That'll be the MO,' and started downstairs.

But it was not the MO. As Lou and Mrs Cresswell came down the stairs a young man stepped hesitatingly through the front door and paused, looking round him with a somewhat bewildered air.

Then, speaking in a pleasant voice that in some way seemed familiar to Lou – perhaps it had a family resemblance to Miss Greenshaw's – he asked:

'Excuse me, does – er – does Miss Greenshaw live here?'

'May I have your name if you please,' said the

sergeant advancing upon him.

'Fletcher,' said the young man. 'Nat Fletcher. I'm Miss Greenshaw's nephew, as a matter of fact.'

'Indeed, sir, well – I'm sorry – I'm sure –'

'Has anything happened?' asked Nat Fletcher.

'There's been an – accident – your aunt was shot with an arrow – penetrated the jugular vein –'

Mrs Cresswell spoke hysterically and without her usual refinement:

'Your h'aunts been murdered, that's what's 'appened. You h'aunt's been murdered.'

III

Inspector Welch drew his chair a little nearer to the table and let his gaze wander from one to the other of the four people in the room. It was the evening of the same day. He had called at the Wests' house to take Lou Oxley once more over her statement.

'You are sure of the exact words? *Shot – he shot me – with an arrow – get help?*'

Lou nodded.

'And the time?'

'I looked at my watch a minute or two later – it was then twelve twenty-five.'

'Your watch keeps good time?'

'I looked at the clock as well.'

The inspector turned to Raymond West.

'It appears, sir, that about a week ago you and a Mr Horace Bindler were witnesses to Miss Greenshaw's will?'

Briefly, Raymond recounted the events of the afternoon visit that he and Horace Bindler had paid to Greenshaw's Folly.

'This testimony of yours may be important,' said Welch. 'Miss Greenshaw distinctly told you, did she, that her will was being made in favour of Mrs Cresswell, the housekeeper, that she was not paying Mrs Cresswell any wages in view of the expectations Mrs Cresswell had of profiting by her death?'

'That is what she told me – yes.'

'Would you say that Mrs Cresswell was definitely aware of these facts?'

'I should say undoubtedly. Miss Greenshaw made a reference in my presence to beneficiaries not being able to witness a will and Mrs Cresswell clearly understood what she meant by it. Moreover, Miss Greenshaw herself told me that she had come to this arrangement with Mrs Cresswell.'

'So Mrs Cresswell had reason to believe she was an interested party. Motive's clear enough in her case, and I dare say she'd be our chief suspect now if it

Agatha Christie

wasn't for the fact that she was securely locked in her room like Mrs Oxley here, and also that Miss Greenshaw definitely said a *man* shot her –'

'She definitely *was* locked in her room?'

'Oh yes. Sergeant Cayley let her out. It's a big old-fashioned lock with a big old-fashioned key. The key was in the lock and there's not a chance that it could have been turned from inside or any hanky-panky of that kind. No, you can take it definitely that Mrs Cresswell was locked inside that room and couldn't get out. And there were no bows and arrows in the room and Miss Greenshaw couldn't in any case have been shot from a window – the angle forbids it – no, Mrs Cresswell's out of it.'

He paused and went on:

'Would you say that Miss Greenshaw, in your opinion, was a practical joker?'

Miss Marple looked up sharply from her corner.

'So the will wasn't in Mrs Cresswell's favour after all?' she said.

Inspector Welch looked over at her in a rather surprised fashion.

'That's a very clever guess of yours, madam,' he said. 'No. Mrs Cresswell isn't named as beneficiary.'

'Just like Mr Naysmith,' said Miss Marple, nodding her head. 'Miss Greenshaw told Mrs Cresswell she was going to leave her everything and so got out of paying her wages; and then she left her money to somebody else. No doubt she was vastly pleased with herself. No wonder she chortled when she put the will away in *Lady Audley's Secret*.'

'It was lucky Mrs Oxley was able to tell us about the will and where it was put,' said the inspector. 'We might have had a long hunt for it otherwise.'

'A Victorian sense of humour,' murmured Raymond West. 'So she left her money to her nephew after all,' said Lou.

The inspector shook his head.

'No,' he said, 'she didn't leave it to Nat Fletcher. The story goes around here – of course I'm new to the place and I only get the gossip that's second-hand – but it seems that in the old days both Miss Greenshaw and her sister were set on the handsome young riding master, and the sister got him. No, she didn't leave the money to her nephew –' He paused, rubbing his chin, 'She left it to Alfred,' he said.

'Alfred – the gardener?' Joan spoke in a surprised voice.

'Yes, Mrs West. Alfred Pollock.'

'But why?' cried Lou.

Miss Marple coughed and murmured:

'I should imagine, though perhaps I am wrong, that there may have been – what we might call *family* reasons.'

Agatha Christie

'You could call them that in a way,' agreed the inspector. 'It's quite well known in the village, it seems, that Thomas Pollock, Alfred's grandfather, was one of old Mr Greenshaw's byblows.'

'Of course,' cried Lou, 'the resemblance! I saw it this morning.'

She remembered how after passing Alfred she had come into the house and looked up at old Greenshaw's portrait.

'I dare say,' said Miss Marple, 'that she thought Alfred Pollock might have a pride in the house, might even want to live in it, whereas her nephew would almost certainly have no use for it whatever and would sell it as soon as he could possibly do so. He's an actor, isn't he? What play exactly is he acting in at present?'

Trust an old lady to wander from the point, thought Inspector Welch, but he replied civilly:

'I believe, madam, they are doing a season of James Barrie's plays.'

'Barrie,' said Miss Marple thoughtfully.

'*What Every Woman Knows*,' said Inspector Welch, and then blushed. 'Name of a play,' he said quickly. 'I'm not much of a theatre-goer myself,' he added, 'but the wife went along and saw it last week. Quite well done, she said it was.'

'Barrie wrote some very charming plays,' said Miss

Marple, 'though I must say that when I went with an old friend of mine, General Easterly, to see Barrie's *Little Mary* –' she shook her head sadly, '– neither of us knew where to look.'

The inspector, unacquainted with the play *Little Mary*, looked completely fogged. Miss Marple explained:

'When I was a girl, Inspector, nobody ever mentioned the word *stomach*.'

The inspector looked even more at sea. Miss Marple was murmuring titles under her breath.

'*The Admirable Crichton*. Very clever. *Mary Rose* – a charming play. I cried, I remember. *Quality Street* I didn't care for so much. Then there was *A Kiss for Cinderella*. Oh, *of course*.'

Inspector Welch had no time to waste on theatrical discussion. He returned to the matter in hand.

'The question is,' he said, 'did Alfred Pollock know that the old lady had made a will in his favour? Did she tell him?' He added: 'You see – there's an archery club over at Boreham Lovell and *Alfred Pollock's a member*. He's a very good shot indeed with a bow and arrow.'

'Then isn't your case quite clear?' asked Raymond West. 'It would fit in with the doors being locked on the two women – he'd know just where they were in the house.'

The inspector looked at him. He spoke with deep melancholy.

Agatha Christie

'He's got an alibi,' said the inspector.

'I always think alibis are definitely suspicious.'

'Maybe, sir,' said Inspector Welch. 'You're talking as a writer.'

'I don't write detective stories,' said Raymond West, horrified at the mere idea.

'Easy enough to say that alibis are suspicious,' went on Inspector Welch, 'but unfortunately we've got to deal with facts.'

He sighed.

'We've got three good suspects,' he said. 'Three people who, as it happened, were very close upon the scene at the time. Yet the odd thing is that it looks as though none of the three could have done it. The housekeeper I've already dealt with – the nephew, Nat Fletcher, at the moment Miss Greenshaw was shot, was a couple of miles away filling up his car at a garage and asking his way – as for Alfred Pollock six people will swear that he entered the Dog and Duck at twenty past twelve and was there for an hour having his usual bread and cheese and beer.'

'Deliberately establishing an alibi,' said Raymond West hopefully.

'Maybe,' said Inspector Welch, 'but if so, he *did* establish it.'

There was a long silence. Then Raymond turned his head to where Miss Marple sat upright and thoughtful

'It's up to you, Aunt Jane,' he said. 'The inspector's baffled, the sergeant's baffled, I'm baffled, Joan's baffled, Lou is baffled. But to you, Aunt Jane, it is crystal clear. Am I right?'

'I wouldn't say that, dear,' said Miss Marple, 'not *crystal* clear, and murder, dear Raymond, isn't a game. I don't suppose poor Miss Greenshaw wanted to die, and it was a particularly brutal murder. Very well planned and quite cold blooded. It's not a thing to make *jokes* about!'

'I'm sorry,' said Raymond, abashed. 'I'm not really as callous as I sound. One treats a thing lightly to take away from the – well, the horror of it.'

'That is, I believe, the modern tendency,' said Miss Marple. 'All these wars, and having to joke about funerals. Yes, perhaps I was thoughtless when I said you were callous.'

'It isn't,' said Joan, 'as though we'd known her at all well.'

'That is *very* true,' said Miss Marple. 'You, dear Joan, did not know her at all. I did not know her at all. Raymond gathered an impression of her from one afternoon's conversation. Lou knew her for two days.'

'Come now, Aunt Jane,' said Raymond, 'tell us your views. You don't mind, Inspector?'

'Not at all,' said the inspector politely.

Agatha Christie

'Well, my dear, it would seem that we have three people who had, or might have thought they had, a motive to kill the old lady. And three quite simple reasons why none of the three could have done so. The housekeeper could not have done so because she was locked in her room and because Miss Greenshaw definitely stated that a *man* shot her. The gardener could not have done it because he was inside the Dog and Duck at the time the murder was committed, the nephew could not have done it because he was still some distance away in his car at the time of the murder.'

'Very clearly put, madam,' said the inspector.

'And since it seems most unlikely that any outsider should have done it, where, then, are we?'

'That's what the inspector wants to know,' said Raymond West.

'One so often looks at a thing the wrong way round,' said Miss Marple apologetically. 'If we can't alter the movements or the position of those three people, then couldn't we perhaps alter the time of the murder?'

'You mean that both my watch and the clock were wrong?' asked Lou.

'No dear,' said Miss Marple, 'I didn't mean that at all. I mean that the murder didn't occur when you thought it occurred.'

'But I *saw* it,' cried Lou.

'Well, what I have been wondering, my dear, was whether you weren't *meant* to see it. I've been asking myself, you know, whether that wasn't the real reason why you were engaged for this job.'

'What *do* you mean, Aunt Jane?'

'Well, dear, it seems odd. Miss Greenshaw did not like spending money, and yet she engaged you and agreed quite willingly to the terms you asked. It seems to me that perhaps you were meant to be there in that library on the first floor, looking out of the window so that you could be the key witness – someone from outside of irreproachable good faith – to fix a definite time and place for the murder.'

'But you can't mean,' said Lou, incredulously, 'that Miss Greenshaw *intended* to be murdered.'

'What I mean, dear,' said Miss Marple, 'is that you didn't really know Miss Greenshaw. There's no real reason, is there, why the Miss Greenshaw you saw when you went up to the house should be the same Miss Greenshaw that Raymond saw a few days earlier? Oh, yes, I know,' she went on, to prevent Lou's reply, 'she was wearing the peculiar old-fashioned print dress and the strange straw hat, and had unkempt hair. She corresponded exactly to the description Raymond gave us last week-end. But those two women, you know, were much of an age and height and size. The housekeeper, I mean, and Miss Greenshaw.'

'But the housekeeper is fat!' Lou exclaimed. 'She's got an enormous bosom.'

Miss Marple coughed.

'But my dear, surely, nowadays I have seen – er – them myself in shops most indelicately displayed. It is very easy for anyone to have a – a bust – of *any* size and dimension.'

'What are you trying to say?' demanded Raymond.

'I was just thinking, dear, that during the two or three days Lou was working there, one woman could have played the two parts. You said yourself, Lou, that you hardly saw the housekeeper, except for the one moment in the morning when she brought you in the tray with coffee. One sees those clever artists on the stage coming in as different characters with only a minute or two to spare, and I am sure the change could have been effected quite easily. That marquise head-dress could be just a wig slipped on and off.'

'Aunt Jane! Do you mean that Miss Greenshaw was dead before I started work there?'

'Not dead. Kept under drugs, I should say. A very easy job for an unscrupulous woman like the housekeeper to do. Then she made the arrangements with you and got you to telephone to the nephew to ask him to lunch at a definite time. The only person who would have known that this Miss Greenshaw was *not* Miss Greenshaw would have been Alfred. And if you remember, the first two days you were working there it was wet, and Miss Greenshaw stayed in the house. Alfred never came into the house because of his feud with the housekeeper. And on the last morning Alfred was in the drive, while Miss Greenshaw was working on the rockery – I'd like to have a look at that rockery.'

'Do you mean it was Mrs Cresswell who killed Miss Greenshaw?'

'I think that after bringing you your coffee, the woman locked the door on you as she went out, carried the unconscious Miss Greenshaw down to the drawing-room, then assumed her "Miss Greenshaw" disguise and went out to work on the rockery where you could see her from the window. In due course she screamed and came staggering to the house clutching an arrow as though it had penetrated her throat. She called for help and was careful to say "*he* shot me" so as to remove suspicion from the housekeeper. She also called up to the housekeeper's window as though she saw her there. Then, once inside the drawing-room, she threw over a table with porcelain on it – and ran quickly upstairs, put on her marquise wig and was able a few moments later to lean her head out of the window and tell you that she, too, was locked in.'

'But she *was* locked in,' said Lou.

'I know. That is where the policeman comes in.'

'What policeman?'

'Exactly – what policeman? I wonder, Inspector, if you would mind telling me how and when *you* arrived on the scene?'

The inspector looked a little puzzled.

'At twelve twenty-nine we received a telephone call from Mrs Cresswell, housekeeper to Miss Greenshaw, stating that her mistress had been shot. Sergeant Cayley and myself went out there at once in a car and arrived at the house at twelve thirty-five. We found Miss Greenshaw dead and the two ladies locked in their rooms.'

'So, you see, my dear,' said Miss Marple to Lou. 'The police constable *you* saw wasn't a real police constable. You never thought of him again – one doesn't – one just accepts one more uniform as part of the law.'

'But who – why?'

'As to who – well, if they are playing *A Kiss for Cinderella*, a policeman is the principal character. Nat Fletcher would only have to help himself to the costume he wears on the stage. He'd ask his way at a garage being careful to call attention to the time – twelve twenty-five, then drive on quickly, leave his car round a corner, slip on his police uniform and do his "act".'

'But why? – why?'

'*Someone* had to lock the housekeeper's door on the outside, and someone had to drive the arrow through Miss Greenshaw's throat. You can stab anyone with an arrow just as well as by shooting it – but it needs force.'

'You mean they were both in it?'

'Oh yes, I think so. Mother and son as likely as not.'

'But Miss Greenshaw's sister died long ago.'

'Yes, but I've no doubt Mr Fletcher married again. He sounds the sort of man who would, and I think it possible that the child died too, and that this so-called nephew was the second wife's child, and not really a relation at all. The woman got a post as housekeeper and spied out the land. Then he wrote as her nephew and proposed to call upon her – he may have made some joking reference to coming in his policeman's uniform – or asked her over to see the play. But I think she suspected the truth and refused to see him. He would have been her heir if she had died without making a will – but of course once she had made a will in the housekeeper's favour (as they thought) then it was clear sailing.'

'But why use an arrow?' objected Joan. 'So very far fetched.'

'Not far fetched at all, dear. Alfred belonged to an archery club – Alfred was meant to take the blame.

Agatha Christie

The fact that he was in the pub as early as twelve twenty was most unfortunate from their point of view. He always left a little before his proper time and that would have been just right –' She shook her head. 'It really seems all wrong – morally, I mean, that Alfred's laziness should have saved his life.'

The inspector cleared his throat.

'Well, madam, these suggestions of yours are very interesting. I shall have, of course, to investigate –'

IV

Miss Marple and Raymond West stood by the rockery and looked down at that gardening basket full of dying vegetation.

Miss Marple murmured:

'Alyssum, saxifrage, cytisus, thimble campanula . . . Yes, that's all the proof *I* need. Whoever was weeding here yesterday morning was no gardener – she pulled up plants as well as weeds. So now I *know* I'm right Thank you, dear Raymond, for bringing me here. wanted to see the place for myself.'

She and Raymond both looked up at the outrageou pile of Greenshaw's Folly.

A cough made them turn. A handsome young ma was also looking at the house.

'Plaguey big place,' he said. 'Too big for nowadays – or so they say. I dunno about that. If I won a football pool and made a lot of money, that's the kind of house I'd like to build.'

He smiled bashfully at them.

'Reckon I can say so now – that there house was built by my great-grandfather,' said Alfred Pollock. 'And a fine house it is, for all they call it Greenshaw's Folly!'

Lord Edgware Dies

POIROT

Agatha Christie

When Lord Edgware is found murdered the police are baffled. His estranged actress wife was seen to visit him just before his death and Poirot himself heard her brag of her plan to 'get rid' of him.

After all, how could Jane have stabbed Lord Edgware to death in his library at exactly the same time she was seen dining with friends? It's a case that almost proves to be too much for the great Hercule Poirot.

'The whole case is a triumph of Poirot's special qualities.'
Times Literary Supplement

ISBN-13 978-0-00-712074-1

Five Little Pigs

POIROT

Agatha Christie

Beautiful Caroline Crale was convicted of poisoning her husband, but just like the nursery rhyme, there were five other 'little pigs' who could have done it: Philip Blake (the stockbroker) who went to market; Meredith Blake (the amateur herbalist) who stayed at home; Elsa Greer (the three-time divorcee) who had her roast beef; Cecilia Williams (the devoted governess) who had none; and Angela Warren (the disfigured sister) who cried all the way home.

Sixteen years later, Caroline's daughter is determined to prove her mother's innocence, and Poirot just can't get that nursery rhyme out of his mind...

'Mrs Christie as usual puts a ring through the reader's nose and leads him to one of her smashing last-minute showdowns.'   *Observer*

'The answer to the riddle is brilliant.'
                                          Times Literary Supplement

ISBN-13 978-0-00-712073-4

Murder on the Orient Express

POIROT

Agatha Christie

'The murderer is with us – on the train now…'

Just after midnight, the famous *Orient Express* is stopped in its tracks by a snowdrift. By morning, Hercule Poirot knows that the millionaire Simon Ratchett lies dead in his compartment, stabbed a dozen times, his door locked from the inside. One of his fellow passengers must be the murderer.

Isolated by the storm and with a killer in their midst, detective Hercule Poirot must find the killer amongst a dozen of the dead man's enemies, before the murderer decides to strike again…

'Very real, and keeps readers enthralled and guessing to the end.'   *Times Literary Supplement*

ISBN-13 978-0-00-711931-8

The ABC Murders

POIROT

Agatha Christie

'Let us see, Mr Clever Poirot, just how clever you can be.'

There's a serial killer on the loose, working his way through the alphabet, and the whole country is in a state of panic.

A is for Mrs Ascher in Andover, B is for Betty Barnard in Bexhill, C is for Sir Carmichael Clarke in Churston. With each murder, the killer is getting more confident – but leaving a trail of deliberate clues to taunt the proud Hercule Poirot might just prove to be the first, and fatal mistake...

An entirely original idea.' *Daily Telegraph*

Christie is to be congratulated on the perfection of her invention.' *The Times*

ISBN-13 978-0-00-711929-5

The Mysterious Affair At Styles

POIROT'S FIRST CASE

Agatha Christie

Peril to the detective who says: "It is so small – it does not matter…" Everything matters.'

When Emily Inglethorpe is found murdered, Captain Hastings calls for help from an old friend: a certain Belgian detective who has grown bored of retirement.

A shattered coffee cup, a splash of candle grease, a bed of begonias – only Poirot could unravel an ingenious crime from these few intriguing clues.

'Almost too ingenious.' *Times Literary Supplement*

ISBN-13 978-0-00-711927-1